SPECIAL MESSAGE TO READERS

This book is published under the auspices of

THE ULVERSCROFT FOUNDATION

(registered charity No. 264873 UK)

Established in 1972 to provide funds for research, diagnosis and treatment of eye diseases. Examples of contributions made are: —

A Children's Assessment Unit at Moorfield's Hospital, London.

•

Twin operating theatres at the Western Ophthalmic Hospital, London.

•

A Chair of Ophthalmology at the Royal Australian College of Ophthalmologists.

•

The Ulverscroft Children's Eye Unit at the Great Ormond Street Hospital For Sick Children, London.

You can help further the work of the Foundation by making a donation or leaving a legacy. Every contribution, no matter how small, is received with gratitude. Please write for details to:

THE ULVERSCROFT FOUNDATION,
The Green, Bradgate Road, Anstey,
Leicester LE7 7FU, England.
Telephone: (0116) 236 4325

In Australia write to:
THE ULVERSCROFT FOUNDATION,
c/o The Royal Australian and New Zealand
College of Ophthalmologists,
94-98 Chalmers Street, Surry Hills,
N.S.W. 2010, Australia

Raymond Haigh was born, educated and has lived in Doncaster, South Yorkshire, all his life. He is married with four children and six grandchildren.

THE DOLL DOCTOR

Benjamin is missing. And he's no ordinary six-year-old. Bonds of blood and family link him with the highest echelons of the establishment and the murky depths of organized crime. Despite his mother's frantic appeals and the tireless efforts of the police, hopes of finding him are fading, and fear gnaws at the heart of a man who has everything to lose. Samantha Quest is searching. Dismissed from the security services, she is free from constraints to try and recover the child, alive or dead. Her search involves her with a family tormented by secrets. It plunges her into a vicious underworld where the death toll is rising. Ruthless killers stalk her while they, too, hunt for this strange child they are so desperate to find.

Books by Raymond Haigh
Published by The House of Ulverscroft:

COLDER THAN THE GRAVE
CRIPPLEHEAD
DARK ANGEL
KISS AND KILL

RAYMOND HAIGH

THE DOLL DOCTOR

Complete and Unabridged

ULVERSCROFT
Leicester

First published in Great Britain in 2008 by
Robert Hale Limited
London

First Large Print Edition
published 2009
by arrangement with
Robert Hale Limited
London

British Library CIP Data

Haigh, Raymond
The doll doctor.—Large print ed.—
Ulverscroft large print series: adventure & suspense
1. Kidnapping—Fiction 2. Organized crime—Fiction
3. Suspense fiction 4. Large type books
I. Title
823.9′14 [F]

ISBN 978–1–84782–551–3

Published b
F. A. Thorpe (Publishing)
Anstey, Leicestershire

Set by Words & Graphics Ltd.
Anstey, Leicestershire
Printed and bound in Great Britain by
T. J. International Ltd., Padstow, Cornwall

This book is printed on acid-free paper

1

Samantha drew a gloved hand over the misted windscreen of the Ferrari and gazed at the apartment block beyond the trees. Forest Heights: eleven storeys of blood-red brick and bone-white stone, rising out of the crest of a hill against a backdrop of dark, snow-laden clouds. The suave, pin-stripe-suited estate agent who'd shown her the plans had assured her they were the most luxurious apartments ever built in Leeds, splendidly appointed, with panoramic views over the city. He'd noted the fictitious address she'd given him in a bulky, leather-bound Filofax, and promised to contact her immediately he had one to sell.

Lights glowed behind high windows, blurred and remote in the misty gloom of the winter afternoon. Closer, beside the main road, a gatehouse overlooked the entrance to the walled grounds. It was in darkness. Probably unmanned, Samantha mused: the residents would control the steel barrier remotely, from their cars. She'd have to leave the Ferrari in the side street and enter on foot.

The dashboard clock was showing 2.45.

Rather early in the day for the kind of services she was going to offer, but she had to make progress and her feet, in her delicate suede and snakeskin shoes, were becoming cold. Shivering, she drew her fur coat around her. Fashioned from the winter pelts of Siberian wolves, its silvery softness seemed to fill the car. The Russian Minister of the Interior had been effusively charming when he'd presented it. He'd lifted its floor-trailing length from the crimson and gold box and draped it over her shoulders like a cloak. If she lived through this, if she succeeded, would Lawrence Cosgrave show his appreciation in such an extravagant way? Probably not. She suspected he was a man not much given to displays of gratitude.

Other places, other times. Samantha took a deep breath and brought her thoughts back to the man in the high apartment. He'd expect her to be perfectly groomed. She flicked open her bag, found her lipstick amongst the clutter beneath the gun, then, dipping the rear view mirror, deftly defined the shape of her mouth and refreshed the vermilion on her lips. She lowered her head. Huge green eyes, lids delicately shaded, gazed at her from beneath a thick fringe of gleaming black hair. If he was heterosexual and his heart was beating, he'd invite her up.

Dropping the lipstick back in her bag, she plucked out the Exclusive Escorts visiting card she'd concocted before starting out, found a pen, and wrote on the back: *Vincent Bassinger, Flat 20, Forest Heights, Kirkstall Road, Leeds. 3.00 p.m.*, then tucked it behind her collection of ID wallets. She lifted out the gun, checked the movement of the breech and ejected the magazine: nine rounds. When she pushed the clip back the weapon's oily-blackness gleamed in the subdued light; she found the weight and feel of it in her hand more comforting than her furs. About to return it to her bag, she had second thoughts and slid it into a holster sewn inside the pocket of her coat. A final glance at her reflection in the mirror, then she pushed at the door and swung her legs out of the low car.

The air was suddenly cold on her cheeks and her breath made clouds as she walked up the side street. At the junction with Kirkstall Road she glanced left and right. There didn't appear to be any traffic surveillance cameras, but she could see cameras on the gatehouse and on some ornamental lamp standards that bordered the winding driveway to the apartments. She'd deal with that problem later, after her encounter with Vincent Bassinger.

* * *

Marcus gazed through the bare branches of trees that fronted Thames House while he warmed his hands on the radiator beneath the window. Snow was falling in big flakes now, obscuring his view of the city beyond the river. He wasn't happy. He didn't care for the way Samantha Quest was being treated. She'd served them well. She didn't deserve to be placed in this position. And why do it to her now? She'd always been bold and decisive, acted on her initiative. They were the qualities that had made her such a . . . He heard a brisk rapping and turned towards the opening door.

'Did you get my note, Marcus?'

'I did, but I can't agree with the action you're taking, ma'am.' He eyed the tall woman defiantly.

Loretta Fallon's white silk blouse had an oriental collar. It made her navy-blue suit with its pencil skirt seem almost like a uniform. She stepped into the room and closed the door. 'And what don't you like about it?'

'Persuading Quest to accept the assignment, then removing her from the payroll.'

Loretta began to cross the expanse of brown carpet. 'I had to, Marcus. She agreed to find the child, but only if she could take whatever measures she considered necessary. Lawrence Cosgrave can't risk being associated with activity like that, nor can we. If things go wrong, we've got to be able to look press and Parliament in the eye and say we had no part in it.' Loretta joined him at the window and folded her arms beneath her breasts.

'You've actually discharged her from the service?'

'A letter terminating her employment, her P45, and a cheque for outstanding pay and expenses were sent to her yesterday.' Loretta's lips curved in a knowing smile. Would he be as concerned as this about a man? Would he feel so protective if the woman wasn't quite so attractive?

Marcus returned his gaze to the window. Snow was settling on roofs and pavements now. The Thames curled, like a black snake, through the whiteness. 'And if everything goes well with the assignment?'

'We'll reinstate her without break in service.'

'She might not want to be reinstated.'

'She has very expensive tastes in clothes and cars, Marcus. She needs the salary. You'll get your gorgeous Samantha back.' Loretta watched his neck redden. Dark-haired, tall, becoming heavy in middle age, she could tell he'd been home to Charlotte over the weekend; his blue shirt was starched and clean, the stains had been sponged from his Guards Officer's tie, his dark suit neatly pressed.

Marcus frowned. 'What made him ask for Quest?'

'Word gets around.'

'But he was able to ask for her by name, and we've always been so — '

'He asked for Georgina Grey. He must have got hold of the name she uses on her ID documents. The Special Crime Unit probably passed it on.' Loretta shrugged. 'Politicians gossip, and senior politicians would know it was a woman agent at the back of all those resignations from the last government. They know she's deadly, that's been fed back by the Russians through the Foreign Office, and you've been known to wax lyrical about your glamorous little killer.'

Marcus puffed out reddening cheeks. 'I've defended her against detractors, ma'am, but I'd never reveal . . . ' Words eluded him as he struggled to meet Loretta's steady gaze. He studied the generous mouth that was still curved in a smile, the iron-grey hair that was drawn tightly back and secured by a black ribbon. Loretta Fallon was no longer young, but her face radiated intelligence and she was shapely and slender. He found her enormously attractive. She was close enough for him to smell her perfume. Mitsouko? Yes, he was sure it was Mitsouko. He made a show of clearing his throat, then asked, 'Did Cosgrave brief Quest himself?'

'He's a politician, Marcus. He's keeping his distance. Verbal instructions passed on through me. Just the name and address of the mother and a request to take any measures, no matter how extreme, to recover the child. Alive or dead.'

'But why would the Prime Minister be so interested in a missing boy? Do we hear skeletons rattling?'

'Hmm, don't think so. Not the obvious ones, anyway. The Hamilton woman's in her fifties: must have been a very late pregnancy. She was on television last night, making an appeal. Even allowing for all the distress, she's never looked the kind of woman a man like Cosgrave would risk everything for.'

They stood in silence, watching snow fall over the city. Marcus stroked the hot radiator with his hands; Loretta allowed her thighs to rest against it. The heating system still wasn't coping on this floor. She made a mental note to give the surveyor at the Property Services Agency a real dressing down.

Presently Loretta said, 'Her son-in-law was

involved with the Bassinger Brothers. He was the key witness at the trial.'

'That's probably it,' Marcus breathed. 'Christ, what have we done to Quest? Where's the son-in-law now?'

'Dead. The police and Special Crime dealt with the Bassinger investigation, so there's not much material on the files. I've had what information and images we have put on a disk and sent to Quest.'

'If you remember, ma'am, we offered to keep the Bassinger brothers under surveillance, but Special Crime didn't want us involved. They made a hash of it in the end: months in court and only one conviction.' Marcus's tone was scathing.

'Ronald,' Loretta said.

'Ronald?'

'Ronald Bassinger: he's the brother who was convicted. Government is adopting a very aggressive approach to the sequestration of assets. Been discussed at cabinet level. Very high-profile case so the Home Secretary wants to look tough after the pathetic outcome to the trial. Collection agencies have been told to have all cash gathered in by the end of March and to move fast with the seizure and sale of his property.'

'What do Bassinger's lawyers have to say about that?'

Loretta laughed. 'Quite a lot, I gather, but they're getting nowhere. The government's determined about this one, and there's universal revulsion for the Bassingers. When he passed sentence the judge said he was confronting pure evil in human form. All the tabloids used it as a headline.'

Marcus pressed his hands on to the radiator. 'One brother's serving life: that leaves five still on the outside, all mired in violent crime. And there are sons, of course, probably a dozen; all big and vicious like their fathers.' He watched a police launch surge down the river and disappear beneath Lambeth Bridge. Then, in a quieter voice, added, 'Of all the Bassingers, Vincent's the most terrifying. Met him once: huge man, brutish, emanates cruelty, very adept at breaking women's necks. Broke his wife's neck and did the same to at least two other women. And he's supposed to have murdered a child. Cunning, too: police have never been able to charge him with anything. If the judge thought Ronald was evil, he should have had Vincent in the dock.'

'And if Special Crime and the Crown Prosecution Service hadn't botched the job he probably would have been,' Loretta muttered.

'If the Bassingers are involved in this,

ma'am, Quest's going to be in some peril. What support are we permitted to give?'

Loretta gave him a sideways look. His concern for the woman was beginning to irritate her. 'None, Marcus,' she said frostily. 'She's experienced, she's hardened, she's utterly ruthless. The Israelis trained her, for heaven's sake. She's more vicious than the Bassingers! And we don't know they are involved; we're just surmising. It's probably a paedophile.' Sighing out her irritation, she snapped, 'Quest can still access the information systems. I think we should leave it at that. We've got to give this one a very wide berth.'

'And her encrypted phone?'

'It's been reclaimed.'

'Can she use the armourer?'

'I don't think she's going to need the armourer, Marcus. When I told her what we were thinking, she requisitioned a dozen cartons of shells for that huge semi-automatic she uses and three-hundred rounds for a Heckler sub. Ulrick had them couriered to her yesterday.' Loretta pushed her knees away from the warmth of the radiator and began to walk towards the door. When she reached it she turned and looked back. 'Must say, I was surprised she accepted the job. Assisting a politician would have been bad enough, but coming to the aid of the Prime Minister is going to sicken her. It's the boy, I suppose; answering the cry of a child in danger.'

More likely to be a desire for atonement, Marcus reflected. Redemption through good works. He liked to think he understood Quest, that he knew what made her tick. And he wasn't so sure she'd return to the department when this was over. Her investigation business would keep her in some comfort, and there was inherited income.

'Best not to ask questions if she makes contact,' Loretta said, as she stepped through the door. 'If things get out of hand we need to be able to look everyone in the eye and say, 'She's not one of us, and we don't know a thing'.'

* * *

Paula Hamilton unfolded the letter for the hundredth time and read:

Dear Mrs Hamilton,
I've arranged for a woman called Georgina Grey to visit you. If it is humanly possible to find Benjamin, she'll find him. Her discretion is absolute, and you have my authority to tell her everything. Indeed, you must tell her everything if we are to have

any hope of the child being found. Whatever you do, don't inform the police about this. It could prejudice Grey's investigations, and the police are best left to continue to search in their own way.

I urge you, for Grey's sake as well as ours, to burn this letter when you've read it.

Sincerely

Lawrence Cosgrave.

A man from his local office had brought the note to her yesterday. Lawrence Cosgrave had probably told him it was a personal letter expressing sympathy to a constituent. The man didn't ask if there was any news of Ben. People didn't do that anymore. They just squeezed her hand and gave her a compassionate look. And women sometimes burst into tears and hurried away, unable to cope with their perception of her grief and the emotions it aroused.

When the police came to see her they always brought a policewoman to hold her hand and make her a cup of tea. This morning they'd asked her if she wanted the policewoman to stay, but she'd refused. Strangers in the house made her edgy. They wanted her to make another appeal on television tomorrow. The thought of it was making her feel sick: sitting in front of all those cameras, revealing her fear and distress. God knows what she'd be like when she tried to read out what they wanted her to say. Last time she'd been shaking so badly she could hardly make out the words. The police had been so confident at the beginning, so determined. Now, their confidence seemed to be overshadowed by despair. They were always very kind. They were trying to keep her hoping, but she'd heard them say that if a missing child isn't found within twenty-four hours the chances of a good outcome become slim. It had been three days now.

Grey, Grey, Georgina Grey. Events had confused her, made it difficult for her to think and remember things, but she had to remember the woman's name. She'd better burn the letter and the envelope. She'd already kept them too long.

Paula Hamilton passed from living room to tiny kitchen, clicking on the light as she went. Taking a colander from a cupboard, she stood it in the sink, then ignited a burner on the cooker. She tore the letter and envelope into narrow strips, lit them in the flames, then dropped them into the perforated metal bowl, one by one. When they'd burnt to ashes, she powdered them between her fingers and washed them down the drain.

She glanced at the clock on the dresser: it

was almost three. When would the Grey woman arrive? And where was Rachel? Her daughter's leave-taking had been angry and bitter, dreadful things had been said, but this was a time for burying differences. It would be getting dark in an hour. She couldn't face another night alone in the house, trying to stop herself imagining what was happening to Ben, trying to control her fear, trying to retain a little hope.

2

Furs gathered around her face, heels clicking on wet pavings, Samantha strode past the empty gatehouse and headed into the grounds of Forest Heights. The driveway curved up the hill and her breathing had quickened by the time she glimpsed the entrance to the apartments. Her view of it was partly obscured by elm trees growing in the middle of a steeply sloping lawn, but she could see lights behind impressive plate-glass doors. A wide triangle of white masonry on four, plain, circular columns protected the entrance from the weather. Architecture reduced to simple shapes, devoid of embellishment: at a distance the portico looked as if it had been built from a child's toy bricks.

She walked on, followed the driveway round to the rear where garages and small buildings that housed waste bins enclosed a generous parking area. A Rolls Royce, a Bentley, a couple of BMW's and a Mercedes stood in bays along the rear wall of the apartment block. Through the brightly-lit window of the janitor-cum-security man's office she could see the head and shoulders of a grey-haired man in a blue uniform. A rear door allowed the residents to access the parking and service area, and a row of blackened louvers ventilated what she knew from the plans to be a boiler house. Windows above the ground floor were wide and floor-to-ceiling high, no doubt made that way to take advantage of the view across the city.

Returning to the front, Samantha stepped up beneath the porch and peered through the glass doors. Honey-coloured marble lined the walls and covered the floor of an entrance hall that was softly lit by wall lights in opal shades. Behind an unmanned reception counter, brighter light was escaping from the open door of the security man's office. On the opposite wall, a couple of lifts were arranged on either side of a stairway. She shoved at the entrance doors. They were locked.

Push-buttons and name-card holders were mounted on a brass plate beside the doors. There was no card in the holder for Flat 20. Vincent Bassinger wouldn't want to advertise his presence here. She pressed the button, then turned and looked back, beyond the elms towards the more distant trees that bordered the road. The vast bulk of the apartment block was obstructing what remained of the afternoon light, and sensors were switching on the ornamental lamps that bordered the driveway. She gave the button another press. Almost immediately a metallic voice snapped, 'Who is it?'

Samantha moved closer to the grill in the brass plate. 'Is that Vincent Bassinger?'

'I said, who is it?' the voice insisted.

'Suki,' she offered, on the spur of the moment. 'Elegant Escorts of Sheffield. I'm a present from Ronald.'

'Elegant Escorts! You've wasted your time, darling. He's taking the piss.'

'No one's playing games, Vincent. The agency told me to tell you Ronald sent me. The fee's been paid.'

'And he knows you're no use to me. He's taking the piss. He always was a joker.'

'I don't know anything about that, Vincent,' Samantha retorted plaintively. 'But if I don't get my appointment card signed, I won't get paid, and I'll have wasted an afternoon driving over from Sheffield in the freezing cold.'

'Goes with the territory, sweetheart.' There was a sneer in his voice.

'Two minutes,' Samantha begged, becoming desperate. 'Just let me come up for two minutes while you sign my card, then I'll get paid.'

'I'm watching the match,' chimed the metallic voice. 'And skirt's no use to me.

Ronald knows that. He's taking the piss. Bugger off back to Sheffield.'

'So, you like boys? That's fine! But you could at least sign the card so I can get paid. You wouldn't even have to drag your eyes off the footballers' backsides.'

'Don't smart-mouth me in that hoity-toity voice.' The man was angry now. 'And why should I waste my time signing some pay chit for a whore?'

'It's OK,' Samantha said brightly. 'I'll tell the people at the agency to blacklist the Bassingers. I'll tell them you're a bunch of pathetic time-wasters who prefer boys.' She turned away.

'Hey! Come back. Don't you dare . . . '

Samantha began to descend the steps.

'I said, come back. Come back and stand on that star shape in the floor,' the voice demanded.

Samantha paused for a moment, then turned and stepped on to a five-pointed white marble star set close to the doors.

'Look towards the end of the porch and open the coat.'

Samantha tugged at silk tapes, drew her furs aside, and rested her hands on her hips to hold her coat open.

'Jesus,' the voice breathed. 'How much did Ronald pay for you?'

'I've no idea what the agency charges, Vincent, they just pass on my fee. And if I don't get my appointment card signed I won't — '

'Come up. Come right up.' The hissing intercom speaker crackled, then fell silent. A lock clicked.

When she pushed at the door it swung open and she stepped into the scented warmth of the foyer. Walking on her toes to prevent her heels tapping on the marble, she moved towards the lifts. Through the half-open door behind the reception area, she could see the uniformed back of the security man. He was reading a newspaper, his feet on a desk ringed by half-a-dozen monitor screens. Above the lift doors, illuminated numbers showed a compartment at the first floor and another at the seventh. Samantha climbed a flight of stairs and entered the lift. Seconds later she emerged on the tenth.

More wall lights were casting their diffused glow over honey-coloured marble. Panelled entrance doors, made from some dark wood and framed by wide architraves, faced one another across the shared landing. With only two apartments per floor, the accommodation was spacious. A voice rustled out of a grille beside one of the doors: 'Come inside and walk through to the lounge.'

Samantha stepped on to soft, grey-blue carpet that swept down a large hallway. Sounds of chanting and cheering were wafting through an open door at the far end. She walked towards it, stood in the opening, saw a large television set, the image on its screen split to display a football match, the ground floor entrance and the landing outside the flat. Grey winter light, seeping in through the distant floor-to-ceiling window, was too dim to relieve the gloom, but when she stepped forward and peered around the edge of the door, she could see him. His streaky blond hair was combed back over a massive head; his neck was short and thick, his shoulders powerful, his chest broad. His coarsely masculine features were in shadow, and deep-set eyes glittered at her out of the dark. He was sitting in a wheelchair, one huge hand on an armrest the other tucked beneath a red tartan rug that covered his legs. Samantha guessed it was clutching a gun.

'Lights,' he snapped. 'Put the lights on.' He nodded towards a switch by the door.

Samantha did as he asked, then turned to face him. The wheelchair did nothing to diminish his brutish presence. Illuminated, he seemed even more intimidating. And it was more than sheer physical size: it was the chilling remoteness of the eyes that were holding her in an unblinking stare.

'What did you say your name was?' His deep voice was rough and unrefined, a London voice from the East End.

'Suki.'

'I'm not a shirt lifter, Suki.' He nodded at the tartan blanket. 'Had my style cramped. There's no sensation, no feeling, from the waist down.'

Samantha nodded. His disability wasn't on the files. It must be pretty recent. 'Can't they do anything?' she asked.

'They keep trying. I keep paying their bills. Take the coat off.'

'I'm freezing,' Samantha said. 'Can you wait until I get warm?' Pushing her furs aside, she rested her hands on her hips and let him see her short black dress.

A wet tongue glided over fleshy lips and left them glistening. His hungry eyes rose, slowly, from her shoes to the swell of hips beneath pleated silk, to her breasts shaping black velvet, then up to the dense crown of black hair that fell in a neat fringe across her brow. When his eyes settled on hers she held them, challenging him. He scowled and his mouth hardened. He wasn't accustomed to being challenged. 'You said you wanted something signing.'

She let the coat fall back over her dress

while she fumbled inside her bag. When she found the Elegant Escorts card, she held it out and smiled.

'Drop the bag on the floor and come over here.' Blue veins writhed over the back of the hand that beckoned her towards him. Heavy gold rings, one decorated with a sovereign, were clustered on its thick fingers.

Samantha laid her bag on the carpet and walked over.

'Closer,' he growled. 'Come closer.'

When her knees were almost touching the wheel of his chair he grabbed her wrist and drew her down until her face was close to his. Suddenly his other hand was around her throat and moist fingers were choking her. The rug had slipped, exposing the knurled grip and chambers of a revolver.

Shaking her head, he snarled, 'Do you know who I am?'

'Vincent,' Samantha gasped. 'Vincent Bassinger. That's what it says on the card.'

He gave her cheek a vicious slap. 'Show respect.' He slapped her cheek again. 'Show some fucking respect. It's Mister Bassinger to you.' He was still squeezing her throat, holding her in a vice-like grip.

'Mr Bassinger,' Samantha wheezed. 'I'm sorry, Mr Bassinger.'

He moved his huge hands over her body,

fondling her, then slid them under her skirt and began to caress her thighs. Samantha wrapped a fur-covered arm around his head, pressed his face against her, just beneath her breasts and stroked his cheek.

'Ronnie's a sadistic bastard,' he moaned. 'He knew what you'd do to me. It's torture. Sheer fucking torture.' Groping hands made their way up her legs, then his fingers began to knead her buttocks while his thumbs stroked her stomach, pressing deep into the flesh.

'God,' he moaned. 'What I'd give to . . . ' His hands slid up to her waist and he began to fumble with her knickers, tugging at the silk.

Her arm was still cradling his head, holding his face against her body; her fingers were still caressing his cheek. Moving slowly, she slid her free hand inside the pocket of her coat, withdrew the gun, then stabbed its long barrel into his neck, just beneath his ear. 'Don't move,' she whispered huskily. 'Just keep your hands perfectly still.'

'What the . . . ' He bent his head back slowly. Shocked eyes looked up at her through the folds of her coat.

'I said, don't move. And keep your hands on my hips. Do anything to make me nervous and you're dead.' When she took her arm from around his head he began to slide his hands down her thighs. She forced the muzzle of the gun against his throat. He gasped at the pain. 'Keep your hands still,' she snapped. 'Move them again and I'll kill you.' After waiting a few seconds, she reached forward, snatched the revolver from his lap and tossed it across the room.

Malevolent eyes stared up at her. 'Who are you?'

'Suki,' she said. 'From Elegant Escorts. Just a whore for you to slap around.' She forced his head back with the muzzle of the gun and made her husky voice threatening. 'Listen to me carefully, Bassinger. When I say, 'Do it,' I want you to take your hands from under my dress and get them behind the back of the chair. I want you to do it slowly. Don't make me nervous.' Parting her feet to steady herself, she said, 'OK; do it now.'

She kept her eyes locked on his. When she felt his hands slide from her knees, she began to drag the muzzle of the gun beneath his ear while she edged round to the back of the chair. He suddenly lunged forward. She stabbed the gun into his scalp. 'Move and you're dead.' She screamed the words at him as blood began to ooze through his hair and trickle across his cheek. She glanced down. His arms were dangling beside the wheels of the chair. Grinding the muzzle of the automatic into the bleeding wound, she hissed, 'Put your hands behind the chair, Bassinger. If you don't do as you're told, you'll be numb all over.'

He swung his arms around the backrest. 'Higher,' she snapped. 'Get your hands higher, and put the palms together.'

'I'm not a fucking contortionist,' he snarled. 'I can't get them any — '

Samantha rammed the gun into the wound and yelled, 'Higher,' then groped in her coat pocket for handcuffs while he made a futile attempt to raise his arms. Deftly hooking bright metal over a wrist, she pressed the ratchet home, then swiftly captured the other before he could snatch it away.

She moved round to face him. He was glowering up at her, his body hunched forward.

'Who are you?' he snarled. 'Who the fuck are you?'

'A present from your brother,' she said sweetly.

'You're not police,' he muttered. 'They wouldn't dare operate like this. Who are you? Who's sent you?'

Ignoring him, she removed her coat and tossed it over the back of a big white-leather armchair. She found a fresh pair of latex gloves in her bag and drew them on, then picked up his gun: it was a revolver with a short barrel, small, designed for easy concealment. Her crimson lips curved into a mocking smile. 'Boys' toys,' she said. 'You couldn't hit a barn door at ten feet with this thing. It wouldn't stop a chicken.'

'There're a dozen notches on the butt,' he growled. 'And they weren't chickens.' His eyes were burning into her. 'I'll do a deal with you, Suki. Just walk away and call a number I give you, and I'll make sure the family forgets the whole thing. No pain, no retribution.'

Laughing softly, Samantha headed off across springy carpet, striding past the back of a white sofa as she moved towards the far end of the room. On her way she slid his gun on to a dining table made from some pale wood with black inlays, then felt the chill of colder air as she approached the huge window. She couldn't be seen. The nearest properties were more than a mile away, beyond a tree-covered hillside that fell steeply towards distant railway tracks, a road and a canal, all grey and misty in the dismal afternoon. She rested her forehead against the cold glass; felt its faint vibrations as she looked down. Height made the parking area seem no bigger than a tablecloth, but the rear ends of the Rolls Royce and the other luxury cars parked behind the building were visible.

Turning, she glanced around the large room. Its ceiling was a little too low for the dozen or so paintings of horses and greyhounds to be properly displayed. The Bassinger brothers were notorious for their contribution to horse and dog racing; a large bronze of a jockey, riding a galloping horse, was resplendent on a long sideboard that matched the dining table.

She studied the man in the wheelchair. Arms wrapped around the backrest, unable to turn his head far enough to see her, he sat hunched towards the flickering television screen. His dark-blue shirt was open at the neck, its sleeves rolled up to expose massive forearms that were pale and hairless. Incontinence pads were making his biscuit-coloured trousers bulge beneath a belted waist.

Deciding to allow time for his fear and anger to fester, she headed back to the hall and began to wander around. She found a big master bedroom with an en-suite bathroom; a lavish granite and mahogany kitchen, a second single bedroom that was being used for storage, and another bathroom. All of the furniture was plain, modern and high quality; the place was clean and uncluttered. Apart from bathrooms and the kitchen, the same grey-blue carpet flowed through the entire apartment and all of the walls were painted a paler shade of greyish-blue. The effect was restful, elegant and boring.

Something was missing. Samantha tried to recall the plans the agent had shown her. It was a bedroom: a double bedroom. She emerged from the kitchen and walked down the hall towards the entrance, examining the walls and floor as she went. The carpet was plain, and wear patterns showed as a barely perceptible change in its colour outside every door. Halfway down the hall, on her right, were faint signs of wear but no door. She crossed over and took a closer look. Dado rail and skirtings had been joined and extended across what had been an opening. The work had been skilfully done, the wall redecorated, and the carpet relaid, but she could tell there had been a door there.

Walking on, she opened a cupboard near the entrance. A raincoat and heavy winter coats took up most of a rail that stretched across it, and a half life-size bronze of a naked woman, arms curving languorously over her head, occupied what space remained. Parting the coats, she saw a small suitcase and three black-leather attaché cases stacked against the wall. They were locked. She grabbed one and headed for the kitchen.

'Hey, Suki . . . Suki.' Vincent Bassinger called from the sitting room. 'I need tablets, Suki.'

Samantha dropped the briefcase and went through. 'What tablets?'

'For the pain up my spine and across my shoulders. Every two hours. They're in a drawer in the kitchen. Zomax: I take three.'

She smiled. The last things she wanted to give him were tablets to control pain. 'Two minutes,' she said. 'Just give me two minutes,' then headed back to the hall, picked up the case and went into the kitchen.

Tugging open drawers until she found the cutlery, she took out a pair of cook's scissors and used one of the blades to prize up the catches on the case. An unpleasant odour of ink and grime wafted up when she lifted the lid. It was tightly packed with used twenty-pound notes in thousand-pound bundles, held together by brown paper bands stamped Barclays, Lloyds and Westminster. The Bassingers spread their deposits around. She counted the piles. The case held more than three hundred thousand pounds.

A buzzer sounded in the hall. Samantha slammed down the lid, grabbed her gun and returned to the sitting room. One of the frames on the split television screen was showing a blonde woman, wearing a nurse's uniform and carrying a paper package and black leather bag. She was waiting at the main entrance.

Samantha glanced at Vincent Bassinger. 'How do I talk to her?'

'Piss off.' A mocking laugh rustled in his throat.

She rammed the muzzle of the gun against his temple. He closed his eyes, wincing at the pain. 'How do I talk to her?'

'You crazy bitch. The intercom's by the door.'

Striding over, she saw a brass plate with a grille and key pad, set low to accommodate a wheelchair user. The buzzing sounded again. She pressed a key marked 'talk', and said, 'Yes?'

'Nurse Adams, visiting Mr Bassinger.'

Samantha glanced towards the wheelchair and gestured with the gun as she mouthed silently, 'Make a sound, and you're dead.' Then she called out, 'I'm Mr Bassinger's sister-in-law. We've come to collect him for a family party.'

'Would you like me to come up and — '

'It's OK,' Samantha said. 'He's with his brother in the bathroom. He's almost finished getting him ready. We want to get away, to miss the rush-hour traffic.'

'You'll need pads. I've brought a fresh

supply. Should I bring them up?'

'Got some,' Samantha said cheerfully. 'We should have phoned you to save you making the call, but it was a spur of the moment thing.'

'You'll not forget his medication?' The nurse seemed uneasy and concerned.

'He won't let us forget,' Samantha laughed. 'We've gathered it all together.'

'Will Mr Bassinger be away long?'

'Two, maybe three days. We've got the agency's number. We'll let you know when he's coming back.'

'Thanks,' the nurse said. There was still a note of doubt in her voice. Samantha wondered if she'd bought the story about the family visit. 'I'll leave you to it then,' the nurse went on. 'Tell Mr Bassinger I hope he has a pleasant time.'

'Will do.' Samantha lifted her finger off the button and glanced at the TV screen. The nurse descended the steps, then turned and headed for the parking bays at the rear. There was a movement in the frame displaying the landing outside the flat. A plump middle-aged woman, very elegantly dressed, stepped into the lift and its doors slid shut. Samantha went over to the big window and peered down. Seconds later, the nurse came into view, her blonde hair a moving speck of brightness in the gloom. She walked to a red Renault Clio, tossed her bag and the parcel into the back, then climbed behind the wheel. After watching her drive out of the yard, Samantha went and sat on the arm of the white-leather chair, facing Vincent Bassinger. She crossed her legs, allowed her pleated silk skirt to ride up her thighs, and gave him her sweetest smile.

'Prick-teasing bitch,' he growled. 'Eighteen months ago I'd have made you fucking well squeal.'

'Not any more, Binky.'

'Binky! How do you know — '

'I know everything about you, Binky.'

'No one knows what my wife called me when we were in the sack together.'

'Was she moaning, 'Binky! Binky!' when you broke her neck, Bassinger?'

'She was a slag. She was screwing one of Stanley's minders: a handsome bastard called Raines. She — '

'You get off on that, don't you, Bassinger: breaking women's necks. Kitty Flannagan, Mary Summers, Susan Preece. Little girls, too. Little girls like Emma Preece.'

'She saw me. She saw me killing her mother. I had to get rid of her. If the cops had nailed me for that, I'd still be inside.'

'She was only four, for God's sake. You

chased her all over the house. The kid was so terrified she left a trail to the cupboard where she was hiding.'

'I had to,' Vincent Bassinger snarled. 'I couldn't let some tart's little bastard send me down.' He lowered his gaze to Samantha's legs and thighs. Lust began to temper the angry loathing that distorted his craggy features. 'What do you want?' he grated. 'Is it money? Revenge? For Christ's sake, just say what you want.'

'Information,' she said. 'Tell me things I need to know, and I'll leave you in peace.' She waved the gun at him. 'If I think you're lying, if I think you're keeping something back, I'll kill you.'

'What information?' He wasn't sneering now.

'Where's Janos Tyminski?'

'Dead. Don't you read the papers? The bastard's dead.'

'Star witness when they tried your brothers and all their hangers on, the man who made sure Ronald's going to spend the rest of his life inside, and a month after the trial he dies in a car accident — I don't believe it,' Samantha said, and smiled across at him. He seemed perplexed by her; unsure of himself. It was probably the first time in his life that he'd felt perplexed and unsure. He glowered at her venomously while the crowd cheered and chanted on the television. The match was drawing to a close.

'The police never paid your brothers a call after Tyminski's death. That means they knew what had happened to him.'

'Course they knew what had happened to him,' he sneered. 'The bastard had an accident.'

'A month after he'd sent Ronald down, and they didn't come looking for the Bassingers? He didn't die in an accident, Binky. Where is he? Ronald got life. You'd want a lot of retribution for that. Maybe you found someone to bribe, someone in the force who could tell you where he's been relocated, tell you what his new name is. Maybe you've killed him.'

'Tablets,' Vincent Bassinger moaned. 'My back hurts. Being hunched up like this is making it worse. Get me my tablets.' The macho swagger was oozing away. He was almost pleading with her.

'When you've told me what I want to know, I'll get your tablets.'

'Bitch,' he muttered under his breath, then lifted his gaze from her crossed legs to her face and said, 'We had someone at the funeral, one of the undertakers; small affair, only about a dozen mourners. He said they seemed genuine. And we bunged one of the crematorium workers to take a look through the window in the oven door. He said it was a man, about the right build, but the coffin lid collapsed around his face and by the time it had burned off there was nothing to recognize. We think he's dead.'

'What about his wife, Rachel? What's happened to her?'

Vincent Bassinger began a laugh that turned into a cough. 'Give me my tablets. For Christ's sake, give me my sodding tablets.'

'When you've told me what I want to know. 'Rachel Tyminski. Talk to me about her.'

'Austin was screwing her.'

'Austin?'

'Austin Bassinger: James's son. Rachel used to do the books in a little office at the back of the garage. While Tyminski was working on the cars, Austin used to get her down behind the desk. Tall, handsome lad our Austin. And he's got all the smarmy patter. Women can't resist it. Rachel couldn't get enough.' Vincent Bassinger laughed. 'Austin was a reckless young bugger. We kept telling him Tyminski would walk in and catch 'em at it, but he never did.'

'Is Austin still seeing Rachel?'

'Couldn't when he was arrested and held on remand. I think he tried to make contact when he was released after the trial, but as far as I know she wasn't having any. Husband dead: probably guilt. They're Catholics, and Catholics can be serious about guilt. I should know.' Samantha raised an eyebrow and he added, 'Bassingers were a big Catholic family. Mum practised to her dying day. My sister still does. Sons all lapsed.' He grinned mirthlessly. 'Complete load of bollocks.'

'Your back injury?' Samantha asked. 'How did that happen.'

'What's it to you?'

'Just curious.'

'I was visiting some London clubs with Crazy Carson and Alan Hinds, a couple of enforcers we used at the time — pushing the drugs in, collecting the protection, the usual stuff. A bunch of Somali bastards called the Boulder Road Boys had joined up with the Kingston Crew, they're Caribbeans, and they were waiting for us at a place in Brixton. They said we were invading their turf, got agitated and started shooting. They killed Crazy and put a couple of bullets into me, but Alan managed to drag me out.' His lips twisted in a chilling smile. 'Two days later Ronald had the tenement the Somali's were living in burned down. Killed the black bastards and most of their wives and kids. Then he sorted the Kingston Crew; a couple went back to

Jamaica, but we've got contracts out.'

'And you don't know where Rachel is?' Samantha asked.

'Why would I? Austin might have some idea, but he's probably lost touch.' He glowered at her for a few seconds, then said. 'Who the fuck are you? Why do you want to know all this?'

'Benjamin,' she said. 'I'm searching for Benjamin Hamilton. Rachel's his sister; Janos is his brother-in-law.'

'So?'

'Janos is missing, Benjamin's missing; Rachel seems hard to find. If you'd burn down a house full of Somalis and their wives and kids, God knows what you'd do to the Tyminski's after Janos sent your brother down for life.'

'I've told you,' he snarled. 'Tyminski's dead and Austin was fucking his wife's brains out. Why would we be interested in her or her kid brother?'

'Revenge, or to smoke Janos Tyminski out.'

'The bastard's dead,' Vincent spat. 'No one's going to smoke him out.' He glowered across at her. A presenter was commenting on the match against a background of singing and cheering. 'Please,' he moaned. 'Get me the tablets. Three; Zomax; they're in the kitchen, the drawer next to the fridge.'

'You've not told me anything, Binky. You're a useless time-waster. Tell me what I want to know, and I'll fetch your pills.'

He began to throw his shoulders around, flailing his arms up and down, trying to tug his wrists apart. 'Bitch!' he yelled. 'You fucking bitch. You'll regret this. You think you can trick your way in here and treat a Bassinger like shit? When the family gets you, you'll be meat on a slab. You can't imagine what they'll do to you. You'll beg to die.'

Rising to her feet, she stepped over to the chair and pressed the muzzle of the pistol against the side of his head. 'Keep quiet and sit still, or I'll kill you. All you've got to do is tell me what I want to know.'

'I'm a cripple, you stupid bitch. I just sit here. Twice a day a woman brings me a meal. Three times a day a nurse comes and cleans my arse. I'm like a bloody baby, sitting in my own piss and shit. I'm not the head of the family any more. No one asks me anything; no one tells me anything. Ronald runs things now, and he's inside.'

'When are you breaking him out?' It was an inspired stab in the dark.

Bassinger's eyes narrowed. 'Breaking him out? What do you know about breaking — ?'

'Austin told me,' she began to lie brazenly. 'We met in Manchester, then spent a weekend together in London.' She curved her lips in a smile. 'I can understand Rachel Tyminski's infatuation.'

'And what else did Austin tell you.'

'This and that. He knows Ronald's coming out; he knows it's soon, but he doesn't know when. Tell me, Binky; tell me when Ronald's coming out, and I'll get your pills.'

Vincent Bassinger closed his eyes and sagged forward, his wrists, secured behind the backrest, preventing him falling out of the chair. He'd never been treated with such total disrespect before. He felt humiliated and defeated. And the pain in his arms and back was becoming unbearable. He needed the tablets. Sighing, he mumbled, 'He's taking stuff to make him bleed when he shits. Stomach trouble. When the symptoms start to show, they'll have to ship him out to hospital. When that happens, James will get a call. Everything's lined up: cars, drivers, chopper. We're just waiting for the call.'

She gazed at him. The sports programme had ended and some giggling contestants were playing a word game. Even if he'd not told her everything he knew, she was pretty sure he wasn't going to give her any more information. The woman who provided his meals might be calling soon, and the tapes had to be snatched from the surveillance monitors in the security guard's office. She needed a diversion for that. She ought to leave now. 'Do I have to enter a code to operate the door locks?'

He looked up, his eyes brightening. He sensed his ordeal was coming to an end. 'Just turn the latch and slam the door when you go out. You operate the system to let people in.'

Samantha glanced around. The only thing she'd touched with her bare hands was the revolver she'd left on the table. She retrieved it, gathered up her coat, slid her gun into the pocket holster, and went through to the kitchen. After wiping his revolver with a soapy sponge she jammed it in the waste disposer, then closed the attaché case. When she forced the damaged catches home, one of them held. She carried the case into the hall, left it with her coat by the door, then kicked off her shoes and returned to the sitting room.

Kneeling beside Vincent Bassinger, she unbuckled his belt, slid it from around his waist, and used it to strap his ankles to the footrests. She pulled the chair backwards, towards the door. He probably weighed around two-hundred-and-fifty pounds, but she could move him easily, especially if she pressed down on the handles to balance his weight over the back wheels.

'Where are you taking me,' he moaned.

'Tablets: I need tablets.'

Samantha's back was against the wall. Through the window at far end of the long room she could see lights beginning to gleam across the darkening city. From the television came the sound of clapping; the quiz master was handing out a prize. 'You won't need your tablets any more, Binky.' She heaved herself off the wall and began to propel the chair. 'You're going on a ride to the land of the dead.'

He began to yell and thrash around, but she was running fast now and his movements hardly rocked the speeding chair. She kept pushing until the footrest hit the glass and shattered it, then let the chair go as his weight tipped it forward. An icy wind ruffled her hair and lifted her skirt as she stood on the edge of the floor slab and looked down. Metal crumpled under his weight when his head smashed into the roof of the Rolls Royce. The thud of the impact and the crash of splintering glass were deafening. She had her diversion.

Dashing back to the hall, she pulled on her coat, slid her shoes into its pockets, picked up the attaché case, and stepped out on to the landing. She closed the flat door behind her, made sure it had locked, then pushed through a door beside the lift and began to run down the emergency stairs, swift and silent in her stocking-covered feet.

The foyer was deserted. Cold air was wafting in through an open door to a passage that connected with the rear yard. The guard's brightly-lit office was empty. Samantha moved around the end of the reception desk and stepped inside. On one of the monitors she could see the guard standing, slack-jawed, amongst splintered glass, staring at the body and the mangled remains of a wheelchair embedded in the roof of the car.

Individual video recorders were stacked under the monitors. She ejected all six tapes and bundled them under her coat. Out in the foyer, lift doors were opening and she could hear voices and footsteps on the stairs. She closed the security room door with her foot, leaned against it, and watched the monitor screens. Seconds later, about half-a-dozen excited residents joined the guard around the car. Some of them were looking up and pointing. There was no sound on the system, but she could see a bald-headed man's mouth shaping the words, 'My car. Look at my car. Look what the crazy bugger's done to my car.'

Samantha eased the door open and peered out into the foyer. It was deserted again. Clutching the videotapes and the attaché case, she ran to the entrance, tugged open one of the doors and stepped out into the dusk. She made her way to the road over the wet grass. It was less painful to her stocking-covered feet, and it kept her away from pools of light cast by the lamps along the driveway. When she neared the trees that lined the boundary, she slid her feet into her shoes, stepped on to the tarmac, and walked the final fifty yards to the gatehouse.

Three minutes later she was nosing the Ferrari out of the side street and merging with the traffic on Kirkstall Road. It was almost four-thirty. She had to find the motorway, then head westwards over the Pennines for her meeting with the mother of the missing child.

3

Paula Hamilton woke with a start and stared into the shadows. How long had she been asleep? She remembered coming up to Benjamin's room. She must have stretched out on his bed and dozed off. Clicking on the lamp, she tried to read the time on his Mickey Mouse clock. Ten past seven. It was late. She swung her legs to the floor and felt for her shoes. The woman Lawrence Cosgrave was sending wouldn't come now. She stood up. The tiny candles were guttering. She'd lit candles every evening since Benjamin had disappeared; set them on either side of the chipped plaster statue of Our Lady of Fatima. She'd had the statue since she was a little girl: a first Holy Communion present from her gran. Benjamin's photograph was leaning against it, his spectacles awry, grinning out at her. Where was he now? The scream started to build up inside her. She tried to close down her mind, to think about trivial things. When she allowed herself to wonder where he was or what was happening to him, an unimaginable frenzy of fear and dread rose up inside her. She wanted to run into the street and let out an endless howl of pain.

Tablets: she'd better take her tablets. She'd be climbing up the wall if she didn't. Heading out on to the landing she switched on the light and began to edge her way down the steep stairs. She could hear the Muslim family in the house next door reciting their prayers, Arabic words rolling off the father's tongue. His voice was the loudest. The mother and the children seemed to follow, creating a fainter drone of incomprehensible sounds.

Two quick knocks startled her. The police! Perhaps they had news of Benjamin. She hurried down the last few steps, turned the latch and dragged open the door.

'Mrs Hamilton? Mrs Paula Hamilton?'

'Yes, I'm Paula — '

'I'm Georgina Grey.'

Paula's hand darted to her throat. She felt a sudden, inexplicable stab of fear. The woman had a low husky voice, a heavy-smoker's voice, and she looked overweight and shapeless in the unbelted raincoat. Large tinted glasses hid her eyes, and a yellow silk headscarf completely covered her hair.

'I think you're expecting me,' the husky voice said softly. 'May I come in. I'd like to get off the street.'

'Sorry,' Paula faltered, 'You startled me. When it got late I thought you weren't coming. I thought it was the police calling.' She stood aside. Samantha brushed past her and stepped into the narrow hallway.

'Let me take your coat.'

Samantha pulled off her scarf, removed the glasses and shoved them into a pocket, then unbuttoned the coat and peeled it off. Paula took it. It was light, despite the layers of quilted padding. Stunned, she hung it over the newel post at the foot of the stairs. The woman who called herself Georgina Grey was transformed. Slender now, her body was shapely in an elegant black dress, her black hair gleaming, her lips a vivid red. And the eyes, those huge green eyes, so luminous. The Grey woman was smiling at her. Beginning to feel foolish, she faltered, 'That's a beautiful dress.'

Samantha allowed her smile to widen and held Paula's hand for a moment. 'You have things to tell me. Are we alone?'

Paula Hamilton nodded. 'I'm sorry,' she said, completely flustered now. 'Come into the sitting room.' She led Samantha into a room that seemed scarcely big enough to contain the small two-seater sofa and armchair that were the only furniture. Gesturing towards the chair, she said, 'Sit down,' then knelt in front of the gas fire and flicked the igniter. Escaping gas plopped and flames began to redden the clays. *Tell her everything*, Lawrence Cosgrave had said in his letter. She'd had nothing to eat all day, she'd not taken her tablets; she didn't feel up to raking over the past, revealing the family's darkest secrets to a stranger. Rising from her knees, she looked down at the elegant young woman reclining in the chair. 'Can I get you something to eat?'

'That would be kind,' Samantha said. She'd not bothered with a meal; just left the car in the hotel car park, disguised herself in the padded coat, and taken a taxi to the end of the street.

'I've not much in. I've not been bothering. I . . . ' The young woman's huge green eyes were holding hers. She suddenly wanted to cry. 'Would a poached egg be all right? Poached egg on toast, and a cup of tea?'

Samantha smiled. 'Poached egg would be fine. Shall I come and make the tea?' She followed Paula Hamilton into a tiny kitchen that contained a gas cooker next to a sink unit, a table with a yellow plastic top, and a yellow and white plywood dresser. A fridge was humming in a recess that had once been a pantry. Everything was spotlessly clean. The woman's lips were trembling. She was close to tears. Samantha began to chatter to distract her, to calm her, so she'd be coherent when she began to tell her story. 'I couldn't poach an egg,' she said. 'And I'd probably burn the toast.'

'You don't do much cooking, then?'

Samantha laughed softly. 'I don't cook, I don't dust or clean, I don't wash or iron clothes. I have a man who does those things for me.'

Mrs Hamilton turned and looked at her. 'Your husband?' she asked. Then added hastily, 'Your partner?' Everybody had a partner these days. It used to be called living in sin, living over the brush. But she couldn't talk. Not any more. She'd had the pride knocked out of her.

'Just a friend,' Samantha said. 'He has a boyfriend.' She'd managed to distract Paula Hamilton; her face was wrinkled in a kind of puzzled disapproval now.

Paula studied the young woman leaning against the dresser. Her scarlet lips were shaped in a smile. It was a generous smile that invited confidences.

'I've shocked you, haven't I?' Samantha murmured huskily, and began to laugh.

Paula felt her lips tugging into a smile. It was the first time she'd smiled since . . . Suddenly her face crumpled and tears began to fall. Lifting the hem of her apron, she covered her face and began to sob. She felt the woman's arms enfolding her. They were soft and warm and she was holding her like her mother used to when she was a child, her cheek nestling against hers. And there was a fragrance about her; some subdued, elusive perfume.

'Everything's going to be fine, Paula,' Samantha murmured, and held her tighter.

'It's not going to be fine,' Paula sobbed. It's been three days. He's been gone too long. The police have lost hope. I can tell.'

Samantha gripped her by the shoulders. 'Look at me,' she insisted. The woman lifted her tear-streaked face. 'I'm going to find him for you, Paula. No matter what it takes, no matter what has to be done, I'm going to bring him home. Don't ever doubt that.'

* * *

High Gables had been James Bassinger's home for more than ten years, ever since he'd abandoned London to the immigrant criminal fraternity. Stockbroker's Tudor, on Baslow Road, heading west out of Sheffield. Isolated, exclusive, but not too remote, Beryl had transformed it. She had taste. She only bought the best. Quality carpets, curtains, furniture: no tat. She had style and flair. Homemaking was what she was good at: that and looking after him and the boys. Pity the expensive frocks couldn't hide her fat arse and sagging tits. But you can't have everything. Christ, after that devious bastard Tyminski had started blabbing he was lucky to have kept what he had and stayed on the outside.

Most of the Bassinger men had responded to his call. They were here now, waiting for him to tell them what it was all about: Henry and his three sons, Morris with his two boys, Stanley with his eldest. Ronnie's boy, here without his father, looked old beyond his years. He watched Beryl slide a silver tray piled with beef sandwiches next to the platter of ham and chicken rolls. She'd laid out slabs of fruitcake for Henry, Madeira cake for Morris. She remembered these things, like a good hostess should. She went back to the kitchen, returned with a cruet and bowls of horseradish sauce. After arranging it all on the low table between the two sofas, she wedged the bottles of beer deeper into the ice-filled plastic box, then turned and looked at him. 'Whisky, fags and glasses on the sideboard: that OK for you, love?'

'Perfect. Just like you, babe. Perfect.'

Laughing, she headed back to the kitchen

and closed the door on the low drone of male conversation. The talk stopped. Ten pairs of eyes turned towards James Bassinger.

'Got some bad news,' he said, unable to keep the shake out of his voice. 'Some seriously bad news. Vincent was murdered this afternoon, around four o'clock.' He watched their faces relax with shock, then harden with outrage. 'Security man at Forest Heights phoned me before he phoned the police. When Vince went into the apartment, I gave the security man a key and asked him to contact me if he had any worries about him.'

'How was he killed?'

'Some bitch pushed him in his chair through that big window. Fell ten floors.'

'A woman? How do you know it was a woman?' Morris asked.

'Videotape. When the security man went back to his office after checking the commotion outside he saw the tapes had been pulled from the monitors, so he went up to the flat to see if a tape had been running in Vince's security system. He found one, in a recorder under the telly. The murdering bitch probably thought it was part of the set and ignored it. I arranged for Alan to meet him at a motorway service station and collect it; give him a grand for his trouble and tell him to keep his mouth shut.'

'Flat's full of Ronnie's stuff,' Henry said. 'Those sequestering government bastards could get their hands on it.'

'Crawling with cops now,' James said. 'Got to leave it. The blokes who sealed up the doorway did a good job. We'll just have to sweat it out and hope they don't find anything. The bitch who murdered Vince knew it was there, though.' He rose to his feet and made for the sideboard. 'Get a drink. All of you get a drink. You'll need one when I start the video.' He brought glasses over and handed them round, poured out generous measures of scotch, then handed bottles of Becks to the beer drinkers. He switched on the set. 'I'm warning you, this is painful.' The screen became blurred as he wound back the tape. 'In fact,' he said, 'I still can't bloody-well believe it.' He pressed the 'play' button, then returned to his seat.

Images, stored on the time-lapse recording, jerked from frame to frame and, every few seconds, switched between cameras in the hall and sitting room. They watched a black-haired woman, wrapped in furs, walk down the hall, then the recording flicked to her standing in a doorway before crossing over to Vincent in his wheelchair. After another look at the empty hallway, the system switched back to the sitting room. She was holding Vincent against her now and his hands were moving under her clothes. When she drew a gun from her pocket and stabbed it into his neck the collective intake of breath was audible.

'Look at the size of the piece,' somebody muttered. 'Gun's almost as big as she is.'

'Large bore Beretta,' Stanley said. 'Or maybe an American army Colt. Mick Manson, that hit man we've used, always carries one. It'd stop a truck.'

It was like viewing an old silent film. Deep male voices muttered curses when they saw the woman prod the back of Vincent's head with the gun; there was a rumble of outraged protest when she secured his hands behind the chair. 'She's humiliating him,' James moaned. 'This is Vince we're looking at. Our brother Vince. He's being pistol whipped by a bloody tart. We shouldn't have let him live alone. We should have — '

'She's found the cash,' Morris interrupted. The equipment had switched to the hall. They watched the woman, skirt swirling, move past the camera carrying an attaché case, then Vincent appeared on the screen again. He was leaning forward, tugging at the restraints on his wrists, making a futile attempt to lift his arms over the back of the chair.

'Bitch!' James was almost sobbing with rage. 'Look how the bitch is treating him. She's treating Vince like a piece of shit!'

They watched her come back through the doorway, cross over to a chair and sit on the arm, facing Vincent. She was closer to the camera now, her face in profile.

'Looks a bit like Stella, Alan Willard's wife,' Morris muttered.

'Stella's gorgeous, but not that bloody gorgeous,' James said. 'And she wouldn't know what to do with a gun. Trouble is, the tape's old and the vid's piss poor. Vincent always was a tight sod. If he'd replaced the gear with something more up-to-date, if he'd just remembered to change the tape now and then, we'd have a clearer picture.'

They fell silent, watched as the scene flicked between the empty hall and the woman talking to their brother. They saw her remove his belt, strap his ankles, then take hold of the wheelchair and pull it back to the wall. Suddenly she lurched off, her image jerking across the screen in great leaps as she propelled a writhing Vincent down the room.

'Vincent! God in heaven, Vincent!' a voice moaned. 'Why? Why would some crazy tart want to kill Vincent?'

'Look, she's taking one of the cases,' Stanley announced. 'Maybe it was the cash.

Maybe she knew about the cash.'

'No one knew about the cash except us,' James growled. 'And why didn't she take the other cases? She could have lifted more than a million quid.'

Henry gulped at his drink. 'What was she doing looking at the wall? Maybe she's involved with the guys who bricked it up, came to see what she could find and left with what she could carry.'

James switched off the set and wiped his eyes. Trying to sound jovial to hide the shake in his voice, he said, 'Get some of these sandwiches eaten, or we'll upset Beryl. Picking up the whisky bottle, he walked around, replenishing glasses, then yelled, 'Beryl . . . More beer. Bring us some more beer from the fridge, love.'

'The dirty little whore's got to be found,' Morris said. 'And we want her alive. We need to know who she's working for and why she was turning Vincent's place over.'

'If we knew what they were saying on the video, we might have some idea.' Stanley offered.

Beryl came in with a dozen chilled bottles on a tray, bent over and tried to find a place for them on the cluttered table. James sighed. The red satin was stretched tight across his wife's hips and backside. He'd always warned her he wouldn't stay married to a fat bird, but she just laughed. She thought he was joking.

'Are you all staying the night?' Beryl asked. She glanced around at the shaking heads. 'You'd better make this the last then. I'll brew up some coffee.' She gathered empty bottles on to the tray, then strutted out her red high-heeled shoes.

Morris uncapped a bottle. 'I've got a deaf and dumb bloke working for me in one of my heel and key booths. Ugly bastard. Looks like Quasimodo. Works in a back room so he can't scare the punters. Got a shoe fetish. Manager keeps finding him fondling the women's shoes.'

'A purve and an ugly bastard,' Henry muttered. There was some muted laughter. James didn't even smile.

'He can lip read,' Morris went on. 'I could get him to take a look at the video and write down what they're saying.'

'We've got to circulate pictures of the woman,' James said. 'Amongst people we can trust, people who get around and keep their eyes open. We could say there's ten grand in it if they lead us to the woman.'

'Pictures aren't clear enough,' Stanley said. He glanced at his son. 'If that studio technician you used to knock about with had a look at this, could he enhance the pictures?

Sharpen them up a bit? Make us some paper copies?' He glanced around at his brothers. 'Shall we say fifty copies?'

'Better make it a hundred,' James said. 'The crazy bitch has got to be found. She's got to be taught respect. Our business is built on respect. Respect through fear. You've got to keep the opposition scared shitless. If it gets out that some little tart's humiliated and murdered a Bassinger . . . ' His voice began to break up. He was close to tears again. Sniffing, he pulled himself together. 'She's got to be broken. I want to hear the bitch begging to die. And when we've finished, we'll dump her where the cops can find her so word can get around about what we did to her before we killed her. We've got to keep the crazy fuckers out there scared shitless.'

'Where's Austin?' Henry asked. 'I thought he'd be here.' He reached for another sandwich. Decent bread, thick slice of beef: Beryl knew how to lay on a spread. And she still looked good. Very sexy in the red satin dress. James was a lucky bugger.

'He's in Carlisle, giving Rachel Tyminski a daily seeing-to.'

'Has he found out anything?'

'Not yet,' James muttered. 'But the randy little devil's working hard at it.' He paused for the laughter. 'Either she really does believe she's a widow, or she's very clever, and Austin doesn't think she's clever.'

Henry chewed and swallowed. 'What about the kid?'

'Same,' James said. 'She knows nothing or she's very smart.'

'We paid that cop ten grand,' Stanley muttered. 'No signs of anyone living at the relocation address, and the neighbours said they'd not seen anybody. House had been sold, but no one was living there.'

'Maybe the cop conned ten grand out of us.' Morris said. 'Maybe Tyminski did get killed, and the cop was stringing us along.'

'Then why did his wife take the job in Carlisle, twenty miles from the house?'

James gave them all a tired glance. 'She told Austin she wanted to get away from Stockport. Make a fresh start where she wasn't known, somewhere he could visit without people talking.'

'You don't think this black-haired piece has anything to do with it, do you?' Henry asked.

'Do with what?'

'With Tyminski, or his wife, or the boy going missing: what's his name?'

'Benjamin,' Stanley said. 'The boy's called Benjamin. They were banging on about it on the telly last night.'

'But why harass Vincent?' James demanded.

'Why should she treat him like a piece of shit for an hour, then tip him out of a tenth-floor window? What can that have to do with a missing kid?'

'Who put Ronnie inside?' Morris asked.

'Tyminski, the bastard.' James snarled.

'And your Austin's fucking his widow, if she is a widow. And her kid-brother's gone missing. It could be connected. It seems crazy, but what else is there?'

'Money,' James insisted. 'She lifted three-hundred grand. The bastards who bricked up the room must have told her some of Ronnie's stuff's hidden there. She knew Vincent was in a wheelchair and she tricked her way in. Maybe she pretended to be a tart; we all watched her letting him have a feel. She killed him to get rid of a witness. Some dames can do more than powder their noses.'

'But she left three cases of cash behind.'

'She got scared. She didn't want to be seen with so many. She'd lifted three-hundred grand and wanted to call it a day.'

Morris shrugged. 'Maybe you're right, but it wouldn't do any harm to keep an eye on Tyminski's mother-in-law's house for a couple of days. What's her name?' He clicked his fingers, trying to remember. 'Paula: Paula Hamilton. Lives in a two-up and two-down in Atherton Road, a couple of streets from the place Tyminski used for a garage.'

James turned the corners of his mouth down. He was emotionally drained. Watching the video had done things to him. He wanted to be alone, not listening to Morris's stupid ideas.

'We ought to cover it,' Morris urged. 'At least until Ronnie gets out and takes control.' He glanced around at his brothers, looking for support. Stanley and Henry were nodding.

James scowled. Until Ronnie was sprung, age gave him seniority; put him in charge. 'Ronnie's not out yet,' he growled. 'And until he is, I make the decisions.'

'No one has a problem with that, James. But just for a night, or maybe a night and a day, put someone in the street to watch the house; see who comes and goes. It can't do any harm, and we can't do anything about the woman until the dummy's watched the tape and we've got some photo's to hand around.' He glanced at his sons. 'You could get there in the early hours, sit it out until dawn, then Mark and Lewis could take over tomorrow.'

The tall, fair-haired young men nodded obediently. Morris turned to James. 'How about it? At least we'll be able to tell Ronnie we covered every angle.'

Cover every angle. James realized it made sense. That's what Vincent would have done before those Somali bastards crippled him, before this crazy bitch murdered him. It's what Ronnie would have done before Tyminski put him inside. 'You're right,' he conceded. 'It can't do any harm. Paula Hamilton never saw your boys, Morris, but she could have seen Mark. He used to keep Austin company when he delivered vans and cars to Tyminski. She might recognize him and we don't want to put her on her guard, especially with the plod visiting the house because of the boy.' He glanced across at Stanley's son, Ian. He was sitting next to his father, their broad shoulders almost spanning the sofa. 'Tomorrow Ian can go with Lewis.' Sliding his glass on to the table, he called, 'Beryl, where's the coffee?'

Morris turned and looked at Ronald's son. 'When's your dad likely to be taken to hospital?'

'When Mum visited last week he told her he'd started passing blood. We had to get the screw to take another pack of tablets in before we got a result. Depends how the prison doctor reacts, but he'll have to protect himself. He daren't let Dad pass blood for long before sending him for an x-ray. I'd guess it's only a matter of days before the screw makes the call.'

James held up the whisky bottle. 'More anybody?' There were no takers, so he splashed a good measure into his own glass. 'How much is this screw costing us?'

Morris laughed. 'Sod all. He used to be a care worker in a home for difficult kids and he's got a thing about adolescent boys. A couple of blokes who spent time in care are working for us in the Manchester clubs. They're willing to make complaints and give evidence if we say the word, and they can find us a dozen others. The screw's seriously scared. He'll do anything.'

James lifted his huge hands and looked around the gathering. 'Respect, brothers. We've built a business on respect, and the only way to get respect is to terrify the bastards.' He stared grimly from face to face, then turned towards the door and yelled, 'Beryl! Where's that coffee?'

* * *

Paula Hamilton felt her eyes closing. The gas fire was making the tiny room uncomfortably warm and the diazepam tablets she'd taken to help her cope with her grief and fear, to help her blur the edges of her shame so she could disclose the family secrets, were making her drowsy.

Samantha leaned forward in her chair, surprised by Paula's revelation, 'Benjamin isn't your child?'

Paula shook her head. She couldn't meet the young woman's gaze: such unusual eyes; they seemed to harrow her very soul. 'He's Rachel's. She'd just finished her A levels. She went to work in Lawrence Cosgrave's constituency office. Three months later, she was pregnant.'

'Cosgrave's the father? The Prime Minister is the father?'

Paula nodded and looked down at her hands. It was so shaming, having to reveal things like this about your own daughter. 'He wasn't the Prime Minister then; he was a shadow something or other. Father Ryan got Rachel the job. Mrs Cosgrave's a Catholic: on parish committees for this, committees for that. She told him her husband needed someone for secretarial work in the run-up to the election, and he mentioned Rachel. She'd got decent A level grades and she wanted a holiday job while she waited to take a place at Durham University. Then she went and got herself in trouble.'

'Surely it was Cosgrave who got Rachel into trouble?' Samantha suggested gently.

'Maybe you're right,' Paula muttered. 'But

she could have said no. She'd been brought up in a decent Catholic home. She could have said no.'

'And you became the child's mother?'

'Cosgrave wanted Rachel to have an abortion and she'd have gone along with it. She was young and stupid; still a child in many ways. She wanted the man so badly she couldn't see what was going on. He was just using her. He wanted it all brushed under the carpet. When Father Ryan talked her out of the abortion, Cosgrave got really worried. Rachel was all for telling his wife, but Father Ryan calmed her down and persuaded her not to; told her she'd done enough already without ruining another woman's marriage. In the end he brokered an arrangement with Lawrence Cosgrave. We'd go away, Rachel and me, and when we came back I'd say the baby was mine; say I'd got caught during the change. That's what we did. Went to Bognor Regis, a little place on the South Coast. Lawrence Cosgrave paid for it all: the rented bungalow, the birth in a private clinic. He dealt with everything. My name and Derry's were entered on the birth certificate; a man at the clinic gave us an envelope with all the papers in on the day Rachel left. She stayed in a week, to make sure she was all right and give her a bit of time to adjust before we came back. Since then Cosgrave's sent me a cheque for a thousand pounds, every month. Well, it was a thousand. He's increased it, year by year. It's almost fifteen hundred now. He's kept his part of the bargain, and we've kept ours. We've lived the lie and told no one. No one until you.'

Samantha gazed at the thin, almost emaciated woman with straggly shoulder-length grey hair. Paula was still looking down at her hands, abject in her shame. 'And how did Rachel feel about it: about you taking the child and everything?'

'She wanted the man,' Paula said. 'She didn't seem to give the baby much thought. Reality began to dawn over the six months we were in the cottage. Cosgrave never got in touch with her; never enquired about the birth. As far as he was concerned, he was doing the honourable thing by paying, and it was all over.'

'What was Rachel like after the birth? Surely . . . '

'The doctor at the clinic knew what was going on. Friend of Cosgrave's I should think. Doctors are like priests, aren't they? They keep secrets. He made sure she didn't have overmuch to do with Benjamin while she was in the clinic. Anyway, by that time she was very bitter. Like I said, all she wanted was the man, not the baby. She even let Derry and me pick his name: Benjamin.'

'Derry, your husband,' Samantha asked. 'How did he react to it all?'

'Heartbroken,' Paula said bitterly. 'Quite literally heartbroken. He was Irish. Came from Galway. Very devout. He was deeply ashamed; overwhelmed by it all. He was a bricklayer: a decent, hardworking, uneducated man. He couldn't deal with the likes of Cosgrave. The man had abused his daughter, and he couldn't do a damn thing about it. If he shamed Cosgrave by making it public, he'd shame his daughter, too. Father Ryan kept telling him it was best for Rachel, and a great charity to avoid distressing Cosgrave's wife and maybe causing a family to be broken up. In the end Derry went along with it.'

'And why was it best for Rachel?'

'She stayed respectable, our family stayed respectable, and she could still make a good marriage.'

'It's England in the twenty-first century, Paula. Not Ireland in the nineteenth,' Samantha said softly.

'Maybe,' Paula muttered. 'But that doesn't change the way some of us feel about things. And it doesn't stop you wanting a decent life for your child.'

Samantha said nothing, just watched Mrs

Hamilton picking at the hem of her pinafore. The hiss of the gas fire was loud in the silence, footsteps trod along the pavement outside the window, a car whispered down the street.

Paula looked up and her shaking voice revealed her bitterness and anger as she said, 'It killed Derry. Heart attack, when Ben was two. I was wheeling Ben in his pushchair and I happened to look down the alleyway that runs across the backs. I saw the soles of these great boots sticking up: Derry always wore brown-leather boots, and I realized it was him. He was still alive when I got to him. When I spoke his name, he kept on saying, 'It's getting dark, Paula. I can't see no more. I'm going into the dark.' I ran and got Molly Braden. She brought her two sons and they carried him in here.' She nodded towards the fireplace. 'He passed away on that rug. Rachel broke his heart.'

'Cosgrave broke his heart,' Samantha insisted. 'He was old enough to be Rachel's father. He should have kept his hands to himself.'

Paula Hamilton shrugged. 'Maybe.' She seemed resigned to the thought that the family of a well-brought-up Catholic girl should bear the guilt and accept the consequences.

'And no one knew the circumstances surrounding the birth?'

'Not a soul. They feted Derry at the Irish Club when I came back holding the baby. Virile at his age and fathering a boy, too. All that sort of silliness. I said I was embarrassed getting caught so late, and the women at church thought it was a huge joke. Late pregnancies aren't unknown in Catholic families.'

'The money,' Samantha said. 'How does he pay you the money?'

'Paid into the bank, every month, by some accountants. Cosgrave's never contacted us, never asked about Benjamin. It's as if we'd ceased to exist. When Ben disappeared I got desperate. I wrote him a letter and sent it to Westminster. Wrote it so only he would understand and know it was me. Reminded him Ben was his child, too, and he had to do something.' Her cheeks had flushed. Anger was beginning to show.

'Janos Tyminski?' Samantha asked. 'How did he come on the scene?'

Paula's expression softened. 'Nice boy,' she said. 'One of Father Ryan's altar servers. Grandparents were Polish. Father Ryan had a do in the Hall to celebrate his jubilee.'

Samantha raised an eyebrow.

'As a priest,' Paula explained. 'Thirty years

as an ordained priest. He introduced them at the party. I think he'd had his eye on Janos for Rachel. Janos is shy, a bit withdrawn, not much idea how to talk to girls, but he's respectful and considerate — kind, too. A girl can't ask for more than that. They were married a year later. He opened a garage, bottom of Spandyke Street, in a place that used to be a furniture warehouse. Specialized in high-performance cars. Henry Bassinger's sons started to bring their cars to him. That's when things went wrong.'

'Went wrong?'

'The other Bassingers began asking him to do jobs. Weld false floors and compartments in vans and cars, things like that. Paid him well. Rachel used to do the accounts. She told me what they made some months. It was more than Derry earned in a year. She wanted a fancy house down Parkside, and Janos let her have it. Spent a fortune on curtains and furniture.' Paula Hamilton lapsed into a thoughtful silence. She was still tugging at the hem of her apron, her shoulders hunched, the sallow skin of her face and hands contrasting with the whiteness of her cotton blouse. Her green cardigan needed straightening; her grey skirt, hanging loosely over her scrawny thighs, was at least two sizes too big.

'You said things went wrong,' Samantha prompted.

'Janos realized they were doing something illegal with the cars and vans he altered. He thought it was drugs. He talked to Father Ryan about it. Father told him it was his duty to go to the police. Rachel didn't want him to. She said it was none of their business. She said the Bassingers could just be wanting the cars and vans strengthening. She'd got used to the money. And they had this great big mortgage to pay and all the credit card debt.'

'So he went to the police?'

Paula Hamilton nodded. 'They watched the garage, followed the vans and cars when the Bassingers drove them away. The police moved Janos and Rachel into a hotel before they made the arrests. When the trial was over, they bought them a house near Carlisle, then staged Janos's death in a car crash.'

'Who knew about that?' Samantha demanded.

'Me, Rachel of course, and Janos's parents. No one else. Janos went to live in the house, and Rachel got a job in a travel agent's in Carlisle and rented a little flat. The police told them they'd have to be careful for a while: they'd expected to convict more of the Bassingers, but the trial didn't go their way. That's what made things so dangerous. The Bassingers were free and they could get back at Janos. Rachel blamed Janos for it all. She said he'd been stupid to listen to Father Ryan. Going to the police had cost them everything: the house, the furniture, the business, their life together. I think she saw him a few times, I imagine that's why she took the job in Carlisle, but the marriage was more or less over. The last time I spoke to Janos's mother, she said he was having mental problems and being treated for depression. She didn't really want to talk to me about it.'

'What does Janos call himself now?' Samantha asked.

'Keating, Brian Keating. As far as I know, he's working in a garage, some dealership for expensive cars. Rachel doesn't come home. I don't think she can bear to after what's happened. Janos did everything the police asked, and after the trial they didn't want to know him anymore.' Paula's voice became plaintive and Samantha could hardly hear her when she said, 'I thought Rachel might have come home and stayed with me when Benjamin . . . '

Voices, raised in prayer, began to chant in the adjoining house. Mrs Hamilton scowled. 'I get sick of it,' she said angrily. 'Several times a day, every day. I've started banging on the wall.' Tears began to roll down her cheeks. 'Everything's changed,' she sobbed. 'I can count on one hand the people I can talk to now. The only things I can buy at the corner shop are milk and bread; the rest's all spicy stuff. Bishop sent a pastoral letter for the priests to read out at mass. 'Be welcoming to our friends from overseas; remember the parable of the Good Samaritan'. The bishop and politicians ought to come and live here; have to listen to the chant, chant, chant all day. You're supposed to love, Miss Grey, but my heart's turned to stone. I tried to talk to Father Ryan about it, but he's busy with his own problems. Catholics are leaving the area and he's losing his congregation. Kids from the council estate keep breaking into the church and threatening him. And I'm so alone,' she moaned. 'Derry's gone, all the people I used to know have gone, Rachel doesn't come to see me any more, and now Benjamin's gone.'

Samantha rose, stepped over to the tiny sofa and sat beside her, holding her hands. They were thin, bony hands, with rough palms, icy cold despite the warmth of the room. 'We can't turn back the clock, Paula. What's done is done. But I'm going to find Benjamin and bring him back to you.'

'You can't,' Paula moaned. 'He's dead. I know he's dead. I can feel it and its driving me insane. God's taken him. No one can bring him back now.'

4

Samantha's eyes opened. She could hear the faint drone of a car above the patter of falling rain. Pushing herself out of the cushions, she peered down into the street. Tail lights were drifting out of view. She glanced at her watch. It was almost five. Paula Hamilton was in the bed, snoring gently; Samantha was in an armchair, by the window, swathed in her padded raincoat. They were sharing the front bedroom. It was Paula Hamilton's sanctuary. The armchair and a television had been brought up from the tiny sitting room. A gas fire in an old iron fireplace provided warmth. The bedroom was more distant from the pavement that ran past the front door; perhaps less affected by noisy neighbours. Paula had been too distraught to leave on her own. Her relief had been palpable when Samantha suggested staying the night, and she'd seemed pleased when Samantha declined the offer of Benjamin's bed in the back room and said she'd sleep in the armchair. With the chair positioned beside the window, she'd been able to watch the street.

The murmur of the car was still audible.

Gears changed, its engine revved, then the murmuring grew louder and headlamp beams approached, glistening on wet tarmac. A black two-door BMW crept into view, slowed to a stop, then reversed into a space on the far side of the road. The driver cut the engine and flicked off the lights. No one emerged from the car. Samantha tried to discern faces through the windscreen, but all she could see was the reflected glare of a street lamp. It was a big, powerful car, almost new; too expensive a thing to be owned by a resident of Atherton Road. She noted the registration number, then watched and waited.

Nothing moved. At six, Samantha took her dress from a hanger hooked over the wardrobe door and put it on; stepped into her shoes then slid her arms into the padded raincoat. Paula stirred, then jerked into a sitting position, her thin body lost inside a pale-blue flannelette nightdress. 'You're leaving! Let me make you some breakfast.' She reached for the bedside lamp.

'Don't put the light on,' Samantha said hastily. 'And thanks, but I've got to go. Can I leave by the back door and walk along the alleyway?'

'It's blocked off. The council are doing the drains or something. It's been like that for a month. Why do you — '

'There's a car parked across the street. Someone inside could be watching the house.'

'Watching the . . . Why would anyone want to watch me?'

'Not you, Paula: me.' Samantha tied the yellow scarf over her hair then groped in her bag for the tinted glasses.

Paula Hamilton threw back the duvet and swung her legs to the floor. 'At least let me make you a cup of tea.'

'No tea, Paula, but I could use a plastic carrier bag and an umbrella if you have one.'

Mrs Hamilton lifted a dressing gown from a hook behind the door, drew it on and stepped out on to the landing. Samantha listened until her footsteps had descended to the hall, then opened her bag and took out the gun. Moving her fingers through compacts and lipstick cases, ID wallets and pens, she found the silencer and screwed it on to the muzzle. The weapon was long and unbalanced now. She reached into the pocket of her coat, tore a hole, and slid the extended barrel of the gun into the quilting. It bumped against her thigh as she climbed down the stairs.

Mrs Hamilton was standing in the narrow hallway, holding an umbrella and a plastic bag.

‘Co-operate with the police and do whatever they ask,’ Samantha said. ‘But don’t mention my involvement to anyone.’

‘How can I contact you?’ Paula Hamilton sounded frightened and bewildered.

‘You can’t,’ Samantha said. ‘I’ll get in touch with you.’ She took the plastic bag and dropped her handbag inside. ‘Where can I catch a bus into town?’

‘Turn right at the end of the street and go up the rise to the main road. There’s a row of shops there. The bus stops outside the post office, every ten minutes. The first one should be along about now.’ Paula handed her the umbrella. ‘Those people, the people in the car outside, they won’t come asking questions, will they?’

‘If they are watching,’ Samantha said, ‘they’re watching for me. They’re not likely to bother you, but if they ask, tell them I’m a friend. Tell them I came to stay the night because you were scared and upset. OK?’

Paula Hamilton nodded doubtfully. Samantha tugged open the door, pushed up the umbrella, and stepped outside. When she turned and embraced the frightened woman, she whispered, ‘Close the door and lock it.’ Paula clung to her and began to shake. Drawing away, Samantha strode off into the darkness and the pouring rain. She heard the house door slam, then glanced across the street. A hand was wiping condensation from the windscreen of the black BMW; another hand was clearing the sidelight.

As she neared the end of the terrace she heard a car door open, then thud shut, followed by the heavy tread of a man's footsteps. When she rounded the corner she began to run up the hill that led to the main road. On the far side of the street, an opening in a high brick wall led to an alleyway. Samantha glanced over her shoulder. The man hadn't rounded the corner yet. Dashing across, she ran into the passage, brushing past rubbish sacks and a discarded mattress as she plunged into the darkness.

A gate was sagging open. Samantha peered across a tiny, rubbish-strewn back yard at a derelict house, its windows and door no more than black holes in wet brickwork. Stepping through the gateway, she furled her umbrella, headed down the side of a rear projection and went inside. She groped her way through what had been a kitchen, turned into a narrow hallway that contained the stairs, then stumbled into a back room where a window opening gave her a view of the yard and the gateway to the alley. Drawing the gun from her coat, she released the safety catch.

Footsteps, hurrying along the street, faded

beneath the hissing of the rain and the faint rumble of distant traffic. The sky above the rooftops was becoming lighter, but it was still dark in the house and yard. Someone was hurrying back down the hill. He must have realized he'd missed her. The sound of running feet grew louder, then paused at the entrance to the alleyway. After a few seconds there were rustlings as he struggled past the mattress and rubbish sacks. Samantha risked a glance around the edge of the window opening. He was standing in the gateway, his hair and face a vague blur of lightness above the dark mass of his body.

He entered the yard, tripping over debris as he picked his way down the side of the kitchen. He was close now, standing just beyond the window opening. Samantha could hear his heavy breathing above the patter of the rain. When his feet scraped on the step, she pressed her body into the corner of the room, sagged into a crouching position and gripped the gun with both hands. She could just make out the faded pattern on the wallpaper. Perhaps it had grown a little lighter, or perhaps her eyes had become accustomed to the dark.

Big male shoes crunched over grit and plaster on the kitchen floor, then shuffled along boards in the narrow hall that ran beside the stairs. Raising the gun with outstretched arms, Samantha pointed it towards the doorway. She heard a rotten board snap, the thud of a body falling against the wall, and muttered curses. The gun with its silencer fitted was unbalanced: long in the barrel and tiring to hold. From the passage, heavy breathing was punctuated by more curses then feet began to shuffle over the boards again.

The fingers of a large hand appeared, clutching at the door-frame, steadying her pursuer on the rotten floor as he groped his way past the opening. He turned and glanced inside. He didn't see her at first, crouching in the dark corner. Then his gaze lowered and his eyes widened. 'Hey! What . . . '

Pigeons, startled by the thud of the silenced gun, flew from upstairs windows with a frantic beating of wings. Samantha rose and went into the hall. He was sprawling alongside what remained of the stairs, his eyes still wide with shock. She needed light. Returning to the corner by the window, she dipped inside the plastic carrier, clicked open her handbag, and found a small torch. Back in the hall, she unbuttoned his overcoat and peeled it open. Tall and broad shouldered, his mother's genes had refined coarse Bassinger features and made him almost handsome.

Reaching inside his jacket, Samantha plucked out a wallet. The leather was smeared with blood that had oozed from a dark wound in his chest. She wiped it on his coat, flicked it open and found a driving license: Carl Bassinger. The document gave a Manchester address.

She was certain she hadn't left any trace of herself at Forest Heights. How had they tracked her to Paula Hamilton's? Was it luck, or did the Bassingers know she was searching for Benjamin? Either way, they'd become a threat. She was no longer circling an unsuspecting prey. They were stalking her now, and it would be best if the body remained undiscovered. Shining the torch over the wall beneath the stairs, Samantha found an opening that led down to the cellars. She dragged Carl Bassinger's body over and tumbled it into the darkness.

Damp walls, encrusted with a powdery whiteness, gleamed in the torchlight as she descended stone steps and squeezed past the sprawling corpse. It was damp and musty beneath the house. Ceilings were low and the air heavy with the smell of drains and decay. A coal cellar at the front was connected to the street by a chute. The chute had lost its iron grating and the floor was ankle-deep in litter. In a chamber at the rear, the remains of fuse boxes were hanging from a wall and a stone shelf bridged a recess.

Returning to the foot of the steps, she played the torch over Carl Bassinger's body. Suddenly his eyes were staring at her up the beam of light. The shocked look had gone. Death had made them dull and opaque. Blood, escaping from the corner of his mouth, had formed a dark line down his neck and saturated the collar of his shirt. Samantha grasped his clammy, lifeless hands and somehow managed to drag him into the back cellar. After removing his watch and signet ring, she searched his pockets for a mobile phone and any keys and papers that might identify him.

Exhausted now, she was finding it difficult to bundle the limp, heavy body, bulky in winter clothes, under the stone shelf. Somehow she managed it, aided by an old broom handle that she used to push and prod limbs and torso until they were wedged at the back of the confined space. The floor was strewn with newspapers and rags, a broken doll, bottles, empty beer cans. Gathering most of it up, she heaped it inside the recess to hide the body. Something brushed past her ankle and a dark shape scurried through the beam of the torch. Rats: the winter cold might preserve the body, but rats would make it unrecognizable.

Samantha climbed the steps, retrieved her bag and umbrella, then picked her way across the yard. The dawn sky was streaked with red now; the sound of traffic was becoming louder. Pausing at the mouth of the alleyway, she glanced up and down the street. It was deserted. Carl Bassinger's companion was still waiting in the car. Stepping out, she half-walked, half-ran, up the rise to the main road. She spotted the post office then joined a woman who was carrying a leather bag and an umbrella and some men wearing raincoats and hooded anoraks who were all waiting at the bus stop in front.

She looked back towards the junction. An old Ford saloon struggled to the top of the hill, waited for a gap in the traffic, then chugged out and merged with the city-bound commuters. Seconds later, a bus pulled up at the stop, doors hissed open, and the woman with the bag folded her tiny umbrella and climbed inside. The driver was taking fares and issuing tickets. Samantha reached into her bag, searching for coins as she moved with the queue towards the door. Before climbing the steps, she took a last glance back; a black two-door saloon was waiting to move out. Carl Bassinger's companion had become concerned and decided to take a look around. Passing coins to the driver, she said, 'City Centre,' then picked up her change and ticket and headed down the aisle.

Horns blared when the black car lurched out and overtook the bus. From her high vantage, Samantha could see another broad-shouldered, fair-haired young man behind the wheel. He was glancing at the pavements, searching for a man in a dark overcoat following an overweight woman wearing a yellow headscarf.

* * *

Rachel Tyminski pulled the duvet up to her chin and yawned. 'I loathe these dark winter mornings.'

'Rain,' Austin Bassinger mumbled. It's the rain that's making it so dark. What time is it?'

Rachel lifted her head from the pillow and glanced at the clock. 'Almost seven.'

'Got another half-hour.' He slid his arm around her waist and eased his leg over hers.

'No, Austin!'

'You weren't saying no last night.'

'I need a shower, and I want to brush my teeth.'

He began to caress her breasts and nuzzle her shoulder.

'I said no, Austin. If I'm late for work

again, they'll give me a formal warning and I don't want to lose this job. I get on really well with all the girls.'

'Bet they've not got breasts like these.'

'Austin!' She let out a shocked little giggle. 'Just stop it. I've got to . . . '

He turned his body until his thigh was nestling between her legs. 'I adore you, Rachel.' He kissed her neck. 'I utterly, totally and completely adore you.'

She laughed. It was a low, soft, throaty sound that said how much she liked being adored. She closed her eyes. His hand was caressing her stomach and his lips were gently moving over her breasts. 'There's no one else, is there, Austin? I'd want you to tell me if you started seeing someone else.'

His head emerged from the duvet. 'Someone else? Jesus, would I have the strength for someone else?'

She looked into his pale-blue eyes. His face was very close. God, he was handsome. Such a sexy mouth, such a hard, lean body; and the blond hair, almost as long as hers. Why? Why did he fancy her? She stroked the stubble on his cheek. He was so different to Janos.

Austin lowered his head to kiss her.

'Why?' she said, stopping him. 'Why me? There must be lots of girls — '

'Because I adore you.' He whispered the words in her ear.

'But I'm not even pretty, and I'm pounds overweight.'

'You're not pretty, Rachel, you're beautiful. Beautiful in a very special way.' He was gazing at her intently, his face serious. 'And your figure's perfect. You shouldn't even think about losing weight.' He was being truthful about the weight. He quite liked heavy-breasted, narrow-waisted women, with wide hips and plump thighs. She was gazing into his eyes, searching for reassurance. Austin kissed her, very tenderly, on the lips; he felt her body relaxing under his, her hand slowly caressing his thigh.

He wasn't getting anywhere. It was becoming a joke with the family. They were saying she'd let him fuck her to death before she'd tell him anything. He was going back to Manchester today, then over to Leeds. There'd be more questions and more ribald laughter. But he daren't be too direct, too obvious. He had to keep her trust, catch her when her guard was down. Propping himself on his elbow, he gazed at her for a while, then murmured, 'Marry me, Rachel.'

'Marry you?' She let out a shocked little laugh. 'I can't marry you.'

‘Why can’t you? You’re a widow, aren’t you?’

A blush flared on her throat then touched her cheeks. She seemed flustered. ‘I can’t . . . Not after what Janos did.’ Turning her head on the pillow to avoid his gaze, she stared out at the darkness beyond the half-drawn curtains, listening to the rain peppering the window.

‘It wasn’t you who went to the cops,’ Austin said. ‘You tried to talk the silly bugger out of it.’

‘Your family hate him so much they could never accept me. They’d have nothing to do with us if we got married. You’d lose your family, and that’s something you couldn’t bear.’

‘It wouldn’t be like that,’ Austin said softly. ‘And I don’t understand you. It’s as if Janos were still alive. It’s as if you’re still — ’

Rachel glared up at him. ‘Don’t talk like that,’ she snapped. ‘I don’t like it. And why did you have to mention Janos? You’re always going on about Janos.’

He’d pushed her as far as he could. She was becoming wary of him. Making his voice contrite, he gazed into angry brown eyes and caressed her breast with his fingertips while he murmured, ‘I suppose it’s jealousy, Rachel. I go crazy when I imagine you and him doing things together.'

'You didn't seem bothered when we were in the office at the back of the garage.'

Clever bitch! His mind raced, trying to come up with a retort. 'People change, Rachel. I wanted you the moment I first saw you, but I didn't love you then. Feelings overwhelm me now. I love you,' he made his voice break, 'I love you so much, Rachel. And when I think of Janos . . . ' He felt her hand on his cheek; saw her gaze softening into a deep tenderness.

'Janos isn't like you, Austin,' she whispered. 'He didn't seem to need me the way you do. Don't be jealous. It's silly.' She slid her arms around his neck. 'Come here.' She drew him down and kissed him.

Austin began to make love to her with his body, but his mind was elsewhere. She'd spoken as if Janos were still alive. It could have been a slip, but it wasn't the first time. And she didn't give a shit about her baby brother; she'd turned the telly off when her mother was making the appeal the other night. Maybe she was blocking out old memories, running away from new worries and fears. Hadn't she said she'd come to Carlisle to forget?

Rachel's breathing had quickened. Her hand was no longer caressing his thigh and he could feel her nails digging into his shoulders. Aroused, she was beginning to respond. Thinking was for later. Right now he had to concentrate on the task in hand.

5

The Saint Francis Xavier Primary School was a collection of flat-roofed single-storey classroom blocks arranged around an assembly hall. Samantha studied it through the windscreen of the Ferrari for a few moments, then let her gaze wander beyond the school to a plain red-brick church and presbytery further down the tree-lined road. A hot bath, a change of clothes and a full English breakfast had revived her. The children's mid-morning break should be starting soon. The rain had stopped, the weather was suddenly warmer and the sky less overcast: they'd probably be allowed out into the playground. Suddenly they were emerging, on a wave of happy screams and shouts.

Samantha picked a speck of lint from the skirt of her crimson Versace suit, took her bag from the passenger seat and climbed out of the car. A woman wearing a green smock and grey quilted jacket was watching the children. Samantha trotted over the road, went close to the high wire-mesh fence and beckoned. The woman came over.

'I need to talk to Miss Hibbs, the reception class teacher.'

'You'll have to clear that with the headmistress, Sister Bernadette.'

'How do I get inside?'

The woman pointed. 'Just beyond those bushes, the fence turns and runs up to the entrance. It's locked. You have to ring the bell. Sister's very strict about security.'

The entrance hall smelt of wax polish, plimsolls and school meals. Samantha turned towards the plump, grey-haired woman who'd let her in. 'May I see Sister Bernadette?' She groped in her bag and plucked out a wallet. 'Georgina Grey. Special Crime Unit.'

'Is it about the little boy?'

Samantha nodded. 'I really want to speak to Miss Hibbs, but I understand I have to clear it with the headmistress first.'

The woman smiled. 'If you'll just wait a moment, I'll go and see if sister's free.' She crossed the hallway and disappeared through a door marked 'Private.'

Samantha glanced around. A framed picture of a white-robed Pope Benedict was hanging above a plaque that announced the opening of the school by a bishop, twenty years earlier. In a niche in the far wall, tiny vases of snowdrops and crocuses were clustered around a painted statue of the Virgin and Child. Facing the statue, across the entrance, was a large oak crucifix with a figure moulded from some ivory-coloured material. It all brought back memories.

The door opened and the woman's head appeared around the edge. 'Sister will see you now, Miss Grey.'

Samantha entered a narrow corridor where parquet, untrod by tiny feet, gleamed, and the smell of polish was almost eye-watering. The woman paused beside an open door and gestured for Samantha to pass through.

The only object on the shining surface of the desk was a black telephone. The nun sitting behind it wore a pale-blue linen blouse and a grey cardigan. A white-edged wimple of a lighter grey hid her hair. Eyes that were small and button-black shone out of a pale face that was completely unlined. Dark, bushy eyebrows merged over the bridge of a narrow, rather long nose.

'I understand you wish to see Miss Hibbs.' The nun's quiet voice was cold and refined. She didn't offer the visitor's chair.

Samantha pulled it towards her, sat down, crossed her legs and settled her crimson Gucci bag on her lap. Giving the nun a dazzling smile, she said, 'That's right, Sister. I understand she takes the reception class.'

Paula Hamilton had told her this the night before.

'And you're from the police?'

'From the Special Crime Unit.'

'Benjamin's no longer in the reception class. Mrs Gregory is his teacher now. I think you should talk to — '

'I want to see Miss Hibbs,' Samantha insisted. 'The police have already interviewed Mrs Gregory.' She kept up the smile. It was becoming an effort.

The nun's tiny mouth hardened. She didn't care to be interrupted. 'If you insist, but I really don't see how Miss Hibbs can help you, and Mrs Gregory's the more senior member of staff.' She let out an exasperated sigh. 'I'll have Miss Hibbs brought in.'

'Alone,' Samantha said. 'I want to talk to her on her own. Perhaps I could go through to the classroom?'

'As Headmistress, I think I should be present when matters affecting the school are discussed, Miss Grey. And we're all deeply concerned about Benjamin.'

'His mother's traumatized,' Samantha said softly. 'Time's passing and Benjamin's still missing. Alone, Sister: I'd like to speak with Miss Hibbs on her own.'

Sister Bernadette snatched up the phone,

keyed in a number and fixed the over-assertive young woman in a piercing stare. Did her clothes have to fit quite so well? With a figure like that, the effect was much too provocative. And she'd never seen a member of the police dressed so expensively and so fashionably before. Dear Lord, babies were starving in Africa, and the suit and shoes, the gloves and bag, must have cost . . . 'Mrs Bennet?'

Samantha heard a faint 'Yes, Sister.'

'Would you come through and escort Miss Grey to the reception class for me, then go to the staff room and tell Miss Hibbs Miss Grey's waiting to see her.'

Samantha rose and stepped up to the desk. Holding out her hand, she said, 'Thank you, Sister.'

'The search for Benjamin: how is it going?' Sister Bernadette's handshake was cold and limp.

'Progressing,' Samantha said. 'I'm brushing obstacles aside; slotting missing pieces into the jigsaw.' When the door opened behind her, she smiled at the headmistress, then turned and followed the grey-haired Mrs Bennet down the corridor.

'Sorry I've disturbed your break, Miss Hibbs.' Samantha was sitting on a low table in the reception class. The diminutive teacher was almost hidden behind her desk. Her white hair had been tinted strawberry-blonde; her face heavily, and a little carelessly, made up; and her blue eye-shadow clashed with an emerald-green dress. She reminded Samantha of an exotic tropical bird.

'I don't know how I can help you, Miss Grey. I had Benjamin in reception, but Mrs Gregory's his teacher now.'

'I want to know what sort of child he is: what sort of a person,' Samantha said. 'I've spoken to his mother, but she was too distraught for me to question closely. So, who better than you?'

'You've got an awful cold.'

Samantha smiled and raised an eyebrow.

'Your voice. It's so husky and soft.'

'I don't have a cold, Miss Hibbs. My voice has always been this way. I've learned to live with it. Benjamin,' she prompted. 'Tell me about Benjamin.'

'A very sweet child,' Miss Hibbs said. 'And very affectionate when he gets to know you. Gentle nature, wouldn't hurt a fly. Children with difficulties are often like that, aren't they?'

'Difficulties?'

'You didn't know?' Miss Hibbs seemed surprised.

'His mother never mentioned it.'

'She wouldn't. She's very protective. She's in denial about it. Refuses to believe there's anything wrong. Sister Bernadette didn't want to accept him. She said he ought to be placed in the Council's special needs school, but Father Ryan persuaded her.'

'Benjamin has learning difficulties?'

'Rather more than that. I thought he might be autistic, but the psychiatrist said it wasn't autism. I can't remember what he called it.'

'He was sent to a psychiatrist?'

'Just a few times, after he'd started school. Sister Bernadette insisted. I think she was looking for a way to exclude him. Benjamin's mother was upset, but Father Ryan told her to go along with it. When the psychiatrist said it wasn't autism and that he'd be best educated in a normal school, sister had to give in.'

'Tell me about these difficulties.' Samantha said.

Miss Hibbs pressed her fingers together and frowned thoughtfully at some gaudy artwork displayed on one of the classroom walls. 'He's terribly wary of people before he gets to know them,' she said presently. 'It's more than shyness; he just withdraws and refuses to communicate. When he gets to know you, he can be very affectionate.' She returned her gaze to Samantha. 'Sometimes he doesn't seem to understand what's going on around him. If the children get too excited and boisterous, he becomes frightened, and if it continues, hysterical. And then he suddenly becomes very quiet and stares at the wall. Once he started banging his head, quite hard. I found that rather disturbing.'

'He wouldn't willingly go away with a stranger, then?'

'Not a chance of it. He'd be too afraid. And if they touched him he'd start to kick and scream.'

'Mrs Gregory told the police he was very trusting and affectionate; that someone could easily entice him away.'

Miss Hibbs shook her head. 'Absolutely not.'

'Could he have changed since he left you?'

'He's not really left me. I give him extra reading lessons. He's coming along quite well, but it's still the same old Benjamin.'

Samantha frowned. 'His problem's not below-average intelligence, then?'

'Intelligence is a very elusive and difficult thing to measure, Miss Grey. But I don't think so. He's different. He relates to people and what's going on around him in his own way. He can concentrate, he can reason; sometimes he shows surprisingly mature insights. Order and arranging things in order seem to be very important to him. I gave him an old picture book with beetles and butterflies set out in rows and columns. He was fascinated by it.'

'His mother,' Samantha said. 'Paula Hamilton. How is she with Benjamin?'

'Fiercely protective.' Miss Hibbs let out a mischievous chuckle. 'When Sister Bernadette said she wasn't going to accept him, she ran to Father Ryan and got him to overrule her. And she watches Mrs Gregory like a hawk. Mrs Hamilton's an older woman. She's not some young mother, believing everything the teacher says. And she looks after Benjamin very well: he's always clean, hair washed, spotless uniform, shoes polished. You notice things like that. Some very well-to-do parents don't bother at all. But she's . . . ' Miss Hibbs frowned thoughtfully, searching for kind words.

'She's?' Samantha prompted.

Miss Hibbs smiled. 'There's a time to have children, don't you think, Miss Grey? When you have the energy, the enthusiasm, the hope. Mrs Hamilton must have been well into her forties when Benjamin was born. She always seems so depressed and preoccupied — almost bitter. I'm sure she loves Benjamin dearly, but she doesn't seem able to show him much warmth and affection. I'd go as far as to say tiredness has made her rather distant and cold.'

'Was Benjamin's sister, Rachel, very involved with caring for him?' Samantha said. 'Would she collect him from school?'

'Hardly ever. I could count the times on one hand. Her husband, Janos, often used to bring him and collect him though. Benjamin adored Janos.'

Samantha smiled. 'Really?'

'Janos was a father figure and big brother all rolled into one. He let Benjamin potter around in his garage, made him toys, played football with him. He was a very kind and gentle man. It was shocking that he should die in that dreadful way.'

'Did the family have a routine for collecting Benjamin?'

'Not that I remember. Mrs Gregory might be the best person to ask about that.'

'The evening that Benjamin went missing,' Samantha said. 'Was there anything unusual? Did anyone notice anything different?'

Miss Hibbs shrugged. 'There's a high fence that goes all around the school. The children come in and leave by the tiny yard near the main entrance. There's always a classroom assistant there when the children are being collected, and a lot of mothers too. No one noticed anything strange. No one heard a child screaming or crying. The police have trawled through this endlessly, Miss Grey.'

'No strangers at the gate?'

'No matter what Mrs Gregory told the police, Miss Grey, Benjamin wouldn't go with a stranger, and he'd kick up a fuss if anyone tried to take him. No one saw or heard a commotion, and he certainly wouldn't go out of the gate by himself.'

'When did they realize he was missing?'

'I gather it was when his mother came to collect him. She was a little late and most of the other children had gone by that time.'

'You say Benjamin adored Janos. How did he react to his death?'

'I only have Benjamin for extra reading lessons twice a week, Miss Grey, but when he was with me he didn't seem unduly upset. The week of the accident he told me Janos had gone to Jesus. The next week he asked me when Janos was coming back. A six-year old child has difficulty understanding the finality of death. A child like Benjamin, who interacts with the world in an unusual way, might simply not accept it at all. He may feel deserted and let down when the days go by and the person doesn't appear again.'

Samantha studied the tiny woman with the clear blue eyes and carelessly made-up face. She was a little overweight and not much taller than the children in her care. Samantha couldn't imagine anyone better to have in a reception class.

Becoming uncomfortable in the silence, Miss Hibbs said, 'That's a beautiful suit. Such a vivid red, yet it's so perfect for you. And the fit! May I ask where you got it?'

'Milan,' Samantha said, and smiled. 'Versace. They have their main boutique along the Via Montenapoleone, and an angel of a seamstress who took it in here and there.'

Miss Hibbs laughed. 'What it is to be young. Most of us need things letting out here and there. But I still prefer bright colours. I hate drabness. Sister Bernadette gives me looks. She thinks I'm a frivolous old woman.'

'You're not the least bit old or frivolous,' Samantha said. 'And you should have seen the look she gave me.'

Miss Hibbs's falsetto giggles mingled with Samantha's husky laughter as they made their way between islands of tiny tables and chairs. When they reached the door, the teacher's face suddenly became grave. Gazing up at Samantha with troubled eyes, she said, 'It's so awful about Benjamin. I can't bear to think about it.'

'I'm going to find him.'

'It's been four days now,' Miss Hibbs

whispered. Her lips were trembling. Out in the corridor, a woman in a green smock was leading the children towards the classroom.

Samantha took Miss Hibbs's hands in both of hers. 'You've been so helpful. More helpful than you realize, and I'm very grateful.'

* * *

Father Ryan bolted the main doors, then walked back down the aisle. The church seemed gloomier, the stained glass less brilliant, since he'd had that wire-reinforced plastic fixed over the windows. There was nothing else he could do; a stone had almost hit Mrs Liddel when she was hoovering the sanctuary, and the insurance company had refused to go on paying for repairs.

He genuflected towards the tabernacle, then slid into a pew. This was a godless place now. The young people weren't immoral, they were amoral. They simply didn't know right from wrong. He could hear them at night, boys and girls, cavorting in the bushes that covered the no man's land between the church and the big housing estate. Heavens knows what they were doing, but what chance did children have when their parents had lost all sense of sin? He'd be sixty-four next month: too old for a parish like this. At the next clergy meeting he'd get the bishop on one side and ask him if he'd move him. It would be the third time of asking. The bishop kept on insisting he needed an experienced priest here because of the school. God knows why. The mostly middle-class parents were all smiles when they were having their children baptised so they could get their names on the list. When they were enrolled, the parents disappeared. He needed them in the pews. Muslim immigrants had taken over the streets of terraced housing, and most of his older parishioners had died or moved away. For the past year, Sunday collections had been so meagre he'd not been able to make the loan repayments on the church and school. The bishop didn't like that. He'd be chiding him about it again at the next deanery meeting. The bishop was always courteous, but he made it obvious he wasn't pleased.

'Father Ryan?' The low, husky voice whispered out of the shadows and echoed around the church.

Startled, he turned towards the sacristy door, saw a black-haired woman dressed in red, her green eyes glittering in the light of the offertory candles.

'I rang the bell on the presbytery door but there was no answer. It was open, so I came through.' She moved out of the shadows.

He could see her more clearly now: red shoes, gloves, handbag; a red suit that fitted like a second skin. 'I was going out,' he said. 'Sick visiting. Then I remembered I'd not locked the church doors and I came back. I must have left the house door — '

'I need to talk with you.' Samantha interrupted, studying him as she approached. His grey hair was cut short, his cheap black suit crumpled, but his Roman collar and black shirt were clean and freshly laundered. He was thin and gaunt and his grey eyes were searching her face in a nervous, worried kind of way.

'Is it a personal matter?' he asked. She was standing close to him now. In the damp chill of the church, he could sense the fragrant warmth of her body. She wasn't a parishioner. He didn't have any parishioners who looked and dressed like this. He couldn't imagine her mopping floors or washing altar linen, but he could picture her lifting John the Baptist's severed head from a plate. He shivered.

'Benjamin Hamilton,' the husky voice explained.

'You're from the police?'

Samantha shook her head. 'I'm acting directly for Lawrence Cosgrave.'

Father Ryan watched her click the big gilt catch on her bag, dip slender fingers inside and pluck out an official-looking wallet. She allowed him a fleeting glance at the photograph and signature.

'Lawrence Cosgrave the Prime Minister?'

Samantha smiled. The old priest was gazing up at her intently now, probably wondering how much she knew. Lowering herself into the pew in front of his, she turned and faced him.

Paula Hamilton was a cunning one, Father Ryan reflected. She must have applied pressure, revived Cosgrave's fears, made him do something. 'The police are searching for Benjamin,' he said. 'It's a massive operation. Why would the Prime Minister want to interfere?'

'I'm not fettered.'

'Not fettered?'

'By the law or any human agency.'

He felt chilled. Power and dominion: it was supposed to be a law-abiding democracy, but behind locked doors . . . And this young woman seemed so calm, so self-assured, so deadly. She wouldn't be intimidated by the bishop, and the bishop wouldn't dare say no to her. He had to think, he had to be careful what he said, but it wasn't easy with those eyes burning into you. 'How is Lawrence Cosgrave?' he asked lamely, struggling for time. 'I suppose you know he was a parishioner of mine; still is when he's in his constituency?'

'No idea. I've never met the man. I've been briefed by a third party; assigned to recover the child, dead or alive.'

'Dead or alive! Surely you wouldn't harm Benjamin?'

Samantha scowled, outraged by the suggestion. 'I took the brief to mean I had to recover the body if the child's been killed. No one could stand in the way of my protecting a child.'

Reassured, the old priest asked, 'You think Benjamin's dead?'

'I'm certain he's alive, but in great danger. I think some people, members of the criminal fraternity, want him.'

'Want a child? Why would criminals want little Benjamin?'

'It's complicated, father.'

He had to slow the conversation down; try and work out what all this meant. He was deeply involved with the family. He had to be careful. 'What did you say your name is?'

'I didn't,' the husky voice murmured. 'It was printed on the ID card. 'It's Georgina — Georgina Grey.'

He tried to smile but his lips seemed frozen. The woman was so remote and intimidating. They should have called her

Salome, not Georgina. Swallowing against the dryness in his throat, he said, 'I really don't see how I can help you, Miss Grey.'

She smiled. He was a keeper of secrets. She'd have to unsettle him. 'Where's Janos Tyminski, father?'

The priest's eyes widened. 'Dead!' He nodded down the aisle. 'His coffin was received into church, he rested for a night before the altar. The next day I said his requiem mass. Then he was cremated.'

'Did you see the body? Did you give him the last rites?'

'No one saw the body. It was too badly mutilated in the crash.'

'Who identified it?'

'The police. They used dental records and DNA; took a swab from his mother's mouth.'

Samantha gazed over the back of the pew at him. His eyes were moving nervously over her face. He was telling the truth as he knew it; she was sure of it. There was at least one family secret Father Ryan wasn't privy to. 'Rachel Tyminski: where is she, father?'

'Carlisle. She took a job in a travel agent's. After all that had happened, she wanted to get away from Stockport.'

'And she hasn't come home now Benjamin's missing. She must have known her mother would be frightened and lonely. I'd have thought Rachel would have rushed home and kept the vigil with her.' Holding Father Ryan's gaze, Samantha added softly, 'After all, she's got more reason than her mother to be distressed about Benjamin.'

He looked at her warily, then stared down at his hands. 'People react differently to the troubles of life, Miss Grey.' Nervous eyes flicked back up, their coolness telling her he'd spoken his last word on the subject.

Something was being kept from her, she was sure of it. Something to do with Rachel Tyminski. Samantha gazed at the priest over the back of the pew for a long moment, then said, 'Is Rachel still friendly with Austin Bassinger?'

'I'm not sure what you mean by that, Miss Grey. The Bassingers took a lot of business to her husband's garage; there's no secret about that. It was all reported in the papers. Rachel used to do the accounts. I suppose she must have met some of the Bassingers.'

'Not that kind of friendly, father. What I meant was: is she still having an affair with Austin Bassinger?'

'You're being fanciful now, Miss Grey: fanciful to the point of being offensive. Rachel Tyminski's a decent, respectable young woman who was devoted to her husband. The last thing I could imagine her doing is having an affair.'

Samantha frowned. Vincent Bassinger could have been misinformed or lying, but it was more likely Father Ryan was keeping secrets again. 'Did Janos have many relatives, Father?'

'Wouldn't it be best if you spoke to his parents about that?'

'I'd rather talk to you.'

The priest sighed. 'His mother and father are still alive and there's an older and a younger sister. They were all at mass on Sunday. His grandfather was Polish. He married a Belgian woman and they settled here in the fifties, just after the war. They're both dead now. Aunts and uncles, of course, on both sides of the family. They haven't left the area; they all still live in and around Stockport. Half of them come here for Sunday mass. His father has an older brother who lives some distance away. He didn't come to the funeral, so I must have met him at Janos's wedding. I remember him because he's tall, like Janos, and looks a lot like him. And he has an unusual job that requires considerable skill: a clockmaker perhaps. Janos's parents would be able to tell you.'

'And his sisters still live at home?'

'The younger one does. The older sister's married, but she lives close by. They're a good-living, respectable family, and Janos was a fine young man, thoroughly decent, very devout. I thought he might enter the priesthood, but he was too interested in machinery and cars.'

'What about Rachel?' Samantha said. 'Does she have any relatives?'

'Only on her father's side. Aunts, uncles, cousins: all living in Ireland. They all came over for her father's funeral, but not so many for the wedding, and I don't remember any coming when Janos died. Her mother, Paula, was an only child. Her parents are dead. I think she's more or less on her own now.'

'And you don't know why Rachel hasn't come home to be with her mother?'

'Perhaps her employers are being difficult, perhaps she's on her way. That's something you should talk to Paula Hamilton about.'

'I think I'll have to,' Samantha said. She gazed at the worried looking man in the crumpled suit. She surmised he couldn't, or wouldn't, tell her any more. Gathering up her gloves and bag, she rose to her feet and held out a hand. 'Thanks, Father. Thanks for talking to me.'

Father Ryan glanced down at the extended hand. It was small, almost delicate, its fingers slender and tapered, the nails long and painted crimson, like her mouth, like blood. When he took the hand in his, it was soft and warm. Surprised to see her genuflect towards the tabernacle before they stepped into the sacristy, he said, 'You're a Catholic?'

Samantha smiled at him over her shoulder. 'Respect for ancient traditions. My mother was an Irish Catholic; my father a Russian Jew.'

'And you?'

'My mother had me baptized in Dublin. I was confirmed by the Patriarch of Jerusalem.'

'That doesn't really tell me anything.'

Samantha paused by a chest of shallow drawers that held vestments. 'The conversation we've just had, father, I expect it to have the seal of the confessional.'

'Of course,' he said, and then, on a sudden impulse, 'Would you like me to hear your confession?' He'd expected her to answer with a laugh, but she seemed to have ignored his question. He followed her across the hallway and watched her step out into the damp stillness of the winter morning.

Turning, Samantha looked back at him. 'You'd need a sedative before you heard my confession, father. I've lost count of the men I've killed, but their faces still haunt me: angry faces, shocked faces, frightened faces.' Crimson lips parted in a smile. 'If I change my way of life, I'll come and find you.'

'It might be too late.'

'For you or for me?'

Father Ryan watched her saunter down the drive towards the low-slung silver car. He answered her wave, then called after her, 'Don't you feel any pity?'

'Pity?'

'For the men.'

'Christ wouldn't feel any pity for the men I've killed, father.'

The car door slammed, its engine fired, began to growl like an animal, then the silver machine snarled out on to the road.

Samantha reached into her bag, found dark glasses and slid them on to hide her face. She motored through an area of bay-windowed semi-detached housing, then crossed a main road and plunged into narrow streets where tiny houses nudged the pavements. She was searching for Paula Hamilton's home. Slowing at an intersection, she saw what must have been Janos Tyminski's garage, its big doors padlocked, its high windows grimy rectangles of darkness. Driving on to the end of the terrace, she turned left and found herself in Atherton Road. The black two-door BMW had gone. She slowed as she approached Paula's house. In the daylight she could see shiny blue paint on the front door, a scrubbed step, snowy net curtains drawn like a bridal veil across the agony and loneliness within.

She decided not to call. She'd phone and arrange a meeting away from the house. It would be safer for Paula Hamilton: safer for her. Picking up speed, she cruised to the end of the terrace and crossed over the junction with the street that rose to the main road. A van was parked outside the derelict house. Beneath a logo on its side were the words, *Manchester Public Works Department*. Men were fixing metal sheets across windows and door openings and bedding a concrete slab over the coal chute. Carl Bassinger's resting place was being secured against intruders.

* * *

Morris Bassinger glared at his son. 'Disappeared? What do you mean, disappeared?

Trevor raised his hands and shrugged. 'Like I said, this weighty bird left the house just after six and Carl got out of the car and followed her. I stayed and watched the house and made sure they weren't working the decoy scam. You know, send someone out for you to follow, then, when you're doing the tail, the person you're looking for creeps out.'

'Smart,' Henry Bassinger said. 'The boys were getting it right.'

'I waited maybe twenty minutes, then started calling him on his mobile. When I didn't get an answer, I drove to the main road and cruised up and down. There were no signs of him or the woman, so I went back to Atherton Road and parked near Paula Hamilton's place. Kept calling Carl on his mobile every ten minutes, but no answer. When it got light, I took another look around. Then Ian and Lewis arrived about noon and the three of us walked the streets, went down all the alleyways, checked yards and empty houses. Council workmen had been and sealed up a couple of derelict places, but I'd looked over the one near Paula Hamilton's earlier. We found nothing. He'd disappeared. Vanished. We decided to come back here.'

'This woman,' Henry Bassinger said. 'She look anything like the woman in the video?'

'Much too meaty, almost fat. It was pitch-black and pissing down so you couldn't see much, but she was wearing a raincoat and a headscarf; carrying a Tesco plastic bag and an umbrella. Gave Paula Hamilton a hug and a kiss when she left. Probably a relative.'

'Keep calling him on his mobile,' Morris Bassinger snapped. 'Give it another couple of hours. Then we'll phone the hospitals around Stockport. Silly bugger could have stepped in front of a bus. If that draws a blank, we'll have a meeting and decide what to do.'

6

Paula Hamilton's nervous eyes darted around Samantha's hotel room. Thick blue and gold carpet, blue striped curtains that matched the bed cover, bedside lamps with black shades. It was nice. It was luxurious. Heaven knows what it cost to stay here for a night; the meal they'd just eaten had cost more than she spent on food in an entire week. 'Thanks for buying me lunch,' she said. 'I enjoyed it.'

'I think you've been skipping meals,' Samantha said.

'Can't seem to be bothered. And when I do make something, I don't want it. Today was nice, though, sitting down to a meal that's been cooked for you.'

Samantha studied the woman sitting in the tiny, empire style chair beside the writing table. Looking old beyond her years, she was wearing a dark-blue winter coat and flat, serviceable shoes. Her thin, wrinkled hands were toying with the strap of a black plastic handbag. 'I have to ask you something,' Samantha said. 'And I decided it was best not to call at your home.'

The woman's restless eyes settled on her

face. 'Not come to my home? Why ever not?'

'We have to be careful,' Samantha said evasively.

'That big black car: it drove off about half-an-hour after you left, then it came back and stayed across the street for ages. It had gone when the police brought me back from making the appeal.'

'Probably just coincidence,' Samantha said, trying to calm Paula Hamilton's fears. 'How did the appeal go?'

'Not very well. I got emotional and the policeman in charge of things had to finish reading it for me. You can keep a grip on yourself most of the time, but when they're all crammed in the room with their cameras pointing at you and you're begging whoever . . . ' Her face suddenly crumpled. Clicking open her bag, she plucked out a tiny, embroidered handkerchief that had been neatly pressed, shook it out, and began to dab at her eyes and nose. 'I don't think I can stand anymore.' The tearful words were muffled, almost impossible to hear. 'My mind and body are numb. I try not to think — '

'We've got to talk,' Samantha interrupted. 'I'm sorry to press you like this, but time's passing and I have to move on.'

'I told you everything last night: names, addresses, phone numbers. I don't know what else I can say.'

Samantha watched her fold the tiny square of cloth and wipe her cheeks. Paula hadn't mentioned Benjamin's problems, and she sensed there was another secret she found too shaming to reveal. 'Rachel,' Samantha opened. 'Why isn't Rachel in the house, keeping the vigil with you? She's Benjamin's natural mother. She's every reason to be even more distressed than you.'

'She works. She has to pay rent and feed herself. I don't think Janos is supporting her anymore. She can't just leave her job and come and stay with me.'

'You're alone, Paula. You're extremely distressed. And it's really her child who's missing, not yours. Why isn't she with you?'

'I don't know.' Paula looked down, unable to meet Samantha's searching gaze. She felt her body begin to shake. 'Does it matter? What could she do if she came home?'

Samantha knelt in front of her, took her hands in hers and looked up at her. 'Why isn't she with you, Paula? You've got to tell me. Every little fact, every detail, is important if I'm going to find Benjamin.'

'It's so awful. God, I'm so ashamed. As if Lawrence Cosgrave wasn't enough.'

'Tell me,' Samantha urged. 'We're different. Nothing you could possibly say would shock or upset me, Paula.'

'It was months ago, before the police made the arrests. I'd had an argument with the man next door about all the noise. I didn't think I'd be able to get to school in time to collect Benjamin, and I went to the garage to ask Rachel to pick him up in her car. Janos and another man were working inside a truck, so I just walked through to the little office at the back. She wasn't there, but I could hear sounds coming from a room where they kept registration documents and stored expensive parts. I should have called out. I wished to God I'd called out, but I was starting to panic about Benjamin, so I just went round the desk and pushed at the door. I didn't expect . . . ' She turned her head, unable to go on, unable to meet Samantha's gaze.

'Didn't expect?'

'Austin Bassinger was doing it to her. She'd perched her backside on a table, yanked her skirt up around her waist and wrapped her arms and legs around him. He was standing with his trousers around his ankles, his great long legs all white and hairy. I was thunderstruck. Even if it had been her husband, it was something a mother should never see, but it was that great big Bassinger boy with hair as long as a girl's. They didn't see me. They wouldn't, would they? They were too busy committing sin and making mischief. I crept out through the yard at the back. My legs were shaking so much I could hardly run to the school. Miss Hibbs had stayed behind with Benjamin. When I got there I must have looked awful because she took me to the staff room and made me a cup of tea.'

Paula Hamilton drew her hands from Samantha's and clutched at her bag. Closing her eyes, she began to gently rock backwards and forwards on the seat, distracting herself while she tried to blot out her anguish and shame.

Samantha listened to her chesty breathing for a few moments, then asked, 'But why isn't Rachel with you now?'

'I couldn't keep my mouth shut, could I?' Paula said bitterly. She opened her eyes. 'Rachel came to the house to collect some shopping I'd done for her. Just sauntered in, bright and breezy, looking as if butter wouldn't melt in her mouth after she'd spent the afternoon damning her soul to hell. I had to say something. I told her I'd seen her, told her she was no better than a common prostitute. I told her she had a decent, hard-working husband and a nice home and she was wicked and crazy to risk it all like that. I expected her to be ashamed and embarrassed, but I was the one who was embarrassed. She was angry and vicious. She said I'd ruined her life with my interference; she said I'd colluded with Father Ryan and trapped her into marrying Janos. And then she started talking about bedroom things, about Janos not behaving like a proper husband. She said if he had she'd never have looked at Austin Bassinger.' Paula Hamilton let out an outraged laugh. 'She said if Father Ryan had kept his nose out, she'd have been married to Cosgrave. I never realized she was so stupid. Cosgrave would never have abandoned his family and career for the likes of her.' She paused, took in a long, shuddering breath, then let it out in a sigh. 'All this was Cosgrave's fault: innocent young girl and an experienced man. He awakened her, made her aware of things and ruined her for her husband.'

'But why isn't Rachel with you?' Samantha insisted.

Paula Hamilton began to weep. 'Too much said, by her and by me — things I'm ashamed to repeat. The long and short of it was, she vowed she'd never come back to the house again. Said I could keep Ben, said it would have been better if he'd never been born, better if Father Ryan had kept his moralizing mouth shut and she'd had an abortion.'

'Did she ever visit you again?'

'Only the once. To tell me about the arrangements the police were going to make to protect her and Janos after the trial. That's when she told me she'd got a job in a travel agent's in Carlisle. And I saw her again when we staged Janos's funeral. I've not seen or heard from her since.'

'She's still in Carlisle, at the address you gave me last night?'

'As far as I know.'

'Is she still involved with Austin Bassinger?'

Paula Hamilton shrugged. 'He spent six months in gaol, awaiting trial. When he got out, she'd gone to Carlisle. She'd be crazy to get involved with him again. And anyway, would he want her after all the trouble her husband caused?'

'Do the police know about Rachel and Austin Bassinger?'

'God, no! You're the only person I've told. And they know nothing about Lawrence Cosgrave. As far as they're concerned, I'm Benjamin's natural mother and Rachel's his sister. They got the police in Carlisle to call on Rachel and make sure Benjamin wasn't there, but it was only a formality.'

Samantha gazed at her for a while, then said 'Thanks, Paula. Thanks for talking to me.'

'Don't see how it can help find Benjamin.'

'It's completing the picture,' Samantha said. She picked up a phone on one of the bedside tables. 'I've got to move out before the traffic builds up. I'm going to call reception. Have them get a taxi for you.'

'I could catch the bus.'

'Taxi,' Samantha insisted. 'It's raining and there's a cold wind, and — '

'Yes, madam?'

'My friend's leaving. Could you call a taxi for me?'

'Certainly, madam. Madam . . . ' He was holding her on the phone. 'Some gentlemen have been asking for you at the desk. They didn't know your name, but they described you and your companion rather accurately.'

'Did the receptionist tell them I was here?'

'Certainly not, madam. The staff are trained to be cautious and discreet. If the men couldn't give your name — '

'Were these men tall? Were they fair-haired?'

'One moment please, madam.'

Samantha could hear a conversation between the staff on the desk, but couldn't make out the words.

'It seems one was tall and reasonably young, perhaps about thirty. The other was an older man, stocky and heavily built. The younger man's hair was short and fairish, the older man's dark and curly. Bear with me a moment, madam . . . A porter's just told me they've had lunch in the Tacoma Bar, and they're still in there, drinking coffee.'

Samantha closed her eyes and tried to order her thoughts. Paula Hamilton had made her own way to the hotel. They must still be watching the house. 'Does the hotel have a car?' she asked.

'A people carrier, madam. We use it mostly for early-morning runs to the airport.'

'Presumably it's parked around the back?'

'That's correct, madam.'

'Would it be possible for your driver to take my friend to Stockport: for her to leave by the back way? I've no idea who those men are and they're worrying me.'

'Of course, madam. Shall I send the driver up to your room? He could escort the lady to the car.'

'That would be kind,' Samantha said. 'And I'd like to see the receptionist who dealt with the men. Could you send her up to me?'

'It's a he, madam. He does the six-till-two shift. He went off duty almost an hour ago, but we could try to find him for you. Shall I have him sent up if we do?'

'If you would,' Samantha said. 'I want to thank him.' She cradled the phone.

‘Something’s wrong, isn’t it?’ Paula whispered. She’d stopped rocking herself and was frowning up at Samantha.

‘Something I’ll have to deal with, but it won’t affect you, Paula.’

‘Is it to do with those men? The men who were watching the house?’

‘Could be,’ Samantha said. ‘But don’t let it worry you. It’s me they’re looking for.’ She reached over and took Paula Hamilton’s hands in hers. ‘If anyone comes asking about me, just tell them I was a relative who came over from Ireland for a couple of days because you were upset, and I’ve flown back now.’

‘But why should men — ’

There was a knock on the door. Samantha asked, ‘Who is it?’ and a muffled voice said, ‘Your driver, madam.’

Paula Hamilton rose stiffly out of the chair, her thin, cold hands still clutching Samantha’s. ‘When will you contact me?’

‘When I bring Benjamin back.’

The woman’s face suddenly looked unbelievably old. ‘He’s dead, Miss Grey,’ she whispered. ‘I can feel it. It’s wrong of you to say things like that just to give me hope.’

Samantha squeezed her hands tightly. ‘He’s not dead, Paula. He’s alive. And when I’ve found him, I’ll bring him home to you.’ She opened the door, led her out of the room, and handed her over to a white-haired man who was wearing a quilted car coat over his maroon uniform.

⋆ ⋆ ⋆

The stream of traffic was drifting westwards out of the city. Samantha checked the rear-view mirror. The black Audi with tinted windows was still close behind. Probably a four-litre engine: the Bassingers seemed to like their cars big, black and powerful.

She'd covered her crimson suit with a heavy military raincoat; changed her elegant shoes for thick-soled black boots that laced up to the knee. After standing in the hotel foyer where she could be seen from the Tacoma Bar, she'd lingered on the pavement while the porter struggled to get her bags into the space behind the seats. It had been impossible for them not to notice her. She'd baited the trap.

Waiting in her hotel room until they'd come looking wouldn't have been a good idea. There were two of them. The younger man was probably a Bassinger, the older a professional killer. Added to that, time was haemorrhaging away. She'd already spent longer in Stockport and Manchester than she'd intended, and she didn't want to linger on in the hotel.

Samantha allowed the Ferrari to coast gently to a stop, trying to make sure the traffic lights didn't separate her from the black Audi. The men were closer now, no more than two cars behind. Reaching over, she slid her hand beneath a rug on the passenger seat and touched the cold metal stock of the Heckler, seeking reassurance. There were two men, both of them adept at inflicting pain and death. The means of disposal had to be swift and profligate in its delivery. And the time and place had to be of her choosing: somewhere remote, in the dark, with freezing rain blurring their vision and dulling their wits.

Lights changed to green. They moved on. After glancing at signs suspended from a gantry above the road, she flicked the indicator and moved into another lane. Horns blared at the driver of the Black Audi when he followed. She'd taken him unawares. They swept along in the stream of traffic, negotiated a large roundabout, then dipped down on to a motorway that sliced into the heart of the city. They were moving faster now. Checking the rear-view mirror, she saw the black car was still following, the driver occasionally drifting out so he could make sure the low-slung Ferrari Modena was still two cars in front.

* * *

James Bassinger glanced around the table in the smoke-filled upper room and did a mental roll-call: brothers Henry, Morris and Stanley; five of his nephews, and his own boy, Austin. Ronnie's son, Luke, wasn't here: he was visiting his father in Wakefield gaol with his mother. Clifford was with Alan Hinds, and Carl had gone missing. There was no one else. Making his voice loud to call them to order, he said, 'I think everyone who's coming is here now.'

'Clifford,' someone at the far end of the table said. 'Cliff's not arrived yet.'

'He's on a job with Alan Hinds. I'll put you in the picture in a minute. What about minders? Have we got minders on the doors?'

'Front entrance and emergency exits on the ground floor; end of the corridor up here. Everyone else has been cleared from the club.'

Satisfied, James nodded, then took a breath and said, 'They've found the black-haired bitch.' His tone was triumphant. 'I got Alan to drive over to Stockport and do a stake-out in a snack bar that overlooks the bus stop

Paula Hamilton uses. When he saw her in the queue, he lined up and went with her on a bus to Manchester: followed her to the Majestic. The bitch was waiting for her in the foyer. Alan said he could recognize her from the video stills we had enhanced. When she took the Hamilton woman into the dining-room, Alan gave Cliff a call and got him to motor over. A couple of hours later she's crossing the foyer wearing a heavy black raincoat and fuck-off boots. Porter put her bags in a Ferrari Modena and she drove off.'

'A Ferrari! It's definite then, she's not police.'

'Never thought she was,' James Bassinger snapped, irritated by the interruption. 'Traffic was moving slow and Cliff had parked the car further along the street, so they managed to slip in behind her. They're tailing her now.'

'Where's she heading?' Stanley asked.

'North.' James licked his little finger and dabbed the glowing tip of his cigar. 'At the last call they'd just joined the M6 and were circling Preston.'

'Carlisle,' Henry said. 'She's looking for Rachel Tyminski.'

'Or the safe house.'

'Wasting her time going there,' Henry snorted. 'Mark and Trevor watched it for months on and off; went inside a week ago and took a look around. Never anyone there.'

James turned to his son, Austin. 'Has Rachel told you anything yet?'

Austin shook his head. 'A few times she's talked as if her husband's still alive, but I'm pretty sure they were just absent-minded slips. I've watched her and followed her, but it's never more than to-and-from work and the occasional night-out with the women she works with. As far as I know, she's never been to the safe house. She's as pissed off about it all as we are. She lost the big house in Stockport and the business. She thinks her husband was stupid going to the police. When they'd got what they wanted, they didn't want to know him any more.'

'You were screwing her long before the husband grassed on us,' Morris Bassinger muttered. 'Trevor told me. Every time you took a car over you gave her a right seeing-to in the back room. But did she warn you the cops were crawling all over the place? No she bloody-well didn't! And most of us have spent six months inside awaiting trial, Ronnie's banged up, and the greedy bastards are sequestering his stuff.'

'Maybe she didn't know,' Austin protested.

'Didn't know! Christ, you really fancy her, don't you, Austin?' Morris sneered. 'You've gone soft on the fat slag.' Laughter sounded through the haze of smoke.

Austin blushed. 'If she didn't know she couldn't tell us. And she's not a fat slag.' The laughter grew louder.

James scowled. They were seriously out of order, laughing at his boy like this. Until Ronnie was out, he was the head of the family; he was running the firm. Taking the piss out of Austin was disrespecting him. 'That's enough,' he barked. He thumped his fist on the table. 'Austin's done OK. If there's nothing to know, there's nothing he can find out. And she's a sexy piece. Nobody round this table would say no if they got the offer. We'd have to have a whip round for some Viagra for Morris, but he'd be in there if there was a chance.' The jeers and laughter were raucous now.

'OK. OK. Back to business.' James raised his hands in a wordless call for quiet. 'We've had the tip-off. Ronnie's being brought out. They're taking him to that new hospital just outside Leeds. Tomorrow morning; in the early hours.'

'The ambush is on, then,' Stanley said.

'Ambush is off.' James scowled at his cigar and reached for his lighter. 'Big police escort. Too risky. He's going to be held in the hospital, under guard, for forty-eight hours. We know the room he's been allocated. We'll give ’em the first day to get complacent, then go in just after dark and snatch him: two guys, dressed as medics. A private ambulance is picking up some old woman to take her back to a nursing home, all legit. Ronnie will leave in it. After the woman’s dropped off at the home, the ambulance takes him to a quiet spot and we pick him up. That way there’s nothing unusual on the cameras covering the hospital yard, or the parking bay at the home, and nothing incriminating on traffic cameras in between. We don’t leave a trace.’

Henry glanced around the table. ‘Who’s going into the hospital?’

‘We’re not,’ James said. ‘The cops are still interested in us after the trial, and they’ll be over us like a rash when they lose Ronnie. Ronnie’s picked a couple of minders, Bruce and Terry: they’re smart boys he trusts. We’re all going to be elsewhere when Ronnie’s pulled. And we’re going to be able to prove it. I’d better go over that now.’

‘Before you do, what about Carl?’ Morris demanded. ‘My boy’s been missing since early this morning. I’ve had to tell Elaine I’ve sent him on a job in London.’

‘He’s not phoned in?’ James’s brow furrowed.

Morris shook his head. ‘Trevor fine-tooth-combed the place with Ian and Lewis this afternoon. Walked every street, checked every alleyway, looked in empty houses. Council had fixed metal sheets over windows and doors in a couple of derelict places. Trevor had searched them earlier, but we got Ian's wife to phone and say she thought her cat had got trapped in, just on the off-chance we could get inside. They weren't having any. Said it was impossible. Said the men always checked the places over before they sealed them up.'

James looked down the table at Trevor. 'Had these houses been sealed earlier, when Carl followed the woman?'

'The one nearest Paula Hamilton's place hadn't. When it got light, I took a look inside. Didn't see anything.'

'And there's nothing from the hospitals?'

'Nothing,' Morris said. 'If he'd been taken in, they'd have got his ID from his wallet and phoned us. This is my boy, James. It's been hours, and there's no trace.'

'We'd best be sure about the house,' James muttered. 'I'll tell Barry and Gavin to put overalls on, throw some tools in a van and drive over. No one looks twice at blokes in overalls with a van. They can open the place up and do a thorough search.'

'Do you want me to go along?' Trevor asked.

'Best not,' James said. 'You've got Bassinger written all over you and you've already spent a lot of time poking around.'

'Carl's getting married in two months,' Morris said. 'Ed Fletcher's daughter. He was supposed to have lunch with the girl and her mother today; talk about wedding arrangements. If we don't find him, they'll start saying he's got cold feet and done a runner, and we've got enough on our plate without upsetting Ed Fletcher.'

There was a faint bleeping. James reached inside his jacket, brought out a mobile phone and held it to his ear. He listened for a moment, then said, 'Does she know she's being tailed?' and after listening again, 'Don't lose her. We've got to get the bitch. And we want her alive. OK? Tell Alan Hinds to go easy. We'll sort her out when you've brought her back here.' He pocketed the phone. 'That was Cliff. She's still heading North, up the M6. Weather's bad, evening traffic's bad, but it's helping them to stay close. And Alan's the best. He'll get the nasty little whore.'

'When's Vince's funeral?' someone asked.

'Police haven't released the body,' Henry said. 'They've done the post-mortem but they're taking their time, pissing us about. We can't fix a date yet.'

'Who identified the body?'

'Me and Morris,' Stanley muttered. 'And it wasn't a pretty sight. Fell on his head and parts of the chair had been embedded in his arse and thighs. Sadistic bastard at the morgue just pulled the sheet off; he seemed to want to shock us. What with the accident and the autopsy, body was a right mess.'

'Been thinking about the funeral.' They all turned and looked at Henry. 'I think we should take him back to London.'

'Can't bury him with Sharon. Not after what he did to her,' Stanley said.

'She deserved it.' There was a sneer in Henry's voice. 'Messing about with one of your minders: that big, handsome bastard. What was his name? Raines . . . Tim Raines.'

'Tim Raines never touched her,' Stanley protested. 'It was Vince being paranoid. He always was a jealous sod. It made him crazy. Anyway, blokes were so scared of Vince they wouldn't dare look at his woman. Sharon got her neck broke and I lost the best minder I ever had, all for nothing.' He scowled across the table at Henry.

'We'll lay him to rest with mum,' James said softly. 'Eldest son, head of the firm until those Somali bastards maimed him. It's fitting. Mum would want him with her; she'd want him back in her arms.' He exhaled a cloud of cigar smoke.

Morris coughed. 'One other thing's got to be sorted before we talk about where we're all going to be when Ronnie goes missing. We've got to find him a woman. Even if Ronnie and Alice are still in business, Alice can't go near him the night he breaks out.'

'Nice arse, well stacked, real tits: Ronnie can't stand silicone tits,' Henry added, glancing around the table.

'Might not be easy,' Stanley muttered. 'Not with his reputation. Women talk to one another.'

'What about an Albanian bird? I could talk to Aslan, see if he can come up with someone decent,' Lewis suggested.

'This is Ronnie were talking about,' James snorted. 'Our brother Ronnie. He's been inside for more than twelve months. We can't fob him off with some scabby Albanian whore.' He looked at Stanley. 'What about that pole dancer at your club in Leeds. What's her name, Tara . . . Sarah?'

'Tanya,' Stanley muttered grudgingly. 'There's no way she'll say yes when she knows it's Ronnie. And she's a big attraction. I don't want her upsetting.'

'This is for Ronnie,' James growled. 'He kept his mouth shut, he looked after us, he got life for Christ's sake.' He scowled at his brother. 'Offer her a grand to stay with him for two nights and a day. Tell her there's another grand for her if Ronnie's pleased.'

Stanley opened his mouth to argue. He'd been sleeping with Tanya, on and off, for the past twelve months. The last thing he wanted was Ronnie . . . Nine pairs of eyes were watching him expectantly. Making his voice more enthusiastic, he said, 'Leave it with me. I'll ask her. A thou' up front and a thou' when she leaves.'

7

The rain was heavier now and big lorries, swaying in the gusting wind, were bathing the Ferrari in a cloud of spray. It was tempting to pull out, to overtake the north-bound trucks, but safer to remain where she was until she began to look for a place for the killing.

A signboard flared in the lights of the lorry up ahead: junction 40 and Penrith were a mere five miles away. She'd head eastwards at Penrith and ride up the A686 towards the high fells that formed the crest of the Pennines. Easing out a little, she checked the rear-view mirror. The black Audi had closed in. It was now no more than a lorry and its trailer behind her.

The darkness was impenetrable; the lights of oncoming traffic blurred by spray and driving rain. She was certain they'd try to abduct her, question her, discover what her business was. There were fewer lorries to huddle close to now. The growing isolation represented a danger: it gave them opportunities to act without being observed.

Samantha turned off the motorway, navigated a couple of roundabouts, then began the long climb. The Audi's lights were glaring in her mirrors. They were staying close, no longer caring whether she knew they were tailing her or not. Up here, on the moors, patches of snow lingered in ditches and beside dry-stone walls, torn ribbons of whiteness twisting in the headlamp beams. She was searching for the minor road linking the scattered dwellings that bordered the desolation of the fells.

The Ferrari's headlights caught a sign: Haresceugh, Renwick, Croglin. Maintaining speed until she'd almost reached the junction, she braked hard, turned, manoeu-vred winding bends, then accelerated hard down the narrow road.

Glancing in the mirrors, Samantha saw only darkness behind her. The Audi had overshot the junction. She'd passed through Haresceugh before its lights appeared again, reduced to pinpricks by distance and blurred by torrential rain. A place had to be chosen quickly. Turning right at the next junction, she swept through a cluster of dwellings called Renwick. The road was narrower now. When she rounded a bend she saw, on a rise, a lay-by, cut into the hillside and enclosed by a wall that retained a steep bank of earth and rocks. A timber post-and-rail fence defined the other side of the road, and there was a crude bench where walkers could rest and take in the view. She braked hard, swung the Ferrari off the carriageway and cut the ignition. When she stepped out the wind snatched at her coat and freezing rain stung her cheeks. Reaching under the rug, she took the Heckler from the passenger seat, flicked on the interior light, then closed and locked the door.

The stone retaining wall enclosing the lay-by was chest high. Samantha found a toehold and clambered over; her boots sending loose shale clattering down as she scrambled up the steep slope. Squeezing between boulders, she found herself on a small, rocky shelf where grass and heather were overlaid by a thin crust of melting snow. She was no more than twenty feet from the lay-by and about the same height above it. She could see the roof of her car and, in the spill of its lights, the sweep of the road and the vague outline of the fence that bordered the far verge. She prostrated herself in the wet grass. Low clouds, as black as the fells they covered, were shutting out the moon and stars. With nothing to mark the transition between earth and sky, she felt suspended in an endless darkness.

The Audi swept around the bend and slithered to a stop, its brake lights turning rain into blood. Samantha drew the cowl of her raincoat around her face and positioned the Heckler. It was important that the men be standing close to one another. They had to die together, killed by a single burst. Killing them individually was too risky. One of them might escape and tell tales; worse, he could stalk her and return fire.

The passenger door of the Audi swung open and a man with tightly-curled black hair, wearing a belted overcoat, climbed out. He strutted over to Samantha's car, peered inside, then looked back towards the Audi and beckoned. A tall, broad-shouldered figure emerged, his dark raincoat flapping in the wind. 'The lamp, Cliff. Bring the lamp.'

An interior light silhouetted the tall man when he opened the boot. He lifted out a powerful looking searchlight, then slammed the lid shut. Rain glistened on his coat as he crossed over to the Ferrari. 'Where is she?' He shouted the words over the gusting wind.

His companion shrugged. 'Call of nature.'

'Can't see her stopping for a piss in this lot.' The tall man laughed. Lank, straw-coloured hair was plastered over his brow. He switched on the lamp. An intense beam of bluish light stabbed at the darkness. Samantha pressed her face into the grass before its glare flashed through gaps between the boulders that concealed her. The tall man walked the length of the retaining wall, shining the beam behind it and up the rocky bank, then he crossed over to the railings on the far side of the road and directed the light into the depression beyond. 'There's a path down here,' he yelled. 'Maybe she got scared, left the car and headed out over the moors.' His companion joined him by the railings and they stood together, staring down the beam of light at the windswept desolation.

Confident, Samantha mused, reckless even, wandering around, waving a lamp, yelling to make themselves heard above the roaring wind. But she was just a woman to them, a silly tart, not something deadly, watching from the darkness.

They were standing side-by-side, gripping the railings to steady themselves while the wind tore at their clothes. The lamp was still being directed over the moors. Raindrops, scintillating in its beam, were reflecting back a circle of light that silhouetted the two men. Perfect, Samantha decided. She sighted along the muzzle of the Heckler, squeezed the trigger, felt the shivering recoil as the sub-machine gun stuttered out a dozen rounds. The lamp disappeared. All she could make out were the faint lines of fence rails touched by the light from the cars.

She remained in the wet grass and melting snow, her eyes straining for any sign of movement. She was cold now, and the trickle of rainwater flowing around the boulders had become a stream. After watching for almost a minute, she rose, dug the heels of her boots into the loose shale and slithered down the slope. Still clutching the Heckler, she climbed over the wall and crossed the road. Two bodies made a single heap in the darkness. Peering over the railings, she saw the lamp had fallen on to rough grass beside a path, its glass wedged against a low wall, imprisoning its light. She stepped through an opening, ran down the steep path and retrieved it. When she returned, its light touched the arms of a signpost: one pointed towards Renwick Fell, the other to Croglin.

Rolling the bodies apart, she tugged open coats, removed wallets, keys, phones, documents, rings, watches: anything that would identify them. A Russian pistol was tucked inside the jacket of the black-haired man. She stored it, along with all the other items, in the big patch pockets of her raincoat. His half-closed eyes had been staring up at her while she groped amongst his clothing. The taller man's eyes had rolled up into his head and white orbs bulged out of rain-glazed flesh. Every kill brought a new vision to haunt her.

The wind moaned down from the fells, gasping and roaring as it flayed her face and coat with icy rain. Struggling against the buffeting, Samantha rolled the bodies under the bottom rail of the fence, then pushed them down on to the path. Sweeping the lamp towards the point where the path headed off across the moors, she saw stones had been graded according to size and stacked in neat piles. Beyond the piles, the ground formed a hollow, then fell sharply to a channel that carried rainwater from a culvert beneath the road. She headed down the steeply sloping path, rolling the dead men along with her. When she reached the bend, she gave them a last push into the hollow, then heaved at the stacks of stones, toppling them over the bodies. She played the beam of light on to the untidy heap. The corpses were well concealed and the covering appeared natural and accidental, not recent and contrived. If the men who repaired the dry-stone walls didn't visit their hoard, the Bassinger boy and his enforcer would remain hidden.

Back on the road, she ran over and checked the Audi. Its engine was throbbing and its lights were still stabbing at the dark. The glove compartment held a wallet of servicing documents, a map and a pair of sunglasses. In the rear foot well she found a new-looking leather briefcase. When she lifted the lid of the boot, she saw a set of golf clubs and a couple of overnight bags. Clicking open the briefcase, she emptied the contents of her raincoat pockets into it, all the things she'd taken from the bodies of the men, then carried bags and briefcase over to her Ferrari and tossed them behind the seats.

The lights of the stationary cars had been blazing for too long. They might have been seen from the windows of an isolated house. Samantha slid behind the wheel of the Audi, reversed it into the lay-by, then switched off lights and ignition and locked it. Half-an-hour later she was back on the M6, heading north towards Carlisle.

* * *

James Bassinger listened to the dialing tone until the recorded answering service came on the line, then cradled the phone.

'Anything?' Stanley Bassinger asked.

'Nothing. I left a message for Clifford an hour ago. No point leaving another.'

'What about Alan's phone?'

'Same,' James said. 'No answer. And I left a message for him, too. Been calling both numbers every ten minutes. Last message was from Alan, saying they'd turned off the M6 at Penrith and were driving east, over the Pennines. He thought she might be heading for Newcastle.'

James and Stanley eyed each other in silence for a while, then James tried to make his voice reassuring when he said, 'They'll be OK. Alan Hinds is a real pro. One of the best we've ever used. No one's going to put one over on Alan. Christ, he got Vince out of that club when the Boulder Road Boys staged the ambush. And Clifford's handy. If the black-haired bitch thinks she can — '

The phone began to bleep. James snatched it up and listened. Stanley grew concerned when he saw his brother's face harden, his shoulders sag. James put his hand over the mouthpiece, stared at Stanley with angry eyes, and said, 'They've found Carl.'

'Is he — ?'

'Dead. In the boarded-up house. They found him in the cellar, under a stone shelf, hidden behind a pile of rubbish. He'd been shot in the head. Rats have eaten half his fucking face off.'

'Jesus,' Stanley breathed. 'How are we going to tell Morris and Elaine?'

James closed his eyes and tried to think. 'What are we going to do with the body? We can't give him a funeral without a death certificate, and we can't get a death certificate without involving the cops.'

'Morris has got to be told,' Stanley insisted. 'He can decide what to do with the body. He's already having trouble with Elaine. She didn't believe that story about Carl being sent to London on a job. There was a hell of a row when he didn't turn up for lunch with the girl and her mother.'

'Day after tomorrow Ronnie's being snatched from hospital,' James said. 'We don't need any distractions. Most of all, we don't need the cops asking endless bloody questions about what Carl was doing in Stockport and why his body's been found a few doors from where the Hamilton woman lives. I say we leave Carl where he is for forty-eight hours, then have the police tipped off so they do a search and find him.'

'This is Morris's boy,' Stanley protested. 'Lying in a cellar with rats feeding on his face.'

'He's dead,' James retorted. 'He can't feel the rats. And Morris can't do anything with the body if he collects it. The police have got to find it, set the legal wheels turning so we can get a death certificate.'

'We can buy a death certificate.'

'And you don't think the cops are going to

be interested when Morris buries a thirty-year-old son who's never been sick?' James's tone was scathing. 'It's too risky, Stan. The cops are still breathing down our necks after the trial, and they're going to be over us like a fucking rash when we spring Ronnie. Anything the least bit dodgy right now could bugger everything up. We've got to wait until Ronnie's safely out of the country, then pay a grass to tip the cops off, maybe spin 'em a tale about one of the Boulder Road Boys killing him.'

'There aren't any Boulder Road Boys. We roasted the bastards.'

'So? We'll blame it on someone else whose troubling us.' James put the phone back to his ear. 'Anyone see you when you broke into the house?'

Stanley heard a faint voice saying, 'Parked the van at the end of the alley and went in the back way. It's dark, we've only been here ten minutes; even if we've been noticed, nobody's going to be interested.'

'Put him back under the shelf,' James said. 'And seal the place up again. I'll get someone to tip off the police. Meanwhile, don't say a word to anyone. Most of all, don't say a word to Morris and Elaine. OK?' He cradled the phone.

'Morris is going to go crazy,' Stanley said.

'He doted on the boy. Shit! How are we going to break the news?'

'We might not have to,' James said. 'If we play it right the police will, after they've found him.'

'Vince, now Carl, and no message from Clifford and Alan. Ronnie might be safer inside,' Stanley muttered.

'Talking about Ronnie, did you have a word with that lap-dancer?'

'Tanya? Yeah, talked to her. She was willing, but she can't.'

'Can't?' James laughed. 'Two-grand for a couple of nights and a day; what does she mean, she can't?'

'Menstruating,' Stanley said. 'When Ronnie gets out it'll be her period.' He was lying. He hadn't even mentioned it to Tanya. He didn't want Ronnie mauling and frightening her. She was a sweet kid. And anyway, there was something unnatural about sharing a woman with your brother. 'Don't worry,' he went on. 'Found him a stunner. Stripper at a club in Manchester. Exotic piece called Ingrid Umbassa.'

'Ingrid Umbassa?' James gave him a questioning look.

'Half and half: Swedish and black South African. Beautiful face, great arse and tits.'

* * *

Samantha slid the card in the lock, withdrew it, then pushed at the door and stepped inside her room. The late dinner at Carlisle's Millbank Hotel hadn't been the finest meal she'd ever eaten, but it had been comforting, and she was no longer cold.

She picked up the briefcase, carried it over to the dressing table and tipped out the contents. A hundred and fifteen . . . No, a hundred and thirty thousand pounds in bundles secured by rubber bands; rings; a gold Rolex; a steel-cased watch with a lot of dials; a solid gold Dunhill lighter; a Saint Christopher medallion; an almost full packet of cigarettes; mobile phones; keys; a semi-automatic pistol and some wallets. An engraving on the back of the Rolex watch told her Clifford Bassinger had been given it on his twenty-first birthday.

There was a slim cash-book, the edges of its pages soiled by repeated fingering. It contained a list of clubs in Liverpool and Manchester, with cash amounts entered in dated columns. Clifford Bassinger and his enforcer had probably been collecting protection money when they'd been diverted to follow her. Flicking open the wallets, Samantha thumbed through the contents: cash, credit cards, receipts for small purchases, a driving license identifying the black-haired man as Alan Hinds. Tucked behind the banknotes in Alan Hinds's wallet was a postcard-sized photograph. Sliding it out, Samantha looked down at a grainy black-and-white image of a woman sitting on the arm of a chair. She'd missed a security camera in Vincent Bassinger's flat! She was becoming careless. She studied the picture. They'd worked on it, enhanced it as much as they could, but it was still blurred and indistinct. Even so, if they showed it to someone who'd seen her recently, they'd probably detect a likeness. She gave a resigned sigh. There was nothing she could do about it now. Holding the open briefcase beneath the edge of the table, she swept everything inside, then clicked it shut.

The men's overnight bags were lying at the foot of the bed. She unzipped them and groped through toiletries, dirty socks and underwear that was mostly soiled. One of the bags held a couple of clean shirts and an almost full bottle of Scotch. She dragged the zips shut, then headed for the bathroom, feeling a sudden compulsion to wash her hands.

8

Rachel Tyminski eased her haunches towards the back of the seat, parted her thighs, and released her first pee of the day. She held the test strip in the flow, counted to ten, then withdrew it and shook off the drops. The instruction leaflet had said wait five minutes, so she laid it on the rim of the basin and rose to her feet. Suddenly her stomach heaved, then heaved again, and her mouth filled with foul-tasting vomit. She spat it into the pan and pressed the flush.

She felt too fragile to go into work today, but she knew she must. The manager had already warned her a couple of times about attendance and timekeeping. Crabby old bitch! If she woke every morning to Austin trying to get between her legs, she'd be late now and then. She probably wouldn't bother going in at all! Rachel let her robe fall to the floor, stepped over the side of the bath and turned on the shower. When the water was running hot, she moved under the spray, shampooed her hair, then began to soap herself. The sensation of hot water flowing over her body was pleasant. She stood there for quite a while, her eyes closed, her mind blank. When the shower began to run cool, she stepped out, dried herself, and made a turban of the towel.

It had been more than five minutes: probably more than ten. She couldn't put off looking at the strip of plastic for ever. Reaching out, she snatched it up. Two pink bands. Shit! She let out a resigned sigh. The test was only telling her what she already knew. She'd been pretty sure for a couple of days. Her bouts of nausea hadn't been caused by that Chinese meal she'd had on Melanie's hen night. Her breasts weren't tender because of Austin's enthusiastic fondling. It was just like it had been with Benjamin. Recollections faded, but you never really forgot. She was carrying Austin Bassinger's baby! Lawrence Cosgrave, now Austin Bassinger. She really had messed up. All right, maybe she had forgotten to take the pill sometimes, but when Austin's hands and mouth were all over you, taking pills was the last thing on your mind.

The nausea was welling up again. When her stomach began to heave, she bent over the pan and vomited. Shit! Two, maybe three months of this, then the birth. Did she want to go through with it? She should be worried, scared even, but she felt dreamily calm and relaxed. Bloody hormones! This was no time for calm and relaxed. She had to get her mind around the situation, do some serious thinking, decide what she was going to do. And this time there wouldn't be her mother going on and on at her and Father Ryan telling her what she ought . . .

The ding-dong of the door chimes startled her. Austin must have finished his business early and forgotten to take his keys when he left the flat. She needed to be alone right now, not frying him bacon and eggs and slapping his hands away. Picking up her bathrobe, she drew it on as she padded down the hall. She opened the door.

'Mrs Tyminski?'

Nodding, Rachel let her gaze wander over the black-haired woman in the fabulous fur coat.

'Is Austin Bassinger here?'

Rachel's breath caught in her throat. She'd been dreading this. 'You his wife?' she asked, in a shocked voice. She tried to shake off the dreamy lethargy that was dogging her and get her brain working. Glancing down at the woman's hands, she saw they were sheathed in tight black gloves that buttoned beyond the wrists. There was no swelling beneath the leather where a ring might have been. She moved her eyes back to the woman's face and added, 'Or his partner?'

Ignoring Rachel's questions, Samantha repeated, 'Austin Bassinger: is he here?'

Rachel shook her head. 'He's not here. You'd better come in.' She led Samantha along the dark hall and into a sitting room where she began to snatch newspapers and magazines from the sofa and stack them on a coffee table. 'The place is a bit of a mess. I haven't — '

'Don't worry. It looks fine to me.'

When Rachel straightened up the woman was holding out a wallet, opened to show an identity card and a badge. It flicked shut before she could take a proper look. She felt a rush of relief. She wasn't going to be confronted by an outraged wife or partner after all.

'Are we alone?' Samantha asked.

Rachel nodded.

'I have to be sure. Do you mind?' Samantha flashed her a smile, then stepped back into the hall and began to open doors. She checked a room containing an unmade double bed and a wardrobe that held dresses and a man's suit and shirts; a tiny bedroom with a computer on a flimsy desk that was hemmed in by boxes and suitcases and a vacuum cleaner. The bathroom was still steamy after Rachel's shower: a box and foil wrapper from a pregnancy testing kit had been tossed on the window sill; one of the plastic strips, crossed with tell-tale pink bands, was lying in the soap recess at the back of the basin. Unwashed dishes and the remains of yesterday's evening meal cluttered the tiny kitchen. Apart from the wardrobe in the double bedroom, there was nowhere for a man to hide. They were alone. Samantha checked the lock on the outer door, then returned to the sitting room.

'Satisfied?' Rachel demanded irritably.

'I had to be sure.'

Rachel nodded towards the sofa. 'Have a seat.'

Samantha untied tapes and her coat fell open, revealing a green woollen dress with a band of darker green silk around its square neck and bands of silk around the hem. She relaxed back on the sofa.

'How did you get in?' Rachel demanded.

'You let me in.'

'I mean the entrance lobby downstairs; the door on to the street has a lock.'

'Postman,' Samantha said, suddenly understanding. 'He was sorting letters into pigeon holes. His trolley was holding the door open.

Rachel sniffed. 'So much for the security we all pay for.'

'Benjamin Hamilton,' Samantha opened.

'Have you any idea — '

'The police called three days ago,' Rachel interrupted when she realized what the woman's visit was about. 'I can only tell you what I told them. I've not seen him for months and I've no idea where he is. They searched the place even though I'd told them that.'

'You don't seem very concerned,' Samantha said. 'Your mother's demented.'

'I'm trying to put Stockport behind me. Forget the place and everyone in it.' Rachel lowered herself into an armchair she'd brought from the home she'd once shared with Janos; the armchair and the matching sofa were much too big for this smaller room.

'Perhaps you're not concerned because you know where he is; you know he's safe.'

Rachel let out an outraged laugh. 'That's stupid. I've absolutely no idea where my brother is.'

'He's your son, Mrs Tyminski, not your brother,' Samantha said softly.

They eyed one another through an icy silence, then Samantha said, 'I've been fully briefed about the circumstances surrounding Benjamin's birth.'

'My mother told you?' Rachel sounded shocked.

'I'm acting for Lawrence Cosgrave, Benjamin's father,' Samantha answered evasively.

'If you know where Benjamin is; if you've an idea where he might be — '

'I've told you, I've not the faintest idea where Benjamin is. And I might be his biological mother, but he was never my child. I wanted a termination, but my mother stopped me having one. She took him the moment he was born. Couldn't have any more kids after she'd had me. He was the boy she'd always longed for.'

'He was your child.'

'He gave me the creeps, always looking at me in that funny way. It was as if he'd been born wise, as if he knew things. He isn't normal, did they tell you that?' Rachel was trying to meet Samantha's unsettling gaze. She had more than enough to worry about without this poised, beautiful, every-fucking-thing-she'd-ever-wanted-to-be black-haired tart questioning her and freaking her out like this. Her stomach lurched; the nausea was stirring again.

'Not normal?' Samantha murmured huskily.

'He's autistic. The psychiatrist said he isn't, but I'm sure he is. And strange with it. I should never have told my mother I was pregnant. I should have kept it quiet and had the termination. Lawrence would have paid. I could have said I was going on a university interview or something. If I'd had the termination, I'd be married to Lawrence now. He said we'd have to wait until the end of the parliamentary term, then he'd resign, leave his wife and politics, and go back to being a barrister. We'd start a new life together. But my mother couldn't keep her mouth shut, could she? She had to involve Father Ryan and his moralizing. He even went to see Lawrence and lectured him about his obligations to his wife and family. What about his obligations to me?'

Smiling, Samantha asked gently, 'What did you expect a Catholic priest to do?'

'Didn't expect him to do anything because I didn't expect him to be told. It was my mother's fault. She buggered up my entire life making sure she got the baby boy she'd always wanted.'

'Where's Janos?'

'Janos? Janos is dead.'

'Mrs Tyminski, I've been very thoroughly briefed. I know what happened after the trial.' Samantha allowed irritation to show in her voice.

'Don't know,' Rachel muttered truculently. 'Saw him once, at the house the police bought for us in Rosley. They said we had to be very careful about meeting. Janos was going to move the furniture in, a few pieces at a time, then get the place ready so we could live together again when things had settled down. He was really scared; he kept going on about the Bassingers looking for him and what they'd do if they found him. I think he was starting to have mental problems. To be honest, he didn't seem all that bothered whether he saw me again or not. I never tried to contact him after that.'

'Is he still at the safe house?'

Rachel shrugged.

'Austin Bassinger,' Samantha said. 'When did you last see him?'

'My mother tell you about Austin, did she?' Rachel's tone was bitter.

'Vincent Bassinger told me. Your little trysts in the office at the back of the garage were all they talked about.'

'Austin wouldn't . . . ' Rachel looked shocked and disbelieving.

Samantha smiled. 'Men aren't discreet about their conquests, Mrs Tyminski. They boast about them; entertain their friends with the intimate details. The Bassingers were amazed how reckless you both were. They expected Janos to find out.'

Rachel had been hurt by what she'd just heard. She'd never imagined Austin would talk about her and laugh about her behind her back. Maybe the woman was lying, deliberately trying to upset her so she'd reveal things about Austin. Frowning, she said, 'Janos is like a child: naïve and trusting. He wouldn't dream of going with another woman, so he couldn't imagine me doing it with another man. All he was interested in was working on cars and trucks. He hardly ever stepped into the office. He left that side of things to me.'

'Austin Bassinger still sees you?'

'We're together. He comes and goes on business, but he spends a lot of time with me.'

'Has he ever asked you about Janos — asked you about Benjamin?'

Rachel's frown deepened. 'Suppose he does talk about Janos sometimes. We had a bit of a tiff about it yesterday. He passed it off as jealousy; said he couldn't bear to think of me having slept with another man.'

'Strange, don't you think,' Samantha said softly. 'A man like Austin Bassinger being jealous of a dead husband.'

'Why shouldn't he be jealous at the thought of me with another man?' Rachel's tone was indignant. 'He's told me he loves me. He's asked me to marry him.'

'After what your husband did to the Bassingers?'

'That's what I said, but he told me it didn't matter. He said it would be OK.'

'He doesn't know Janos is alive?'

'Christ, no! I'm not that stupid. I keep reminding him I'm a widow. I owe Janos that much.'

'You don't think he could be trying to find out about Janos?'

'I did wonder, but if he has, he's been taking his time about it.' Rachel suddenly became defiant. 'He comes here to see me, that's all. Is there any reason why he wouldn't want to be with me? I mean, he has asked me to marry him.'

'Benjamin,' Samantha said, changing tack. 'Do you think he'd like to know where Benjamin is?'

'We'd all like to know where Benjamin is,' Rachel snapped. 'But what can I tell him? I probably know less than you do.'

Samantha said nothing, just studied the plump woman in the blue bathrobe with a towel around her hair. She wasn't pretty, but she wasn't plain. And she hadn't changed: she was still recognizable as the girl in the wedding photographs her mother had shown her.

Rachel suddenly smiled. 'Men are so very different, aren't they?'

Samantha returned the smile.

'I mean, Lawrence Cosgrave will always be the one as far as I'm concerned. I suppose I was lucky he was the first. He really cared about me, truly loved me, loved me like a mature man. And he was tender and romantic, very gentle with me. He could get carried away, though, really passionate.' Rachel laughed throatily. 'I liked it when he got passionate.' She looked down at her hands and began to toy with her wedding ring. The smile had faded from her lips and her voice was little more than a whisper when she went on, 'I never really wanted to marry Janos. There was something about him that made me uncomfortable. I used to watch him serving on the altar at mass, all got up in his cassock and surplice, handing the priest the censer, carrying the cross. I think he was too religious for me: too devout. His parents were worse than mine; his mother had a very tight hold on him. Mothers! The thing was, everyone seemed to think it was a good idea: Janos and me, I mean. Father Ryan was all smiles about it, and I could tell my mother was desperate for me to marry him. She really liked him.'

'And how did it turn out, being married to Janos?' Samantha asked. 'Were you right to be uneasy?'

Rachel nodded. 'All he did was work and worry. He'd let me have anything I wanted, and then he'd start worrying about paying for it. Scared stiff about starting a family. Kept going on about clearing the debt and getting the business established first. I said I'd go on the pill but he wouldn't hear of it. He said it was wrong in the eyes of the Church and he didn't want me to have it on my conscience.' She laughed. 'I didn't give a damn. I went on it anyway, just as soon as I realized how up-tight he was about getting me pregnant.' She stared out of the window at the grey winter dawn, then sighed and said, 'But he cared about me, really cared in his own worrying kind of way. I always knew that. Like I said, men are so very different. Austin doesn't give a damn about anything; doesn't know what the word worry means. Life's something to be enjoyed as far as he's concerned. Good times and lots of sex.' She laughed. 'Austin does his best to give you a good time. But I couldn't trust him, not with all the women in the clubs he has to visit. And he often works at night. When he goes out, I never know where he is.'

'Do you know where he is now?' Samantha asked.

Rachel shrugged. 'Went out yesterday morning. Said he was going to Manchester then on to Leeds; one of his uncles is coming out of hospital.'

'Did he say which hospital.' Samantha

felt she might be learning something useful at last.

'A new place, just outside Leeds. It's not been open long. I can't remember the name. Austin said there were things he had to sort out before they collect his uncle and take him to a private nursing home tomorrow night. I know it's tomorrow night because I asked him when he'd get back and he said his uncle wasn't being discharged until Thursday and he'd come back here Friday. They're a very close family, the Bassingers.'

'Did he say which nursing home?'

Rachel shook her head. 'He only told me as much as he did because I was giving him grief: accusing him of two-timing me with other women. He was trying to convince me he was telling the truth.'

'Janos,' Samantha said. 'Have you any idea where he is?'

'He could still be living in the house the police found for us, but I don't think so. He was terrified about the Bassingers finding him. I think he'll have moved on.' Rachel frowned. 'Why are you so interested in Janos and the Bassingers? I thought you were looking for Benjamin.'

'The Bassingers could be interested in finding Benjamin,' Samantha said. 'You should be careful what you say to Austin; be careful what you do.'

'I've no idea what you mean,' Rachel snapped. ' 'Be careful what I do'.'

'Be careful you don't lead the Bassingers to Janos when you go and see him.'

Rachel felt a stab of alarm. The woman must be psychic. How did *she* know she was thinking of visiting Janos? And those eyes: so still and remote, always watching, just like a tiger on the prowl. It was as if she'd been reading her mind. 'I've no idea where Janos is,' she snapped. 'So there's no chance of them finding him through me.'

'Does Janos visit you?'

'It'd be the first time.' Rachel watched as Samantha uncrossed her legs and rose to her feet. 'That's a beautiful dress,' she said enviously.

Samantha smiled, 'Thanks. Balenciaga's autumn collection.'

Balenciaga! Who or what was Balenciaga? Some fancy fashion house, no doubt. And the bag and shoes looked expensive, too; not to mention the fabulous fur coat. She could have been dressed like that if her mother and Father Ryan had kept their noses out of her business. If she'd had the termination, if she'd hung on until Lawrence could leave politics and go back to being a barrister, he'd have married her, she was sure of it. How many times had he told her he loved her?

Samantha stepped out of the living room and headed down the hallway. When they reached the door she turned, and said, 'Your mother told me you work in a travel agent's.'

'That's right. *Going Places*.'

'In Carlisle?'

Rachel nodded and tugged open the door. Samantha stepped out on to the deserted landing. 'Be careful,' she said softly. 'The Bassingers are ruthless and your husband caused them a lot of pain.' She reached into her bag, tore a sheet from a notebook and scribbled down a mobile phone number. She handed it to Rachel. 'If you hear anything about Benjamin or Janos, or if you just want to talk, call that number.'

Rachel watched her descending the stairs, waited until the gleaming black hair had bobbed out of sight, then closed the door. She returned to the bathroom. Her nausea had gone. She dropped the lid over the toilet and sat down. Lawrence must be worried if he'd arranged for someone to do an independent search. It was the first time in six years that he'd shown an interest in Benjamin. He didn't know a thing about him: didn't know what he looked like, didn't know he wasn't normal. She shivered, remembering the way she used to catch Benjamin staring at her, his head tilted back a little, that knowing smile on his face, the light reflecting off the lenses of his glasses, obscuring his eyes.

Why was a woman searching? Why not a man? She'd only allowed her a fleeting glimpse of the identity card and it hadn't been possible to read her name or check the organization she worked for. Rachel tried to recall their conversation. She couldn't remember having told the woman anything useful. With hindsight, she'd been a bit too free with details of her love-life, but when the woman had looked at her with those eyes and given her encouraging little smiles, she'd wanted to confide.

Rachel picked up the test strip, stared at the tell-tale bands of pink across the blue and suddenly realized she'd been doing more than confide in the woman. She'd been thinking things through, speaking her thoughts out loud, reaching conclusions. Austin Bassinger wasn't father material. He was fun to be with, a great lover, but apart from the family business he wasn't serious about anything. He just fooled around. He didn't know the meaning of the word responsibility. If she decided to keep the baby, he'd be playing fast and loose with other women while it was making her shapeless.

Rising from the toilet, she padded across

the hall and stepped into the tiny bedroom she used as an office and lumber room. God, it was almost nine! She'd be late for work again. She'd tell the manager she'd had a dodgy meal and she'd been vomiting her heart out. It was partly true. Tugging at a drawer in the flimsy desk, she reached towards the back, groped around until she felt the matchbox, then took it out. She flopped down on the swivel chair, slid the box open, tipped the matches on to her lap, then read the number written inside. Picking up the phone, she dialled it, then relaxed back, listening to the bleeps. When she was about to give up, the line opened and an apprehensive voice, like a ghost from the past, said, 'Hullo . . . Hullo. Who's calling?' She could hear hammering and whistling and footsteps echoing around a big space.

'Janos?'

'Rachel!'

'I need to see you.'

'It's Brian: Brian Keating.' Then his voice lowered, and she could hear the fear in it as he added, 'It's too dangerous.'

'It's been a long time, Brian. I want to see you.'

'Is it important? Just a minute.' He'd removed his mouth from the phone and she could hear him shouting instructions across the big space. 'It's the gasket. There's water in the oil. The cylinder head's got to come off. OK?'

She caught a workmate's muffled reply, then Janos was saying, 'You there, Rachel? You still there?'

'I'm here. I need to see you.'

'Need to see me?'

'Want to see you.' She made her voice tearful. 'It's been a long time. I want to see you again.'

'It's dangerous. You know how — '

'I don't care.' She was choking back sobs. 'I have to see you.' When she heard him sigh, she said, 'Are you at the same address?'

'I've moved. I'm working in Brampton now. Could we meet somewhere in Brampton? It might be safer in public.'

'I'm your wife, Ja . . . Brian, not some woman from a dating agency. I want to see you in private.'

'*Don't* write this down. You've got to remember it. Promise me you won't write it down?'

Rachel promised, then reached for a pad and ballpoint pen.

'Friary Road: number twenty-seven. Are you coming on the bus?'

She scribbled down the address. 'I've got a little car.'

'If you're coming in from Carlisle, drive through the town centre and follow the signs for Haltwhistle and Corbridge. You'll pass a big Victorian church with a spire, about a quarter-of-a-mile out of town. Friary Road's the second turn-off after that, on the same side. When will you come?'

'Tonight, after work.' She was adding his directions to the address. 'I could get there just after six.'

'I don't usually get in until — '

'I need to see you, Brian.'

A resigned sigh came down the line. 'OK, six. I'll make sure I finish early. And for heavens sake be careful, Rachel. Remember what the police told us.' The line went dead.

* * *

Lawrence Cosgrave glanced up when he heard the door open. Florid features, framed by neatly barbered grey hair, appeared around it and beamed across the room at him. 'You wanted a talk, Lawrence?' The nasal voice had a slight lisp.

'I did, Ted. Thanks for dashing over. Come and sit here.' Cosgrave pulled out the chair next to his while the bulky figure waddled towards him. Cosgrave glanced over his shoulder at a black-cased pediment clock on an ornate mantelpiece. Quarter-to-ten. They'd got a good half-hour before the other members of the Cabinet Select Committee were due to arrive.

Panting a little, Edward Ashton dragged the heavy chair clear of the table and sat sideways on it, facing Lawrence Cosgrave. The material of his blue pinstripe suit was stretched tight over his paunch and shoulders, and there was a sheen of perspiration on his face. After sliding an armful of papers onto the gleaming table, he took a handkerchief from his sleeve and patted it over his cheeks and throat. He felt apprehensive. He was wondering what all this was about. Old Lawrence looked grey, really under the weather. He'd never seen him looking so shattered before.

'How long have we known each other, Ted?' Lawrence Cosgrave allowed the tiredness to show in his voice. Alone with his friend in the Cabinet Room he wasn't bothering to project the relentless energy and commanding presence his office demanded.

Edward linked his fingers over his paunch. Was old Lawrence thinking of a Cabinet reshuffle? He didn't want to lose Education, not after he'd just got nicely bedded in. He patted his cheeks and throat with the handkerchief again, then said breathlessly,

'For ever, Lawrence. We were at Oxford together: Eton before that. Must be more than thirty years.'

Lawrence Cosgrave nodded slowly. 'It's been a long time, Ted.'

This didn't sound like reshuffles. Frowning at the Prime Minister, Edward asked, 'What's the matter, Lawrence? Are you ill? Tell me what — '

'I'm thinking of resigning.'

'Christ! You can't be serious?'

'I'm completely serious.'

'But things are going so well. Poll ratings are good; better than we could expect. You've been a very popular prime minister, Lawrence. Everyone's hoping you'll see us through to another term.'

'Sooner could be better than later,' Cosgrave said. 'For Helen's sake as well as for the sake of the Party.'

'For Helen's sake . . . '

Lawrence Cosgrave leaned towards his friend and squeezed his arm. 'I've never told a soul about this, Ted, but I've reached the point where I've got to confide in someone I can trust.'

Woman trouble, Edward guessed. A sexual indiscretion. Curiosity began to infuse his concern as he studied his friend's face. Lawrence's once piercing blue eyes had become dull, the flesh on his cheeks pallid and grey, the lines around his mouth darker, more deeply etched. He'd suddenly aged ten years. Edward listened to a few ticks from the old pediment clock, then said softly, 'You'd better tell me what's worrying you, Lawrence.'

Cosgrave closed his eyes and turned away, trying to collect his thoughts. 'It was seven years ago,' he began. 'When we were canvassing for the election. I didn't think we'd get in. In fact, I thought I might lose my seat. And after being in opposition for a couple of terms, I can't say I was all that bothered. No power, too much constituency hassle, other opportunities going by the wayside, and we both know the pay and perks are pathetic.' He straightened himself in his chair and pushed his shoulders back. He seemed to be bracing himself, gathering the last reserves of his nervous energy before revealing things that might lose him the respect of an old friend. 'Anyway,' he went on, 'we needed an extra pair of hands in the constituency office — you know how it is at election time — and Helen found me a girl. She was bright, hard-working, enthusiastic — '

'Was she very pretty?'

'Not particularly. But she was attractive,

had an emphatic figure; and she was young, just turned eighteen. Something clicked. There was suddenly a rapport between us. She was attentive, interested in what I'd got to say; wives grow accustomed to you, don't they? Perhaps become a little bored with you.' He laughed wryly. 'One even begins to detect an affectionate contempt.' Leaning forward, he rested his elbows on the table and linked his fingers under his chin. 'I must have been mad, Ted. She was only a couple of years older than my eldest son. But she was up for it. And such a ravishing body. I knew it was being offered, and I took it; took the opportunity to hold and caress a sweet young girl again. I was feeling pretty low at the time, disillusioned with politics, the way my life was going. She was the excitement, the diversion, I needed. She gave me the energy to go out and fight the election.'

Edward Ashton ran his finger around his collar. He wanted facts, not reminiscences. And young girls, sweet or otherwise, were something that had never interested him. Lawrence knew that. 'Have the papers got hold of it?' He pressed the handkerchief against his cheeks and throat. Heavens, it was hot in here.

Lawrence Cosgrave shook his head. 'Not yet. It's more complicated than that, Ted.' He took a deep breath. 'She became pregnant. I talked her into getting rid of it, but she must have told her mother, and her mother told the parish priest and the abortion was off. In the end we decided she'd go away with her mother and have the baby and when they came back the mother would say it was hers.'

'You said, 'We decided'. Does Helen know?'

'God, no. Rachel, that's the girl, kicked up a fuss and threatened to go and see Helen, but the priest persuaded her to keep quiet. I paid for everything, of course. Got old Alexander Myers to examine her and attend the birth. He sorted out the paperwork, too. The girl's mother's name was entered on all the medical documents, and her mother and father are named as parents on the birth certificate.'

'Harley Street: physician to the aristocracy!' Edward chuckled. 'You took good care of the girl.'

'He's a first cousin. His name went on the honours list the following year: a knighthood.' Lawrence Cosgrave sighed dolefully. 'Since the birth I've paid the girl's mother an allowance. Drew on a trust fund my parents set up for the boys. Didn't feel very good about that, but there was nothing else I could do.' He closed his eyes.

Edward studied his friend's face. Recounting the events seemed to have drained him. This explained his lack-lustre performance in the House: why Donovan had been able to run rings round him at Question Time. 'It seems you dealt with it very deftly, Lawrence. I can understand you feeling threatened, but time's passing and if anyone had been going to say — '

'It's more complicated than that,' Lawrence Cosgrave interrupted. 'Let me finish, Ted.'

Edward settled his bulk against the table and mumbled an apology.

'The girl got married. Somehow that made me feel better. She wouldn't want her own marriage unsettling, so she wasn't a loose cannon any more. And I'd become PM and was able to trickle money back into the trust.'

'How much do you pay the girl's mother?'

'Fifteen hundred a month. Was a thousand, but I've kept increasing it.'

'Eighteen thousand a year. Hmm . . . '

'Not a small sum to pay out covertly, especially in the beginning when I was finding money for the boy's school fees. And Helen's never maintained what you'd call a frugal lifestyle.' Lawrence Cosgrave turned and looked Edward full in the face. 'The girl married Jacob Tyminski.'

'Key witness at the Bassinger Brothers'

trial that went belly up?'

Lawrence nodded. 'I'd started to forget it, consign it all to the past, then the media reports began to bring everything back.'

A frown settled on Edward's florid features. 'I'm still not with you, Lawrence. Why should her husband's involvement in the Bassinger trial change anything?'

'The girl's maiden name was Hamilton,' Lawrence said softly. 'She lived in my constituency: Stockport.'

'Hamilton . . . Hamilton . . . ' Edward drummed on the polished table with stubby fingers, trying to jog his memory. 'The kid who's gone missing in Stockport is called Benjamin Hamilton. He's not . . . '

'He's my son,' Lawrence Cosgrave whispered.

'Jesus!' Edward breathed. His beady brown eyes flickered over Lawrence Cosgrave's face while his mind raced. 'You think the Bassingers had something to do with his disappearance?'

'It had occurred to me.'

'Retribution?'

Lawrence shook his head. 'Leverage. They want to stop the sequestration of Ronnie Bassinger's assets.'

'You think the Bassingers know something, know about your being the father of the child?'

‘If they don’t know, they might suspect. The Bassingers and their hangers-on must have spent a lot of time in Tyminski’s garage. They could have overheard something, seen something, might even have noticed a resemblance. They could use the knowledge, or use the child, to coerce me into stopping the sequestration. We’re talking millions, possibly billions, Ted: there’s property, an ocean-going yacht, a private jet, art works, bank deposits. If I didn’t co-operate they could ruin me, ruin my marriage, badly damage the party we’ve both devoted our lives to.’

Frowning, lost in thought, Edward Ashton had sucked in his cheeks and his tiny mouth was pouting like a girl’s. He could understand Lawrence’s worries and fears now. Things didn’t get any more serious. It was amazing he’d been able to function at all with this hanging over him. He cleared his throat. ‘Forgive my asking, Lawrence, but do you feel any great attachment to the child?’

Lawrence Cosgrave didn’t speak. He was staring blindly at a large and rather inept portrait of The Queen that was hanging on the far wall.

Edward did some more throat clearing. ‘The child, Lawrence: Benjamin. Do you feel a strong attachment to him?’

Lawrence shook his head. 'Not really. And it's not something I'm proud of. When the girl's mother involved the priest, when the girl said she wouldn't have an abortion and began to get difficult, it was all over for me. Never contacted her again; never saw the child. Alexander Myers told me there were no problems at the birth and confirmed he'd dealt with the paperwork. Didn't hear another word from the girl or her mother until the boy went missing. Mother wrote to me — a careful letter no one else would understand. She reminded me the missing child was mine and insisted that I did something.'

'And did you?'

'Did I what?'

'Do something?'

'Had a word with Fallon, head of MI5. Asked her if she'd assign someone to search and find; recover the body if the child was dead. Told her I wanted that ruthless female the Israeli secret service trained, the woman who impressed the Russians and caused all that bother for the last government. Hudson at Serious Crime told me one of the names she uses is Grey: Georgina Grey. Fallon made the arrangements. The Grey woman said she'd accept the assignment on condition she could act without restraint, so Fallon cut her loose, dismissed her so there'd be no come backs if things got out of hand. She started searching a couple of days ago.'

'You met this Georgina Grey? You briefed her?'

Lawrence Cosgrave laughed wryly. 'I've been stupid, Ted, but I'm not that stupid. I just gave Fallon the name and address of the girl's mother. When I replied to the mother's letter, I told *her* to tell Grey everything.'

'Any feedback?'

'Not yet, but it's early days. Police have got absolutely nowhere. No witnesses to an abduction, no sightings, no response to the mother's appeals on television. Nothing. And Fallon might not have any information to pass on. Grey's acting independently, so she won't feel under any obligation to report back. I'm presuming she was responsible for the murder in the headlines yesterday: Vincent Bassinger. God knows why she pushed him out of a tenth-floor window.'

'I take it this Georgina Grey is unaware of your thoughts about the Bassingers?'

'Completely. But she's reached the same conclusions and started interrogating and killing the evil buggers. She's thinking along the same lines.'

'What about the police? Do they think there's a connection?'

'I had a word with Malcolm Squires the day after the boy went missing: he's the Chief Constable for the Greater Manchester Police. Stockport's one of his divisions and I've contacted him before about crime in the constituency, so he wouldn't think my interest unusual. Seems the first thing they did was eliminate the Bassingers. The man leading the team that's doing the investigation is sure it's a paedophile. He's certain the Bassingers aren't involved.'

They eyed one another through a silence disturbed only by the slow ticking of the big, black clock. Eventually, Lawrence Cosgrave said, 'What do you make of it all?'

'It's a mess, but I don't see what else you could have done.'

'But should I resign, Ted? Resign now, before anything gets out, before the Bassingers find the boy, confirm I'm the father, and apply pressure?'

'Confirm you're the father? The birth certificate names the girl's parents as the parents of the child. How could they claim you're the father?'

'DNA. Get hold of a strand of my hair; saliva on a cup.'

Edward frowned. Worry was making poor old Lawrence irrational.

Sensing his friend's disbelief, Lawrence

Cosgrave added, 'That's why I've started using hair fixative; drinking bottled water from a paper cup at meetings and keeping the cup. And I've had security run fresh checks on the staff: down here and upstairs in the residence. I'll ask you again, Ted. Do you think I should resign?'

'Sit it out,' Edward said thoughtfully. 'They're being quick and ruthless with the sequestration. If the Bassingers had the boy, they'd have made approaches by now. Anyway, we don't know for sure that the Bassingers are involved. The police could be right: he could have been snatched by some paedophile.'

'The police don't know about the boy's paternity, Ted. If they did, they might have looked closer at the Bassingers.'

'I still say we sit it out. Let's watch and wait; see what this Georgina Grey comes up with.'

9

Retrieving Clifford Bassinger's black Audi hadn't posed any problems. Samantha had taken a taxi to Renwick, the last human habitation she'd driven through before ambushing Clifford Bassinger and his enforcer, then walked the remaining mile to the lay-by. The black car had been too close to the place where she'd hidden the bodies. It had been a grave marker. She'd had to move it. But what should she do with it now? Park it on a double yellow? Leave it in a multi-storey? Take it to a crusher?

She was cruising towards the centre of Carlisle. Weak sunlight was glinting on car windscreens; making the small shops and endless brick terraces seem a little less drab. London Road flowed into Botchergate. She was closing on the city centre. Rachel Tyminski had given her the name of the travel agent's where she worked, but Samantha needed the address. Turning off the main road, she pulled into a gap in a line of parked cars, called directory enquiries, and got the phone number. When she dialled it, a female voice with a broad Scottish accent told her

Going Places was in Lowther Street, and Mrs Tyminski was with a client.

'Don't disturb her,' Samantha said. 'I'll call in. Does the agency have any parking?'

'In a yard at the rear, but that's only for the staff. You should be able to find somewhere in the street outside.'

'And what time do you close?'

'Five-thirty sharp. Can I tell Mrs Tyminski who called?'

Samantha switched off the phone and settled herself in the black leather. Faint odours of male sweat and deodorant still lingered inside the car, and the smell of tobacco smoke was strong. She pressed a button on the armrest and lowered the side-light an inch. Traffic sounds from the main road were louder now. Closing her eyes, she tried to shut out the relentless noise and focus her thoughts.

Rachel had probably been lying when she'd said she'd no idea where her husband was. They had a shared interest in what was left of their property, and they'd been through a lot together. Rachel would know how to get hold of Janos, and a visit from someone acting for Lawrence Cosgrave would have alarmed her. She'd want to warn Janos as soon as she could that someone who knew he was still alive was trying to find him. And things the priest, things the teacher, Miss Hibbs, had told her, had convinced her she must locate Janos Tyminski. Feeding his new name into the information system had revealed he'd worked in the service bays of garages specializing in luxury cars. There'd been some changes of address and then, six-months ago, he'd walked out of his job at a Mercedes garage in Penrith and disappeared from the system.

She'd checked out Janos's last recorded address on her way into Carlisle. The Lebanese who'd taken over the tiny flat had no knowledge of the dark-haired young man who'd been renamed Brian Keating. Perhaps Rachel had been telling the truth when she'd said she hadn't made contact with him for months. If that was so, Janos could be dead, the victim of a revenge killing. Or fear could be keeping him on the run, forever trying to stay one step ahead of the Bassingers. And he could be working outside the tax and social security system. The Bassingers had limitless resources. Janos would be smart enough to realize they could pay to have him traced through it.

Rachel's revelation that Austin Bassinger had gone away for a few days because an uncle was being moved from hospital to a nursing home probably meant they were planning to spring Ronald. Tonight she'd follow Rachel Tyminski when she left the travel agents; tomorrow she'd journey south to Leeds. And she'd leave the Ferrari in the hotel car park and use Clifford Bassinger's black Audi. The tinted windows were a useful feature, and if Ronnie was being sprung she might want to ram his transport; much more sensible to use a Bassinger car rather than her own. If she didn't wreck the Audi, she'd dispose of it later, when an opportunity presented itself.

* * *

Paula Hamilton perched herself on the edge of the chair and arranged her tweed skirt over her knees. The presbytery never seemed like a home to her. It was more like an extension of the church and sacristy. And it was cold in Father Ryan's sitting room. There was never a fire and he only lit the boiler on Sundays and holy days when the church had to be heated for morning and evening mass.

She glanced around. Mary Nolan was right: no matter how much the place was cleaned and polished it would never look nice. It needed decorating, and the carpet had worn through by the door and in front of father's chair. An oak bookcase, an oak coffee table, a small television and three wing chairs were the only pieces of furniture in the large room. It seemed almost empty, as if removal men were in the middle of taking things out.

Father Ryan pushed at the door and struggled in with tea things rattling. He lowered the tray on to the small table. 'Here we are, Paula. We'll just let it mash for a minute. There's biscuits; I hope you'll have a biscuit.' He retreated to his chair and braced himself. He'd offered to make tea so he could escape to the kitchen for a few minutes while he tried to think of something wise and sensitive to say. It was at times like this that he felt so inadequate. He should be able to offer words of consolation to a grieving mother, but the passing of the years had left him just as inept and tongue-tied as he had been when he was a curate. He was more comfortable with men. They expected so little of you: a brief condolence, some brisk words of encouragement. Asking them how they were getting on didn't trap you in an hour-long conversation about their troubles and woes.

'Shall I pour, Father?'

He nodded. 'A little milk, just show it the jug. And no sugar.'

Paula Hamilton tried to control her shaking hands. The shaking had got worse. If she didn't resist it, it spread to her shoulders, then to her whole body. She splashed in too much milk, so she began again with the second cup and when she poured that, the tea dribbled into the saucer. Father Ryan rose and took it from her, selected a couple of biscuits, then returned to his chair. She poured herself half a cup for politeness' sake, then said, 'Did she come to see you, Father?'

Some of his tension ebbed away. Perhaps she wasn't going to go on-and-on about death and loss. 'Did who come to see me?'

Paula Hamilton eyed him. Secrets: priests kept secrets. He knew very well who she was talking about, but he wouldn't say a word until she'd told him who the woman was. 'The black-haired woman Lawrence Cosgrave sent?'

Father Ryan emptied the contents of the saucer into his cup then sipped at it noisily. 'The cool one with the looks of a film star? She did, Paula. She did.'

Paula settled back in her chair. The shaking had subsided. Talking to Father Ryan comforted her. His voice, his accent, were so like her husband's. Hadn't he and Derry both come from Galway? And she could trust him. He never gossiped; there was always kindness and acceptance; never a hint of criticism;

never any talk of blame; always an encouraging word. 'Did I do right, Father? Did I do right to ask Lawrence Cosgrave to do something for Benjamin?'

'Sure you did, Paula. He's the boy's father, after all.'

'But sending that slip of a thing who looked as if she'd stepped out of a fashion magazine.'

Father Ryan took another noisy sip at the hot tea. He was beginning to wonder what Paula Hamilton wanted of him. 'You can be sure he'd send his finest, Paula. He's the Prime Minister of England, no less. Power and dominion, dark forces; there'll be things done that you and I would never dream of.'

'She just took hold of my shoulders, Father, stared at me with those huge eyes and said she'd bring him back to me. She said she was certain he was alive. She . . . ' Her voice began to break and the shaking returned. She rattled the cup and saucer back on to the tray before they toppled over.

Father Ryan put his cup down beside his chair and searched through his pockets for the handkerchief he should have known wasn't there. It was going to be the waterworks after all. Rising, he went through to the sacristy, pulled open a narrow drawer and took out a white linen purificator. He returned to the sitting room and offered it to her. She pressed the square of cloth to her face, then snatched at his hand and clung to it. He hated this. He found it almost impossible to cope with. But losing a child? The woman's grief and anguish were incomprehensible.

'How could she say that to me, Father?' Paula Hamilton sobbed.

'She'll know things,' Father Ryan said. He couldn't take his hand away, and he couldn't bend over her like this, so he knelt beside her chair. 'As I said, Paula. A man as important as Cosgrave, a man with all that power, wouldn't send just anyone to search for his child.'

'He's never been bothered about his child before,' Paula sobbed. 'He's never enquired about him. He's — '

'A parent's always bothered about a child. And silence, on both sides, was part of the arrangement. Hasn't he always been good with the maintenance? Hasn't he kept on increasing it without being asked?'

Paula Hamilton dragged in a shuddering breath and nodded.

'So, he wouldn't send just anyone, would he? I never saw the likes of her: the clothes, the car. Did you see her car now?' He suddenly remembered the woman's eyes.

They'd unnerved him: such a luminous green. Looking into them was like falling into the abyss. Eve must have gazed at Adam with eyes like that. He tried to ease his hand from Paula's but she went on clinging to it.

'I think she was being wicked, Father. Just saying things to console me, to shut me up. Things she knew couldn't possibly be true. She can't bring him back to me. He's gone to God. And I hope he is with God. I can't bear the thought of someone hurting him and doing things to him.' The shaking was violent now. She wiped her eyes and blew her nose, then took the square of white linen from her face, exposing sallow skin, furrowed by age and exhaustion, glistening where it had been washed by tears. 'I think I'm going mad, Father. I'd rather he'd died in my arms of some sickness, been run over by a car, than taken from me in this way. At least I'd have known what had happened to him; at least I'd have had his little body to bury.'

Father Ryan's shoulders drooped. He hung his head. What could he possibly say? What use were words? He squeezed her hand. 'God never sends suffering without giving us the strength to bear it, Paula.'

Paula Hamilton tried to sniff back her tears. She knew that wasn't true. Sometimes people couldn't bear sufferings. Like Mrs

Carver's husband who took one look at their Down's baby, walked out of the maternity ward, and was never seen again. Or that woman in Archer Street who committed suicide because she'd got in so much debt. She looked up at Father Ryan. 'Is it because he was a child conceived in wickedness and sin, father?' Her voice was hushed, not much more than a whisper. 'Cosgrave was a married man and he cheated and lied, and Rachel lied, and Derry and I lied. So much wickedness; so many lies. Surely we're paying for our sins.'

'A kind lie can be worth more than a thousand truths,' Father Ryan said softly. 'We made the best of it, Paula, didn't we now? We spared Cosgrave's wife and children all the heartbreak and anguish; Rachel kept her reputation and made a good marriage; and you had a child to love.'

'Much better if I'd never known and loved him,' Paula moaned. 'Then I'd never have suffered like I'm suffering now.'

'Tell me again,' Father Ryan insisted, trying to distract her. 'Tell me again what the black-haired woman said.'

'She said Benjamin is alive. She said she is certain of it. She said she'd find him and bring him back to me.' Paula's body was convulsed by a fresh wave of sobbing.

Father Ryan squeezed her hand. 'The woman knows something. That's why she's been sent. Don't lose hope, Paula.'

'The police have lost hope,' Paula Hamilton moaned. 'I heard them talking. If they don't have a result within the first twenty-four hours, there's not much chance of a good outcome. It's been days now, Father.'

'Did this woman say how you could contact her?'

'She said I couldn't. She said she'd contact me if she needed to.'

'And has she?'

Paula Hamilton shook her head.

'Don't lose hope,' Father Ryan whispered. 'And forget this silly notion about punishment for sin. Would our Blessed Lord have an innocent child harmed to inflict pain on its mother?'

She hardly heard him. She was taking deep breaths, trying to control herself, trying to stop shaking and crying. She'd forgotten to take her pill again. That wasn't helping. She'd go home and take two; try and catch up on her sleep. Releasing the priest's hand, she swayed to her feet and handed him the soggy square of cloth.

'Nine o'clock mass tomorrow,' Father Ryan said. 'I'll offer it for you and for Benjamin.'

'Thank you, Father.' She moved to the

hallway and headed for the front door. Father Ryan opened it and her trembling legs carried her down the steps into the watery, winter sunlight.

'Shall I see you at mass tomorrow, Paula?'

She nodded, then turned and walked off down the driveway.

'You're in my prayers,' he called after her. 'Both of you.' He watched her disappear behind the overgrown hedge that bordered the road. What more could he have said? He wasn't at his ease with women; wasn't good with the comforting words. A priest should be. It was his job, his vocation. Where it mattered, he was a failure. He glanced down at the damp, crumpled cloth in his hand. A purificator: one of the squares of fine linen that wiped sacred things from the chalice. Blood of Christ and a grieving mother's snot and tears.

* * *

Samantha gazed across Lowther Street at the travel agent's. *Going Places* was spelled out in red neon and light from the display windows shone across the pavement, relieving the early darkness of the winter evening. It was impossible to see inside. Racks of cards advertising holidays in warmer places formed an almost solid screen behind the glass.

She'd spent the previous half-hour driving around Carlisle, acquainting herself with the pattern of one-way streets and checking the landmarks. There was a place with round turrets called The Citadel, The Lanes shopping precinct, the cathedral, and the vast iron framework of an old gasholder in Rome Street that some enthusiast for Victoriana had painted cobalt blue: a colour more suited to a Mediterranean summer than a Cumbrian winter. Rachel Tyminski's car was parked in a shared area behind the shops, accessed through an archway next to a bakery. Samantha had checked the registration number and model. It was a yellow Fiat Punto.

Shoppers and workers were bustling home now, hunched against the cold, and traffic was busy beyond the junction with Spencer Street. Cars began to emerge through the archway, turn right and move off along the one-way system. Presently the yellow Punto appeared. Samantha keyed the ignition and eased out. Horns blared, then a driver, less aggressive or more courteous than the rest, held back and she moved off. Rachel Tyminski had seized her opportunity and surged out. Samantha followed, almost bumper to bumper, and they made their way across Spencer Street, heading towards Warwick Road.

Commuter traffic thinned in the suburbs and remained light through Warwick and the tiny villages beyond. Rachel seemed to lose her way in Brampton. They made two uncertain assaults on the network of streets before leaving the town on the Corbridge road. Rachel was driving slowly, looking for landmarks, too engrossed to notice the big black car cruising along close behind her. They passed a red-brick church, a corner shop, then Rachel turned right into Friary Road and began to drive between rows of bay-windowed terrace houses built against the backs of the pavements.

The yellow car had slowed almost to walking pace; Rachel was checking house numbers. Samantha glanced in her rear-view mirror. The road behind was deserted. She allowed the Audi to roll to a stop and watched. Brake lights suddenly blinked, then Rachel did a neat manoeuvre and parked the Punto in a gap in the line of cars. Moving forward again, Samantha saw Rachel emerge from her car, walk back a few paces and knock on a faded green door. Samantha swung the Audi into a space some distance beyond the house. A segment of light showed when curtains at the side of the bay were tweaked aside. Seconds later the door opened and Samantha glimpsed a man, just short of six-feet tall, with dark curly-hair. Rachel climbed the step and pushed past him. The door closed.

Janos Tyminski: the man was clearly recognizable from his wedding photographs. Samantha re-parked the car so she could watch the house through the windscreen, settled back in the seat and contemplated the search for Benjamin. The Bassingers could have taken him as an act of revenge, but that was unlikely. His relationship with Janos was fairly distant and there was no blood tie. They probably knew, or suspected something, of the circumstances surrounding his birth. If they did, they'd be racing her to find him. They'd arrange a DNA test. If it confirmed their suspicions, they'd apply pressure, have the sequestration of Ronald Bassinger's assets called off. Perhaps this was what Lawrence Cosgrave feared. It would explain his request for her to search for Benjamin and the instruction to recover the child's body if he'd been killed. And the fear of exposure would probably motivate Cosgrave more than any feelings he might have for a child he'd never seen; a child he'd wanted aborted. Benjamin's disappearance could be the work of a paedophile, but the things she'd learned at his school had persuaded her otherwise. She had to confront Janos Tyminski, and when she did he had to be on his own. His wife was with him now. It could be a long wait.

* * *

'You don't seem very pleased to see me.' Rachel's tone was reproachful. She ran her tongue over rather full lips and pouted up at him.

'It's dangerous,' he retorted gruffly, then tried to squeeze past her in the narrow hallway.

Swaying out her hip, she held him prisoner against coats hanging from a rail on the wall. 'It *was* dangerous, Janos. Time passes and the police said we could relax a little after a while.'

'It's still dangerous,' he retorted bitterly. 'And you can't trust the police; you can't believe a thing they tell you.' He made another attempt to pass her. 'Shall we go through?'

'Aren't you going to kiss me? It's been months: so long I can't remember.' She frowned up at him petulantly.

Blushing, he lowered his head and touched her lips with his.

'Is that the best you can do, Janos?'

He pressed his lips against hers again, longer this time, then said, 'We can't stand here. Let's go through to the sitting room.'

Rachel gave him a disparaging look, then let her pout fade into a smile. 'Take my coat first. She tugged at the belt of a bright-red winter coat Austin Bassinger had bought her, unfastened the buttons and drew it open. Janos was gazing down at her blouse now: a filmy, peach-coloured silk creation, gathered into frills around a deep V neck. His blush was deepening. She felt a sudden satisfaction: something about her seemed to have caught his attention at last. When she drew the coat over her shoulders she pushed out her breasts and made them shake as she struggled free of it.

Unable to meet her gaze, he took it from her, mumbling, 'Let's go through to the sitting room,' as he hung it over a hook on the rail.

She contrived to brush her breasts and buttocks against him when she turned in the confined space beside the hanging coats, then moved down the hallway and stepped into a small front room. Wine-red velvet curtains were drawn around the bay window. A lamp with a big shade, standing on a shelf that spanned a recess beside the fireplace, was shedding its light over an armchair and casting soft shadows around a sofa and coffee table. Sofa and chair were covered in some dark-red material that matched the curtains. The oatmeal-coloured carpet and Turkish pattern hearth rug looked fairly new. She recognized the clock on the mantelpiece above the grey tiled fireplace: it was a cheap, glass-cased thing with a tiny pendulum that swung furiously. His mother had given it to them and she'd annoyed him by laughing at it. Car magazines were stacked in neat piles on the low table, and a small brass crucifix was hanging from the wall above the fireplace. The television had a wide screen and the cables behind it had been carefully bundled and tied. Everything was fastidiously neat and tidy; not the least bit like the cluttered sitting room in her own flat. She suddenly remembered how irritating Janos's obsession with tidiness had been.

'Nice,' she said, gesturing around the room.

'I rent it furnished. Took a couple of weekends to get it clean and tidy, but it's not bad now.'

Moving to the far end of the sofa, she sat down, pressed her legs together and arranged her black skirt demurely over her knees. She'd decided to wear stockings rather than tights. She had to make him do what she wanted and a bit of naked thigh between stocking-tops and knickers was one of the few things that aroused him. If he'd been a different kind of man she'd have crossed her legs, let her skirt ride up and allowed him a glimpse, but louche behaviour offended Janos. How many times had he ranted on at her about his cousin, Trudy, sitting with her skirts up, showing her underwear?

She relaxed back on the cushions, folded her hands on her lap and glanced up at him. She caught him looking at her breasts again. He blushed and glanced away. What had happened to make him so repressed? Patting the cushion next to hers, she said, 'Come and sit down, Janos.'

He made for the sofa, had second thoughts and lowered himself into the chair beside the lamp. 'Is it warm enough for you? Can I get you — ?'

Rachel patted the cushion again. 'Come and sit next to me, Janos. Please.'

Still blushing, he crossed over, sat at the other end of the sofa and turned towards her, his eyes chastely fixed on her hands.

'Aren't you pleased to see me?'

'Of course.' He risked a quick glance at her face. He didn't sound very convincing.

'You don't seem to be.'

'I'm scared: really scared.'

‘It was more than a year ago. A year’s a long time, Janos.’ Rachel lowered her voice and made it urgent. ‘I’m your wife and I’m a normal woman. It’s not just men who have needs.’

She saw him flinch. He looked away, then leaned forward, rested his elbows on his knees and stared down at the imitation Turkish rug. She’d almost forgotten how handsome he was: all that dark curly hair and the blue eyes with long, dark lashes any woman would envy. He’d lost weight. His face seemed longer and leaner. It was as if a boy had finally become a man.

‘The police were wrong, Rachel.’ His voice was so low she could hardly make out the words. ‘Wrong or they just didn’t care. Time makes no difference. People like the Bassingers never forget. I left the safe house because it was being watched. One of the neighbours told me some tall, fair-haired men had been looking around the place while I was at work. I cleared out, got a job and a flat in Penrith. A couple of weeks later, someone followed me when I drove home from work; parked in the street outside and watched the flat. God knows how they found me. Maybe they were using the National Insurance system to track me from job to job. So I left Penrith and came up here to Brampton, got a job in a tin-pot garage owned by an Asian who has a taxi firm. I'm paid cash on a piecework basis: no deductions for tax or NI contributions. In effect, I'm self-employed. That way I'm not logged into the system. I've been here about six months. They've not found me yet, but they will, and when they do . . . ' He closed his eyes and his voice dropped to a whisper. 'Dear God, I daren't think about it.' He'd not told her everything; not told her what had happened a week ago when they'd almost caught him; not told her about the drastic thing he'd had to do. She'd been stupid coming here. They could be watching her. If she'd been followed she'd have put them both at risk, acting on this silly whim.

Rachel didn't speak; she just gazed at her husband for a while then shuffled along the sofa and slid an arm around his shoulders. 'It's going to be OK, Janos,' she said softly. She pressed her thigh against his, hard enough for him to feel the fastener on her suspender. 'Things might take a little longer, but they'll settle down.'

He shook his head. 'The Bassingers won't forget, Rachel. I'm a dead man. And you're in danger just being with me like this.'

She sagged back on the cushions. Her arm was still resting on his shoulders, her fingers brushing the curls at the nape of his neck.

She suddenly decided not to tell him about the black-haired woman who was searching for Benjamin. This was going to be even more difficult than she'd expected. It would be unwise to burden him with more worries and fears. Janos had never been very interested in sex. In his present state, sex would be the last thing on his mind. But she had to entice him to make love to her. Doors would close if he didn't. And it had to be tonight. He might be afraid to see her again, and too much delay and even Janos would suspect. 'I'm here for you, Janos,' she said softly. 'You've given them the slip, you've been clever, staying out of the system. Didn't you say it's been six months now?'

He didn't answer. He didn't want to tell her what had happened when he'd gone to the so-called safe house to collect a duvet and some pillows. It was better she didn't know. There was no point frightening her.

'We could go away, Janos. A long way away: Australia or New Zealand, like the police suggested after the trial.'

'Police! Don't talk to me about the police. And the Bassingers are powerful. They've got money and resources. They'd find us if we went to the moon.'

'Let me cook you a meal,' she said. She had to stop him thinking and talking about the

Bassingers. Her fingers were still moving through his curls.

'Later maybe.'

'I've missed you, Janos,' she said softly. 'I've missed being your wife.' She felt his shoulders tense. He didn't speak; just sat there, his elbows on his knees, staring down at the imitation Turkish rug.

'Have you missed me?' she asked.

'Course I've missed you.'

'I mean, missed me as a wife?'

He didn't respond. He didn't like the way the conversation was going.

'Haven't you missed making love to me? It's been more than a year since — '

'Don't, Rachel. Don't start going on at me. If you were being hounded by the Bassinger brothers, in constant fear for your life, the last thing you'd be thinking about is making love.' He turned his head and, for the first time, looked directly into her eyes. 'And I'm worried sick about you. They might come looking for *you* if they don't find me.'

'Nobody's going to come looking for me, Janos.'

'How do you know the Bassingers aren't watching you? Maybe they've been watching and waiting, hoping you'd lead them to me. Maybe they've followed you here.'

She thought of Austin and the baby inside

her, then gave Janos a reassuring smile and said, 'I've not seen a Bassinger since they were in court, and no one's tried to contact me. They don't operate this far north; isn't that why the police got us the safe house here? I'm not even thinking about it any more.'

'You can't trust the police, Rachel. After they'd had me on the witness stand, they didn't want to know.'

She snuggled closer, pressing her thigh against his. 'Make love to me, Janos.' She breathed the words into his ear. 'It'll calm you, make your fears go away, bring you some peace for a while.'

Turning his face from her again, he muttered, 'We mustn't. What if you got pregnant? It would have been difficult before, but it would be a disaster now with me having to live and work like this. I can't look after you and support you. I could be dead before it was born.'

'It's the safest time of the month. You needn't worry.' She sagged back into the cushions and let out a bitter little laugh. 'And tell me something new. You were always scared stiff about getting me pregnant.'

'It was the debt,' he muttered. 'We had a hell of a mortgage and all the furniture and other stuff was on credit. It was the first thing that hit me when I woke up in the morning; the last thing I thought of before I went to sleep at night. All I could think about was work and the business and earning money to pay it off. I dreaded you having a kid when we were in so much debt.'

'Babies don't cost anything.'

'Don't you believe it. You wouldn't have been able to spend so much time in the office; I'd have had to pay someone to do the books and clerical work. And we'd have had to buy a lot of stuff for the kid.'

'I thought you really liked children,' Rachel said. 'You liked Benjamin and he adored you.'

'Course I like kids. And I understand Benjamin. He isn't stupid: he's very clever. He's just different, that's all.'

'You never really wanted me, did you, Janos?' Rachel made her voice tearful.

'I don't know what you mean.'

'Wanted me like a man wants a woman: wanted to undress me, look at me with my clothes off, wanted to touch me, to fuck me.'

'Don't talk in that dirty way,' he snapped angrily. 'You're my wife. I don't like you saying things like that. And I don't like you using filthy language.'

She'd shocked him; provoked a reaction. He wasn't whinging about his worries and fears now. She ploughed on, 'It's the truth you don't like, Janos. You can't stand being confronted by the truth. God knows why I bothered keeping myself pure before we were married. And why should I bother keeping myself for you now? You don't want me. You've never wanted me.'

'I'm only asking you not to talk like that. It's not decent. It's not the way I expect my wife to talk.'

'You've never been interested in women, have you, Janos?'

'What's that supposed to mean?'

'I should have read the signs,' she went on, ignoring him. 'You were only happy, only truly yourself, when you were on the altar with the other boys, wearing your cassock and surplice, all got up like a woman in white lace and a black dress.'

'Don't talk like that,' he snarled. 'It's ritual. It's the celebration of the mass. The robes conceal the man. It has nothing to do with sex. You're being blasphemous.'

'I think you're gay, Janos. It's men you're attracted to, not women. You can hardly bear to look at me, let alone touch me.'

'Shut up.' His voice was a warning growl. 'If you know what's good for you, you'll shut up.'

Laughing, she placed her hands under her breasts, lifted them, almost pushed them out of her blouse, taunting him. 'I used to catch Denis Wharton, that solicitor, the president of the Catenians, looking at me, Janos: looking at these. And that big black boy who carried the censer, the one with hot, hungry eyes. He'd have liked to — '

Janos suddenly lunged forward, grabbed a handful of her hair and forced her down on the cushions. 'I asked you to stop this crazy, disgusting talk.'

She laughed in his face. He'd startled her, but she didn't feel afraid. She was getting a reaction. She felt elated. 'You're a poof,' she sneered up at him. 'A queer. Mincing around the altar like a girl in a dress.'

'I'm not like that,' he yelled. 'You know I'm not. Why are you talking like this?'

She began to unfasten tiny pearl buttons on her blouse. 'Fuck me then. Prove it. Act like a man and fuck me.'

'Stop it! Stop it!' He was almost sobbing with anguished rage. 'And no more swearing. You're my wife. I don't like my wife talking and acting in a dirty, vulgar way.'

'It's because I'm a woman, isn't it Janos? All women are dirty to you. I'd have to be a man to — '

Rage suddenly made his face ugly. His hand swung down and slapped her cheek. She could feel him fumbling around her legs, trying to pull up her skirt. 'Bitch!' He gasped the word out through clenched teeth. She heard his zip slide; felt his knee thrusting between her thighs. He slapped her again, viciously this time. 'You foul-mouthed, dirty little bitch.' He tugged her blouse open, freed it from the waistband of her skirt, then drew straps over her shoulders and released her breasts.

He was thrusting harder, trying to force her legs apart, but the sofa was narrow and Rachel too shocked to co-operate. Losing patience, he grabbed her arm and dragged her on to the floor. She felt his weight fall on her. She'd taunted him until he'd snapped. He was showing her. He was going to prove he was a man. She closed her eyes, turned her face from his and submitted to the angry violence of it. He began to grunt, then his grunts became groans, the groans became louder, and suddenly it was over and his gasping mouth was making roaring sounds in her ear. She felt his body relax. Her cheeks were stinging and there was a dull ache in her jaw, but she'd got what she wanted. All she had to do now was choose: Austin or Janos or a termination.

His raucous breathing became erratic, then fractured into sobs that made his chest heave against her breasts. Combing her fingers into his hair, she kissed his cheek and murmured, 'What's the matter, Janos?'

'I'm sorry,' he moaned. 'God, I'm so very sorry.'

'Sorry?'

'For hitting you and using you like that. I'm disgusted with myself. I feel so ashamed.'

His weight was lifting from her. She curved her hands around his buttocks and drew him close. 'Don't go away from me. Stay. I want you to stay where you are.'

When he fell back he forced the breath out of her. Between sobs and moans he kept muttering, 'I'm sorry, Rachel. God, I'm so sorry.'

'It's OK,' she whispered. 'It's what men and women do together.' This was how it had always been with Janos: a brief coupling, a frantic rush for sexual relief, followed by guilt and self-loathing. 'Father Ryan married us, Janos. It made sex OK. It's a sacrament. When you fuck me, it's a sacrament.'

'Don't,' he sobbed. 'Please don't talk like that. It's filthy and blasphemous. A good Catholic wife should know better.' He made another attempt to draw away from her, but she squeezed his hips between her thighs and held on to him.

She found his mouth, forced it open with hers, felt him recoil when she pushed her tongue between his teeth. ‘I’m going to cook you a meal,’ she breathed after she’d kissed him. ‘Then you can take me to bed and do the sacrament again. But slower next time. A lot slower.’

10

Samantha lifted her head, suddenly roused from a doze. A door had opened, the sound barely audible beneath the steady drumming of the rain on the roof of the car. She drew the back of her hand through the condensation on the sidelight and peered across the dimly-lit street. A woman wearing a red coat was standing in the doorway of number twenty-seven, pushing up a large black umbrella. When she stepped out, a dark-haired man with an anorak over his blue overalls followed. He slammed the door. After a brief exchange of words, he made to walk off, but she snatched at his sleeve, drew him under her umbrella and kissed him. He was straining to get away. When she let him go, he climbed into a battered pick-up truck and drove off. The woman in the red coat stood there until he'd turned right on to the main road, then she walked to her yellow Fiat Punto, furled her umbrella, slid behind the wheel and pulled out. Samantha followed, saw her turn left at the bottom of the street, heading back to Carlisle.

Janos Tyminski was probably driving to his

place of work: a useful address to have. Samantha made a right at the bottom of Friary Road. After rounding a bend, she chose a right fork. Two minutes later she realized she'd guessed wrongly. There was no pick-up truck on the dark stretch of highway. After reversing into a lane, she headed back to Friary Road and parked outside number twenty-seven.

Janos had tugged the door shut. He hadn't used a key. It was secured on a cylinder latch. Taking a square of springy plastic from her bag, she pressed her knee against a panel, eased the flexible sheet into the gap between door and frame, and pushed back the latch. When she turned the knob, the door swung open and she stepped inside. She did a quick reconnoitre of the modest house, switching lights on and off as she went: small sitting room at the front, kitchen and bathroom at the back, two bedrooms off the top of a steep flight of stairs.

Returning to the kitchen, she made a cup of coffee, then carried it up to the smallest bedroom where suitcases and boxes of what looked like personal things had been stacked on and beside an unmade single bed. She knelt on the floor, took a couple of sips at the coffee, then lifted the flaps on the first box. It was filled with books on car servicing and car wiring, there was a bible and *The Collected Works of Saint John of the Cross*. Samantha smiled — hardly a light read. She flicked through pages, found an old tax demand and a picture of St Jude with a prayer for lost causes. Another box held a battered toy train and some die-cast toy cars. There were two small suitcases, both empty; a large case held shirts and underwear, pillowcases and sheets, all clean but not ironed. Framed pictures were sticking out of the last box. A wedding photograph of Janos and Rachel posing in front of their families, a photograph of half-a-dozen men and boys with Father Ryan on what looked like an altar servers' outing, a few photographs of his garage, and a sugary Madonna and Child. Insights into a life, but nothing that would help her in her search for Benjamin. Samantha replaced the items in the boxes and folded down the flaps. When she slid the box of books back in position, she heard paper crumple, glanced behind it, and saw a brown paper package trapped under the edge of the bed. Tugging it out, she unwrapped it and found a cardboard folder tied with pink tapes. It was crammed with family photographs, postcards, personal letters.

Samantha glanced at her watch. It was almost 7.30. She needed to get back to the hotel, bathe, change her clothes and have a meal before driving back to Yorkshire. Deciding to take the package and sift through it later, she crossed the tiny landing and entered the front bedroom. It still smelt of sleep. A double bed with a white headboard, white bedside tables and a white chest of drawers were arranged on a faded purple carpet. The furniture looked cheap but new. The sheets and duvet were tangled, and one of the pillows had fallen to the floor. A painted plaster statue of a resigned-looking St Joseph stood on the chest of drawers; a missal in a worn leather binding and a black-beaded rosary were lying on one of the bedside tables. Ironed shirts and underwear filled the topmost drawer of the chest; the other three drawers were empty. A man without a settled home was travelling light.

Returning to the ground floor, Samantha flicked through a stack of car magazines in the sitting room, searching for letters and papers. She found nothing. Back in the kitchen, she washed her cup and replaced it in a cabinet, then went through a tiny lobby and checked the bathroom. A damp towel had been folded over the end of the bath and a man's toiletries were ranged along a glass shelf above a cracked wash hand basin. It was a cold, bare room, painted blue, with a single row of white tiles above the bath and basin. Like the kitchen, it was spotlessly clean.

Samantha drew bolts, opened the back door and glanced out over a small, rainswept rear yard. A wheely bin and a plastic box for recycling rubbish were standing by a gate in the high back wall. Splashing through puddles, she crossed over. A black plastic sack had been dropped in the bin. She tore it open, found the remains of a loaf and a mound of soggy food scraps. When she lifted the lid on the box she saw bottles, cans and a bundle of newspapers and magazines. Brushing aside the bottles, she flicked through the papers. Advertisements had been ringed in some old copies of the Carlisle Mercury lying at the bottom of the pile. She grabbed the bundle, replaced the lid on the box, then ran back through the rain to the house.

Brown paper parcel and newspapers under her arm, clutching her bag, she opened the front door and glanced up and down Friary Road. An overcast sky was delaying the dawn and the feeble light of the street lamps made the misty darkness seem even more dismal. She waited until a car had swept past, its tyres swishing through the rain, then stepped out, slammed the door, and ran across the road to Clifford Bassinger's black Audi.

* * *

Stanley Bassinger took a long pull on his cigar and allowed his eyes to close. He ached; ached like he had in his boxing days when he'd gone ten rounds and lost on points. It was moments like this that made him realize he wasn't young any more. He let the smoke escape through pursed lips. He could still perform, though. He began to smile. Two times: three for her.

'Darling . . . Stanley, darling . . . Sweetheart . . . '

He opened his eyes and peered through the fragrant mist.

The girl in the bath let out a ripple of laughter. 'You're tired, darling. I'm not surprised. God, you were like a stallion.' Big blue eyes gave him a naughty-naughty look, then the girl laughed again. Her young voice was soft and lilting. It was music to him. 'Could you bring me a towel, darling, I'm going to get out now.'

Stanley rested his cigar on the edge of the wash basin, heaved his tall frame upright, then tugged a towel from a rail and set out across pink marble.

She rose from the water in one smooth, flowing movement, lifted her arms above her head and rested her fingertips in long blonde hair that had been gathered up and tied with a blue ribbon. Her smile widened, became a little wicked, as she watched his gaze settle on her breasts before gliding down to her hips and thighs. 'Lift me out, darling. Lift me out and dry me.' She closed her eyes and puckered her lips, tasted the bitterness of his cigar when he kissed her, then let out a giggly scream as he gathered her in his arms and swept her up and out of the bath. 'Gosh, you're so strong, darling, like a young bull.'

Stanley laughed his gruff, rustling laugh and she held her arms above her head while he stroked her body with the warm softness of the towel. Jesus, she was beautiful. And the flesh was so firm: her breasts and buttocks were almost hard. Alma's body had never been like this, not even when he'd first caressed it. She'd been seventeen and he'd been twenty-four. She'd let herself go since then, especially after Hugh was born: chocolates, cake, Italian food, too much day-time television. James was always banging on about Beryl being overweight, but she was slender compared to Alma.

'Penny for them, darling.' The girl turned, rested her foot on the rim of the bath and presented her back for him to dry.

He began to dab her gently with the towel. 'Penny for what?'

'Your thoughts, darling. You suddenly looked so sad. I don't like my Stanley to be sad.'

He lifted his gaze from pert buttocks. She was looking at him over her shoulder. When their eyes met, she smiled and shaped her lips in a kiss. 'Just thinking, Tanya.' His throaty voice was deep and tender.

'Thinking what?'

'That you're the most beautiful woman I've ever seen.'

Beaming at him, she brushed the towel away, laid her cheek on his chest and wrapped her arms around him. 'And you're the sweetest, sexiest man I've ever known.'

He kissed her hair, took her by the shoulders and gently eased her away so he could look into her face. 'I've got something for you, Tanya. Meant to give it to you last night, but we got carried away.'

'Something for me?' Her face radiated a surprise and excitement that were almost childlike.

Laughing softly, he ambled through to the bedroom, groped inside his jacket, then returned with a black leather case and laid it in her hands.

When she opened it her eyes widened. 'Are they real?'

'Course they're real.'

'I mean, are they really sapphires and diamonds?'

'They're real, Tanya. Completely kosher. Come here and let me put them on.'

'By the mirror,' she said. 'So I can see.' She skipped over to a long, mirrored wall cabinet. Stanley followed, took the necklace from its case and fastened it around her throat. The square-cut stones fell in glittering rows towards her breasts. They stood in silence for a moment, studying her reflection, then he took the earrings from the case and clipped them to the lobes of her ears.

'They're beautiful,' she said, looking at the jewels.

'Perfect,' he breathed, gazing at her breasts.

She'd always known he was sweet on her. He'd always given her a good time; always been gentle and considerate. And he wasn't bad in the sack for a guy old enough to be her dad. But the necklace and earrings! How much had they cost? She met his gaze in the mirror. 'I simply don't know what to say, Stanley darling. Do you want to take me back to bed?'

He laughed throatily. 'I'm going to take you somewhere for breakfast. How about the Hilton?'

'I could make us some breakfast.'

'There's no food in the kitchen to cook.'

'And I've not brought my toothbrush and toothpaste,' she said. 'Are there any in here?' She slid one of the mirrored panels aside, then let out a shocked little scream. 'Is that what I think it is?'

Laughter began to rumble around in Stanley's chest. 'Yeah,' he said. 'It's what you think it is.'

'What's it doing in a sweet jar? What's it doing in the bathroom cabinet?'

'Safe storage. It's valuable.'

'A bit of poo in a jar?'

'Depends who's poo it is, Tanya. That's a two-grand turd.'

She wrinkled her nose. 'But why — '

'No more questions, sweetheart. It's business.' Chuckling at the pun, he took a cellophane wrapper and a box from a shelf, slid the panel shut, and handed them to her.

She grimaced down at the toothpaste and brush. 'Don't know whether I want to use them after they've been in there with that thing.'

He began to caress her buttocks. 'The turd's sealed in a jar and the things are wrapped in cellophane. They're fine.' He gave her a playful slap. 'Hurry up and get dressed. I'm hungry. And after breakfast I've got business to attend to. Then I've got to rest up and get ready for tonight.'

She flashed him her wicked grin. 'Again? Tonight? Will we be staying here?'

'Not you and me, Tanya. It's business. Serious business. I've got to drive over to Leeds.'

* * *

Samantha motored past the old Victorian church and the junction with Friary road, then negotiated a bend. She took the left fork this time. After half-a-mile she was cruising through a ramshackle industrial estate where the buildings had corrugated metal roofs and barbed-wire-topped fencing was stretched between concrete posts to form compounds for equipment and materials. Janos Tyminski had ringed four advertisements in one of the old newspapers she'd taken from his home. Azam Autos was the only one on the east side of town; the only one needing a right turn out of Friary Road. She'd decided to pay him a call before heading south to Leeds.

Driving slowly, twisting and turning between windowless factories and workshops, she saw Azam Autos spelt out in red letters on the grey metal side of a huge shed. She circled a rear yard that was crowded with cars, mostly taxis, then pulled on to a concrete hard-standing at the reception end of the building. Lifting her bag from the passenger seat, she crossed over to a metal door and stepped into a customer area not much bigger than a couple of telephone booths. Beyond a crude wooden counter, a dark-skinned man, with close-cropped black hair and a neatly trimmed moustache and beard, was lounging behind a battered desk. He began to look her over with a studied nonchalance, starting with the eyes and vivid lipstick, before moving down to the black suit with its narrow pinstripe, the black Bulgari bag and black gloves that buttoned above the wrist. He didn't speak, just sniffed and raised an eyebrow.

Samantha said, 'I understand someone called Keating works here.'

He was still holding her in a silent stare.

She laid her bag on the counter and removed one of her gloves. 'I'm told he's good with Audis.'

The man shrugged.

'I've got an Audi,' she said. 'It's making a funny noise. I'd like him to look at it.'

'Funny noise?' His smile betrayed his contempt for women who said cars made funny noises. 'Keating's busy. Leave the car and I'll get him to look at it when he's free.'

'Where's Mr Azam?'

'I'm Mr Azam.'

'I don't want to be stranded in this

God-forsaken hole, Mr Azam. I'd like him to look at it now.'

'He's busy right now. Maybe this afternoon. Leave your phone number and we'll call you when he's checked it over. I'll get a driver to bring a taxi round and take you back to town.'

Samantha clicked open her bag, peeled notes from a roll of Bassinger money, and held them up for him to see. 'I want it looking at now, Mr Azam. Not this afternoon.'

He let out an exaggerated sigh, then, feigning boredom, picked up a grimy telephone and keyed in a number. After a few seconds, he said, 'Brian, there's a woman here who's heard you're good with Audis. She wants you to take a look at hers. Now.' He listened, then put his hand over the mouthpiece and glanced across at Samantha. 'He wants to know who recommended him.'

'Someone I work with at a travel agent's: Rachel Tyminski.'

He relayed the information, then cradled the phone and sauntered towards the counter. Slender brown fingers reached out and took the notes. His eyes were all over her now. They kept returning to the red sweater that was framed by the lapels of her tiny jacket. 'Travel agency must pay well,' he said. He fanned the notes out in his hand and smiled. 'Money, fine clothes, an expensive car.'

'I own it,' she said. 'It's called *Going Places*.'

A door opened at the back of the room. She caught a fleeting glimpse of a big workshop area before it swung shut behind Janos Tyminski. His expression was worried, almost fearful, as he approached.

Azam grinned at him, then inclined his head towards Samantha. 'Her car's making funny noises. She wants you to look it over.'

Janos Tyminski nodded, lifted a flap in the counter, then opened the outer door and stood aside for Samantha to pass. She stepped outside.

'Who told you I'm good with Audis?'

'Mrs Tyminski. We work together: *Going Places* travel agency.'

'And what's the problem?' They were standing by the sleek black car.

'When I'm turning right it makes a funny grating noise. Could you do a test drive with me?' She handed him the keys. 'I could be imagining things.'

Janos followed her round to the passenger side and opened the door for her; averted his gaze while she slid on to the seat and lifted her legs inside. He slammed the door, then studied the wheels as he circled the car, pausing for a moment as he passed the radiator grille. When he opened the driver's door, he lowered his head and eyed her warily. 'My overalls are oily. I'll go and find a seat cover.' His voice was tense.

'I don't mind. It's black leather.'

'Let me get one. The grease could mark your clothes. I won't be a minute.' He began to turn back.

Samantha sensed his fear. He knew something. He was desperate to get away. Reaching inside her bag, she pulled out the gun and pointed it at his chest. 'Get inside the car, Janos.'

'Janos? How do you know my . . . Jesus,' he moaned. 'Sweet Jesus. You've come to — '

'Inside the car,' she snapped. 'All I want is a talk.'

'No.' He shook his head. 'I don't believe you. You're — '

Samantha reached over, grabbed his overalls, and dragged his head and shoulders through the door. His face was close to the muzzle of the gun now. 'In the car, Janos.' She held him until he'd lowered his haunches on to the seat and lifted his heavy-booted feet beneath the wheel.

Hands trembling, he stared at her with fearful eyes.

'All I want is a talk, Janos.' Samantha

groped inside her bag for one of her ID cards. Her fingers touched a plastic wallet and she drew it out. Flicking it open, she held it in front of his face. 'Special Crime Unit. I just want to talk. Put the keys in the ignition, start the car and drive.'

Janos hadn't looked at the ID card. Reaching out with a shaking hand he grabbed the door, slammed it shut, then touched a control at the side of the seat and moved it back to give himself more room. 'Who are you?' His voice was hoarse with fear.

'Grey: Georgina Grey. Start the car and drive.' She jerked the gun.

He did as she asked, swung the car off the concrete hard standing and began to drive through the winter drabness of ugly buildings, cluttered stack-yards and rusting fences.

'Turn right here,' Samantha instructed, when they reached the main road. 'Head back towards town.'

'This is a Bassinger car.' He was accelerating through the gears. 'They run a fleet: Audis, Mercedes, BMWs; all big and powerful, all black. It's one I've worked on. I remember the registration number. Clifford Bassinger used to drive it. They've sent you to find me. They've sent you to — '

'Relax. Clifford Bassinger's dead. I took it.'

Semi-detached housing gave way to older

terraces and small shops. They were closing on the centre of the town. 'That pub up ahead: The Black Swan. Pull into the car park.'

He flicked the indicator, braked, then turned off the road.

'Under those trees. Park it there.'

He eased the bonnet close to the boundary wall, yanked up the handbrake and switched off the ignition.

Gun hand resting on her bag, Samantha turned in her seat and faced him. 'Where's Benjamin Hamilton?'

Startled eyes flickered over her face. 'Benjamin Hamilton?'

'Don't go all stupid on me. Your brother-in-law. The child who's missing. You took him, didn't you?' She studied his expression. He seemed dazed and fearful, but there was no sign of outrage at her suggestion.

'You're crazy.' He let out a jittery little laugh. 'Why should I take Benjamin?'

'The Bassingers,' Samantha said. 'You became worried about what they might do, or you got to know something. You collected him from school and took him somewhere.'

He swallowed noisily. 'Who are you?'

'I showed you my ID,' Samantha reminded him irritably. 'Special Crime Unit. I've been assigned to find Benjamin.'

Janos studied the perfect face spoiled by vivid lipstick and the stuff she'd brushed around her eyes. She smelt nice, more than nice; in the confines of the car her fragrance was mingling with the smell of metal and leather. It was provocative. And the suit she was wearing: hand sewn with tight sleeves and a tight skirt, emphasizing as much as concealing. She made Rachel look dowdy. Rachel! He mustn't forget Rachel. He had to go to confession. The Bassingers, this woman: he could die, and he was mired in mortal sin. Hitting Rachel, raping her, and when they'd gone to bed she'd done things he should have stopped. If he walked away from this he'd find a priest right away. His gaze dropped to the powerful gun, big and black in the slender hand, and his mind froze. 'Don't kill me,' he whimpered. 'Please don't kill me.'

'Tell me about Benjamin. Tell me where you've taken him.'

He dragged his terrified eyes from the gun and stared through the windscreen. The weak sunlight was casting faint shadows of branches on the wall. He had to make a stand; try to behave like a decent person. He daren't trust this woman. Even if she was telling the truth, Special Crime was just another name for the police and the

Bassingers had the police in their pockets. 'You've got it all wrong,' he said. 'I've not seen Ben and I've no idea where he is.'

'You're lying, Janos,' the husky voice whispered. 'And your mother-in-law's demented. She's going crazy wondering what some sick pervert's doing to her child.'

Janos cringed. 'I know nothing,' he insisted.

Samantha studied the man, bulky in his overalls, shoulders sagging, his long-fingered hands clutching the rim of the steering wheel. He'd lost almost everything: business, home, a normal married life. Should she tell him about Rachel's affair with Austin Bassinger, tell him about her pregnancy, rob him of what little life had left him in the hope that the destroyed man would despair and tell her what she wanted to know?

'How did you find me?' he whimpered.

'I interviewed your wife yesterday morning.'

He turned his head and stared at Samantha. 'You saw my wife? She didn't tell me. And she doesn't know where I'm working, so she couldn't . . . '

'I followed her when she left work last night. I followed you this morning.'

He returned his gaze to the shadows on the wall. His lips were pressed together, his expression grim.

'You've put Benjamin in danger,' Samantha said softly. 'Quite apart from the distress you're causing his mother. And she's not young. This could kill her.'

He closed his eyes. His lips parted, but he didn't speak.

Samantha tugged at the breech of the gun and let it snap back with a metallic clatter. His body tensed and began to shake. 'Is it my time?' he moaned. 'Are you going to kill me?'

'I don't like liars who put a child in danger and crucify its mother. Where's Benjamin? I'm going to count to three.'

He sagged over the steering wheel and held on to it like a drowning man clutching at a life belt. 'You're not police,' he reasoned. 'They can't be trusted, but they wouldn't dare threaten me with a gun. You're from the Bassingers. Why do you want Ben? Why do you want to hurt a child?'

'I'm from Special Crime. You saw the badge.'

'The Bassinger's can forge a badge, or buy a badge. They've got people who can get them anything. And you're driving a Bassinger car. Why else would you be driving a Bassinger car?' Janos turned his head and stared at her. He'd sussed her out. Women from the police didn't look and dress like this. It took Bassinger money. She was probably Clifford Bassinger's wife or partner. Sometimes their women had come with them when they'd brought cars to the garage: fancy clothes and made-up faces, strutting around like whores.

Samantha reviled him with her eyes. She'd handled it badly. He wasn't going to tell her anything. 'You're being stupid,' she hissed. 'You're going to get the child killed.' She lifted the gun. His eyes squeezed tight shut and his body became rigid. 'Get out of the car. I gave your wife a telephone number. When you come to your senses, call it and tell me where you're hiding the boy.'

His eyes blinked open. He couldn't believe what he'd just heard. Maybe she'd decided that if she killed him she'd never find out what he knew. Flinging open the door, he dragged his boots over the sill and almost fell on to the tarmac.

11

Ronald Bassinger linked his fingers over his chest and stared up at the ceiling; watched fluorescent lights glide by and listened to the swish and rattle of the trolley's rubber wheels. Easing his head up from the pillow, he peered at the grey-shirted guards. Merit Security: he'd read it on their cap badges. Privatized service, not coppers, not properly trained. Coppers would have walked behind the trolley so they could watch him and the nurses, not strolled along in front and alongside. He felt edgy. This mustn't go wrong. He'd die inside if it went wrong. And back in the ward the doctors had been looking thoughtful, suspicious even, after getting the results of the blood tests. Colonoscopy: that's what they were taking him down for. What the fuck was a colonoscopy?

He risked a glance at Bruce and Terry. They'd completely ignored him. No sign of recognition. He'd not recognized them at first: short haircuts, nametags, white uniforms with elbow-length sleeves exposing hairy forearms. Terry even had a stethoscope hanging around his neck. Fucking poser. They looked cool, calm, alert. He'd made wise choices. If he had any chance at all, they'd deliver it.

The trolley jolted over a threshold and clattered beneath the illuminated ceiling of a lift. Bruce slid a wad of gum from his mouth, snaked his arm up behind the surveillance camera and pressed it over the lens. Understanding flooded the face of the guard standing at the back of the compartment. Terry moved in, began to deliver savage blows with a leather-covered cosh. Before the other guard could turn from the closing doors, Bruce was pounding the back and side of his head with an iron bar. The grey-shirted men hardly made a sound; just a swift intake of breath, a groan, a muffled thud as their bodies collapsed on to the floor.

Snatching the radio from the belt of the guard he'd felled, Bruce pressed 'call'. After a few seconds the hissing stopped and a metallic voice said, 'What's the problem, over.'

'Prisoner's not coming down. He's started haemorrhaging. They're holding him on the ward.' He glanced at Terry and nodded towards the lift controls. Terry pressed the button for lower-ground. 'We'll stay with the prisoner. Do you want to take a break while we're waiting, or do you want to come up and relieve Angus?'

'Been standing here for an hour. I'll slip out and have a fag then I'll come up. OK?'

Bruce tossed the radio down and took a bundle from beneath the pillow. 'We've got to get you dressed, Mr Bassinger.'

Ronald Bassinger swung his legs to the floor. Bruce pulled white cotton trousers over his knees, then Ronald rose from the trolley and yanked them up. Terry handed him a nurse's jacket before kneeling amongst the bodies of the guards and easing Ronald's feet into white trainers.

The lift lurched to a stop. 'This is it.' Terry's voice was taut. The doors rumbled open.

'Cameras,' Ronald Bassinger snapped. 'What about the surveillance cameras?'

'Sorted,' Bruce said. 'The one viewing the lift doors has been covered with a brown paper bag. The cameras in the ambulance bay outside have been nudged out of alignment. They look down the sides of the van, not into the back. Let's go, Mr Bassinger. After we've settled you in the ambulance, we've got to dump the guards somewhere, then get out ourselves.' When they stepped from the lift, Terry pulled the trolley forward to keep the doors apart and stop it rising to another floor.

Fairview Nursing Homes was written in an elegant script across the rear of the ambulance. Bruce swung the doors open, climbed inside and lifted a seat over a narrow locker that ran the length of the compartment. Terry joined him; helped him take out blankets and bandage packs, small gas cylinders and breathing masks. 'Get in, Mr Bassinger,' Terry urged. 'They'll bring an old lady in a few minutes; they're taking her to a home about a mile from here. When they've dropped her off, they'll drive you to the lay-by where the car's waiting.' Ronald nodded, clambered inside the ambulance and stepped into the locker. He stretched out on his side. Bruce and Terry covered him with the blankets, then piled the remaining things back on top. The seat thudded down and the doors closed.

Useless security men had been guarding him in the hospital, but there'd be police outside, watching, checking cars, maybe even searching ambulances. He closed his eyes against the grave-like darkness and began to feel the cold metal side and floor of the van through the thin uniform. If they discovered him, he'd die in gaol.

Doors banged open, Ronald felt the floor sway as someone stood on the rear step, then a voice said, 'Over to me now, Don.' There was a clatter as a stretcher was wheeled inside. The doors slammed. 'There, Mrs Stanhope, you're going home. I told you we'd take you home. You'll be just in time for the evening meal.' The man who'd been speaking flopped down on the seat, just above Ronald's head.

'Home?' came a querulous voice. 'Home? You're taking me to Ashfield Terrace?'

There was a gentle laugh. 'To Fairview, that's your home now.'

'It's not. It's not my home. It's full of the living dead. I hate the place. Take me to Ashfield Terrace: number fourteen.'

The starter whined, the engine began to rumble and they moved off.

Ronald Bassinger felt the ambulance surge up a ramp, round a couple of bends, then lurch to a stop. A voice, faint but jovial, was saying, 'Where to?'

'Fairview: the nursing and residential home.'

'Emergency trip?'

'Booked day before yesterday. Taking a Mrs . . . ' the driver must have paused to check his schedule, 'Stanhope back. Cataract operation.'

'Mind if we check?'

Feet trod down the side of the ambulance, the back doors opened, the floor swayed as someone heavy climbed inside. A deep, slow voice said, 'Sorry to disturb you, madam.'

Ronald held his breath. He could feel boots scraping on the metal floor. If the alarm had been raised in the hospital they'd pull the ambulance apart to make sure he wasn't being ferried out. But it couldn't be any more than five minutes since Bruce and Terry had wheeled him into the lift. Surely they hadn't been discovered yet.

'Make them take me home, officer. Fourteen Ashfield Terrace. My daughter's there. She's getting my tea ready.'

'Got to take you to Fairview, Mrs Stanhope. That's where you live now. We'd be in trouble if we took you anywhere else.'

'Awful place,' sobbed the old woman. 'Hate it. I absolutely hate it.'

'Sorry to have disturbed you, madam.' The policeman sounded embarrassed. 'Better let you get on.' The floor rocked as he stepped down, doors slammed, then they moved off.

Ronald Bassinger clenched his fists. Yes! He'd done it. He was as good as home and dry.

* * *

Fairview Nursing Homes was written on the ambulance and Austin Bassinger had told

Rachel they were moving a relative between a hospital and a home. Samantha had been watching for more than three hours and this was the first private ambulance to enter the facility and emerge at the top of the ramp. She eased the black Audi out of the parking bay and began to follow it. They stopped at a drop-down barrier where a policeman, bulky in his bullet-proof jacket, went up to the cab of the ambulance and began to talk.

Samantha pushed heavy horn-rimmed glasses up to the bridge of her nose and checked her lapel. The identity tag was still pinned in place, telling the world she was Doctor Georgina Grey. She took a stethoscope from the pocket of her white consultant's smock and laid it on top of the dashboard. She'd come prepared to go inside the hospital and search if she had to. She could only hope Austin had got it right, and, if he had, that the police didn't discover Ronald Bassinger. She watched the burly policeman amble round to the back of the ambulance and open the doors, saw a stretcher and a man in a green uniform sitting on a bench beside it. The policeman climbed inside, words were exchanged, then he stepped down and closed the doors. He approached the Audi. Samantha lowered the window. 'Sorry to keep you waiting, doctor.'

Experienced eyes were peering into her car. ‘Mind if I take a look in the boot?’

Samantha smiled. ‘Shall I release the lid from in here?’

‘If you wouldn’t mind, doctor.’

She pulled a lever beneath the dash while the policeman walked around the back. Suddenly the barrier rose and the ambulance moved off. She heard the boot lid slam down and a voice at the window was saying, ‘Thanks, doctor. Sorry to have kept you.’ The barrier was still up. She gave him a tight little smile, then surged on, heading for the gates.

The stretch of dual-carriageway was brightly lit. It curved sharply to the left, but to the right the traffic was visible as far as the crest of a distant hill. There was no ambulance amongst it. She turned left out of the gates, heading towards Marbeck.

* * *

Ronald Bassinger stood in the doorway, gazing across the dark expanse of winter fields. The rain had stopped and it was suddenly mild, almost like a foretaste of spring. He was taking deep breaths. This was clean country air, not air made foul by the stink of cheap soap and sweat on the bodies of confined men.

His brothers and their sons were gathering in the dining-room of the bungalow. One by one they were drifting over from the charity ball in the big house beyond the tennis courts. It would be good to see them. It was good to be free. The steak and French fries had been good, too. The woman could cook a steak. Stanley had made sure she was here, waiting for him, when he arrived. He hadn't been expecting a coloured piece. Swedish and South African. Bloody lovely. Beautiful face and a body you'd stab her husband for. He'd intended to wait until after the meeting, but he couldn't keep his hands off her. Thirteen months and seven days. She'd laughed when he'd chased her into the bedroom, but she'd soon started screaming. He'd fucking-well make her scream tonight.

'We're all here, Ronnie. Come on through. We don't want to be away from the bash for too long.'

He turned. James was standing in the unlit kitchen, smiling at him. James nodded at the door. 'Didn't we ought to close and lock it?'

'Fresh air,' Ronald said. 'I want it wafting through the place so I can breathe. And I know there are minders out there, but an open back door could be handy if I have to do a runner.'

Laughing, James linked his arm in Ronald's

and led him through to a dining-room where gilt-framed pictures of puppies and kittens and flowers hid a good deal of the beige wallpaper. An oak dining table had been extended, and bow-tied, dinner-jacketed men, fragrant with aftershave and deodorants, were sitting on the collection of chairs and stools that had been arranged around it. The talking stopped. As one man they rose to their feet and began to clap: Henry with two of his sons, Mark and Lewis; Morris with Trevor; Stanley with Ian and Hugh: and there was James's son, Austin. His own boy was at the theatre with his mother. Big warm hands grabbed his as he moved down the room; affectionate arms squeezed his shoulders. When he reached the head of the table he waited until they were silent, then his gruff voice was thick with emotion as he said, 'It's good to be back amongst the family. It's good to be free.' Deep-set grey eyes, cold and remote, ranged around the table, resting for a few seconds on every face. He sniffed, settled his dinner jacket across his shoulders, then added, 'But we can't waste time on pleasantries because you've got to get back to the charity do. What's it for?'

'*Save the Children*,' came a voice.

'Respectable,' Ronald chuckled. 'Very respectable.' He glanced at James. 'How did you arrange all the invites?'

'Dexter owes me, and I promised him big donations.'

Ronald suddenly became serious. He was in control again, running the firm. Voice and manner brisk and business-like, he said, 'First things first: I want Terry and Bruce paying quick for what they did tonight. What we agreed plus a ten grand bonus. They were real pros. And when I've left, I want them and theirs looking after, OK?'

There was a murmur of assent.

'The bitch who killed Vincent: has she been found?'

'We're working on it,' James said. 'Clifford and Alan Hinds were tailing her up the M62 but they went off the radar just south of Penrith, day before yesterday.'

'Went off the radar?' Ronald's tone was scathing.

'Disappeared, vanished. Mobiles not answered; no trace.'

Ronald frowned down the table at Morris. 'What about your boy? Have you heard anything?'

Morris's mouth tightened. He didn't speak, just shook his head and looked away.

James took a deep breath. Ronnie was out now; the truth could be told. 'Carl's dead,' he said softly. 'I sent someone to search an empty house. They found him in the cellar. He'd been shot. His body was hidden under a stone shelf.'

Morris glared at James. 'You knew? You've known all this time? My boy, lying dead, in a cellar?'

'We had to concentrate on getting Ronnie out,' James said. 'We didn't need any distractions. And if we'd recovered the body we'd have had to notify the police so we could get a death certificate. Best if we have the police tipped off so they think they've found him. Dangerous doing that before Ronnie's left.'

'My boy was lying dead in a filthy cellar. We could have bought a death certificate.' Morris's voice became an angry wail. 'Christ, we can buy any fucking certificate. You bastard, James. If it was your son — '

'OK, Morris, OK.' Ronald raised his huge hands in a calming gesture and made his voice placatory. 'James was doing some good thinking. The cops are going to be all over you when I've left. You don't want a dodgy death certificate for your boy.' His face suddenly became grim. 'Vincent, Carl, Clifford, Alan Hinds . . . And you've no idea who the bitch is?'

Nine pairs of eyes looked at him bleakly. Morris was staring down at the table. His lips and chin were trembling. He was trying not to weep. Henry's face was gaunt: he'd already accepted that his own son, Clifford, might have to be numbered amongst the dead.

'What about the pictures you circulated: the ten-grand finder's fee?'

'It helped Alan Hinds recognize her in a hotel in Manchester. She took Paula Hamilton into the dining-room for a meal. There's been nothing since,' James said.

'What about the dummy who works in Morris's heel bar? Could he make out what they were saying on the video?'

'Woman's not facing the camera, Vince is too far away from it, and the picture quality's piss-poor. He couldn't lip-read either of them.'

'What about Tyminski? Have you traced him?' Ronald asked.

'We think he's dead.' James looked at his brothers for support. 'It really was his body at the crem.'

'Dead my arse,' Ronald sneered. He scowled down the table at Austin. 'Has his wife said anything?'

Austin shook his head. 'Nothing. And I've watched her and followed her. As far as I know, she's never been anywhere out of the ordinary; she's never been back to Stockport.'

'What's she like?' Ronald asked.

'Nice kid,' Austin said. 'She's lost everything. She's as pissed off as we are.'

'I mean, what's she like in bed?'

Austin blushed. 'She's OK.'

Ronald's eyes narrowed and his thin purplish lips stretched into a humourless grin. 'You fancy her, don't you, Austin?' he said gently. 'You've got quite attached.'

Austin's blush deepened and spread to his ears. 'She's a really nice kid. Watching her, keeping her company: it's not been a chore.'

Ronald nodded, then looked at Morris and spoke his name to attract his attention. Tear-filled eyes turned towards him. 'Those blokes you used, Morris, when you had the whore houses and massage parlours in Sheffield. They were brothers — '

'Thomson Twins,' Morris choked out the name. He was trying to pull himself together.

'Get hold of 'em. Send 'em to Carlisle. Tell 'em to — '

'She doesn't know anything,' Austin protested. She's as pissed-off as we are. She . . . '

Ronald smiled and said gently, 'We've got to be sure, lad.'

Morris glared down the table at James, then looked across at Austin. Ronald was right. Austin really had fallen for Tyminski's wife, fallen for her the moment he first laid eyes on her, and James had left Carl's body to rot in a filthy cellar. The son was a stupid skirt-chaser and the father had treated him and his boy with total contempt. Suddenly rage began to give way to a feeling of anticipation. It was payback time. When Austin saw his fancy-piece again he'd be sick to his stomach. Morris turned towards Ronald. 'How rough do you want the Thomsons to be?'

'Whatever it takes to find out what she knows. You'd better go with them, Morris. We need to know where her husband's hiding, whether that black-haired bitch has paid her a visit, and where the boy is.'

Morris nodded. 'I'll call the Thomsons tonight. If I can make contact we'll motor up through the early hours.' He glanced at Austin. 'What time does she leave for work?'

'Eight, eight-thirty.' He'd added half-an-hour. She'd probably be out of the flat by then. He opened his mouth to protest again, but thought better of it. 'Flat six, Napier House, Brook Street. It's about half-a-mile from the town centre.'

'Why the boy?' Stanley asked. 'He's just a stupid kid. I used to see him pottering around the garage; he always stared at you in a funny kind of way, never spoke, bit of a retard.'

'Boy's probably Rachel Tyminski's kid,' Ronald explained.

Puzzled faces looked at him and someone said, 'Should that concern us?'

Ronald Bassinger rested his elbows on the table. 'Rachel used to work for Cosgrave: a holiday job.'

'Lawrence Cosgrave, the prime minister?' Stanley asked.

'The same. Rachel and her mother went to the south coast and the mother came back with a baby. Some gossip in the neighbourhood about it, but the birth certificate names Derry and Paula Hamilton as the parents. When I was on remand, I got talking to a bloke whose brother's married to the midwife who attended the birth. She swore the daughter had the kid, but when she was going through the files to pull out the medical notes she saw Paula Hamilton's name on all the paperwork.'

'You're suggesting Cosgrave's the father?' Henry asked.

Ronald Bassinger nodded. 'The prime minister: the bastard who's told his fucking cabinet cronies to be ruthless with the sequestration. We've got to find the kid, get some hair, some spit, get a DNA test done.' He turned and looked down at James who was sitting by his side, 'Did you get a sample from Cosgrave?'

James nodded. 'Got a turd.'

'Jesus, we only need a few hairs or a cup he's used.'

'We don't have anyone upstairs at Number Ten, or in any of his other houses. Molly Roach, old Nat's daughter, is on the ground floor cleaning staff and — '

'Nat Donkin?' Ronald asked. 'The Millbank's robbery man? The one who killed a guard and two coppers, died in Strangeways?'

'Yeah,' James confirmed. 'That old Nat.'

'How did she get security clearance?'

'Husband's a Falklands War veteran. Got medals for killing Argies. Silly sods didn't look any further than that. Anyway, Molly followed Cosgrave into the loos with her bucket and mop, went to the cubicle where the cistern was filling, saw it hadn't flushed away and fished it out; shoved it in a plastic freezer bag then put it in a sweet jar when she got it home.'

'Where is it?'

'Bathroom cabinet, the firm's flat in Manchester.'

Ronald's purple lips stretched into a grin and he began to laugh softly. 'How much did that cost us?'

'Paid some bills for her,' James said. 'Two grand.'

'Two grand for a turd,' Ronald muttered.

There were some deferential smiles, but no

laughter. Bassingers were dead; Bassingers were missing, probably dead.

Ronald frowned. 'Can they do a DNA test on a turd?'

'Bloke running a lab in Rochdale that does forensic work for the police says they can. He said it's trickier than blood or spit, but if the sample's collected fresh and stored in ethanol they can get a result.'

'Ethanol?'

'Pure alcohol,' Stanley said. 'Got a bottle from the chemists and filled the jar with it as soon as I got it to the flat. And the turd had just slipped out of the prime minister's arse. It couldn't have been any fresher.'

'Got to get hold of that kid,' Ronald muttered. He turned and looked at James. 'Got to find him in a few hours, not a few fucking days. Because that's why the black-haired bitch is getting amongst us. I mean, if what I've said about Cosgrave's right, he'd do something, wouldn't he? And he'd send someone handy to sort it, someone like this cunning bitch who's stalking us.'

'Makes me sure you are right,' Stanley said.

'You'd best start trickling back.' Ronald took a last look at all the faces. 'Make yourselves seen amongst the great and the good. The cops are probably banging on your front doors right now.'

James relaxed back in his chair. 'Mark had better go first. He's spent most of the night dancing with a heart surgeon's daughter. She'll be missing him.'

Ronald chuckled. 'Take her up to a bedroom, son; make sure she remembers you.' He turned to James and lowered his voice. 'Where exactly is this place? And when do I move out?'

'Frampton Hall, some aristocrat's ancestral home until Charlie Dexter bought it. It's off the Leeds-Wakefield road about five miles from Leeds. You're in a bungalow built for a dowager duchess at the back. Collin and Luke are doing lookout. Tomorrow a gardener called Harris is going to keep an eye open. He'll bring you some milk and the papers before Collin and Luke knock off, so you know who he is. We'll monitor police road checks. If everything's OK, Stanley's boys will collect you just after dark, walk you across the fields at the back to a car, and drive you to Hull. You're going out on the *Alhambra Star*, logged in as a deck hand. It docks in Lisbon on Tuesday.'

'Money's been transferred?'

'Everything we could get our hands on is in three Swiss accounts. Fifty-seven million. Stanley's boys will bring your passport and all the other papers.'

Ronald nodded then glanced around the table. While they'd been talking the others had drifted out of the room, keen to be back at the fund-raiser, working on their alibis. 'Thanks, James,' he said. 'You've done OK. When Morris has calmed down he'll understand you had to do what you did. But you've got to find the boy: dead or alive, I don't give a shit. If the DNA matches, we've got Cosgrave by the balls and he's going to have to call off the sequestration. And find Tyminski and that black-haired bitch. They've got to suffer, James; really fucking suffer for what they've done to us.' Pressing his hands on the table, he rose from his chair. 'I'll get back to the girl.' His lips stretched into a smile.

'She OK?'

'She's perfect. Protests a little, gets upset, but I like that.'

James left by the back door. When he turned down the side of the bungalow he saw the vague outline of a man, standing inside a small, disused greenhouse, keying numbers into a mobile phone. Moving silently, he joined him just in time to hear the faint bleeps of the ringing tone. He reached out, snatched the mobile, dropped it on the floor and crushed it under his foot. 'Family, Son,' he said. 'It's only family that matters: the family and the firm. If we go soft — '

'She knows nothing, Dad. She's just a nice kid who's had a hard time. And the Thomson Twins are sick bastards. I've seen what they do to women. She's done nothing to deserve — '

'Family,' James insisted gently. 'Distance yourself. You'll find plenty more plump little chickens out there to pull off the perch.'

12

Light was shining behind a dozen tall windows and spilling from an open doorway at the top of a sweeping flight of steps. It glinted on cars parked in neat rows across a forecourt and the lawns beyond. Voices and laughter and music were combining in a symphony of happy sounds that wafted around old, ivy-covered walls.

Samantha had followed the ambulance to a nursing home near Marbeck, watched an old lady being taken inside, then stayed close while it continued its journey to a lay-by on a deserted country road. Ronald Bassinger had been transferred to a black Mercedes and driven here. She could see the car now, parked fifty yards away across the grass.

Four men had climbed out: all tall, with hair that was either fair or turning grey, all wearing dinner jackets and black bow ties. They'd avoided the front steps, walked off between the cars that encircled the big house and disappeared around the back. That had been an hour ago; an hour she'd spent watching guests arrive and pass through the doorway; an hour she'd spent considering tactics, contemplating her search for Benjamin and the mess she'd made of interviewing Janos Tyminski. She was certain the Bassingers were searching for Benjamin; pretty sure that Janos had spirited him away to a place of safety. Safety? Would anywhere be safe for Benjamin until she'd seriously crippled the Bassingers?

There were no more late-comers. Everyone seemed to be inside now. The paths and grounds at the front and down the side of the house were deserted. It was time to look the place over, to see if she could discover where they'd hidden Ronald. She stepped out of Clifford's black Audi. The party had moved into a higher gear and the sound of voices and music and laughter was louder now. It seemed to be coming from the back of the house.

Samantha threaded her way between cars, then walked down the side of the old hall. When she rounded the back, she trod over spongy grass, keeping beyond a pool light that poured from a row of French windows and flooded a wide terrace. The windows were open. The sudden mildness, the crush of bodies in the ballroom, would have made the ventilation necessary. A decent band was playing. Women in ball-gowns and party dresses were dancing with men in dinner jackets and black bow ties. She couldn't venture in there wearing a suit, especially one with a tight skirt, and the blonde wig might not be enough to stop the Bassingers realizing who she was.

A point of light brightened and faded, then smoke drifted from a shadowy recess. Moving closer, she made out a woman wearing a dove-grey dress with a white collar and cuffs and a tiny white apron. Samantha's heels began to tap on the pavings and the woman turned and watched her approach. When they were together in the shadows, Samantha said, 'What's the party for?'

'Charity ball: *Save the Children*. A man called Dexter's hosting it.' The woman was thin with short, bleached-blonde hair. Her hand trembled as she dragged at her cigarette. 'You with *Top Table*?'

'*Top Table*?'

The woman exhaled smoke. '*Top Table Catering*.'

Shaking her head, Samantha muttered, 'Looking for my husband. I think he's in there with his brothers and his fancy woman. He's been lying to me for months and tonight I'm going to catch him at it.'

'Men are bastards,' the woman said with feeling. 'I had to come out here for a fag. I've been out ages and I don't want to go back. Told to take drinks to an upstairs room. When I got there a pompous old goat with a chain round his neck said, 'Do you realize you're serving the Mayor of Barfield?' And then his hands were all over my bust and backside. I tipped the tray over him and ran. It shook me up, though.' Her chin started trembling and she began to weep. 'They treat you like dirt. They think they can do what they like. I'd go home if I could. I don't need the money that badly.'

'Why can't you go home?'

'Place is miles from anywhere. They brought us here in a couple of mini-buses. I've got to wait until they collect us.'

'Look at some photo's for me,' Samantha begged. 'Tell me if you've seen my husband and his brothers in there.'

The woman sniffed back tears and took another puff at her cigarette. 'Let's move closer to the light.' She edged along the wall until she was near one of the French windows. Samantha reached into her bag, drew out a swatch of photographs and leafed through them.

The band started playing and the waitress had to raise her voice to make herself heard. 'I've seen three, maybe four of 'em. They're in there, all right. You can't miss 'em. Stand head and shoulders above the crowd. Which one's your husband?'

Samantha flicked through to the photograph of Austin Bassinger.

'Handsome! I remember him. Been dancing with a red-head most of the night. He's not in there now.'

'Not in there now?' Samantha slid the photographs back into her bag.

'They started to leave, about half-an-hour ago. Two walked off while I've been standing here.'

'They didn't all leave together?'

The woman took a last drag at her cigarette, dropped the butt on the path and ground it under her foot. Smoke escaped from her mouth as she said, 'One by one, a minute or two apart.'

'Did you see where they went?'

'The two that left through these windows crossed the grass and went down a path that runs by the tennis courts.' She nodded towards some high mesh fencing, just visible in the darkness. 'I thought they might be setting up the fireworks, but guests wouldn't do that, would they? They'd have a firm in.'

'They're having fireworks?'

'Drinks, dinner, dancing, fireworks, then a buffet supper. If they sent what it's costing to *Save the Children* instead of the donations, the kids would probably do a lot better.'

'I'm going to confront him,' Samantha said. 'Get it over with. You said they went across the grass?'

'And down the path.' The woman sighed. 'I'd better go back in. Good luck.'

Samantha avoided the path and made her way through rough grass and bushes that bordered the far side of the courts. Mesh fencing gave way to a thicket of birch trees. She pressed on, moving soundlessly over a carpet of wet leaves. When she neared the far edge of the narrow plantation she heard voices. A man who looked to be in his fifties, together with two younger men, had emerged from the front door of a large bungalow that squatted beyond a rectangle of neglected lawn. Even in the darkness their height and broad shoulders made the family resemblance unmistakable: they were Bassingers, probably father and sons. The older man called out, 'Night, Luke,' and a voice from the shadows beyond a path replied, 'Goodnight, Mr Bassinger.' Someone was keeping watch.

Maybe the men of the family had gathered together to welcome Ronald home. She screwed the silencer on to the muzzle of her automatic. She should have brought the Heckler. It was in its case, under the seat in the Ferrari parked behind a hotel in Carlisle. Missing the video in Vincent's flat, the botched meeting with Tyminski, not coming here properly armed: she was losing her edge.

Footsteps faded, then a fourth man

stepped out and strode off. After a minute or so another figure emerged. They were drifting back to the big house, returning in ones and twos so they wouldn't be noticed. Still watching and waiting, Samantha saw two men appear from the side of the bungalow and then someone stepped out of the front door and slammed it shut. Eight men had left in as many minutes. She kept within the narrow belt of trees as she crept towards the path. The look-out was visible now, bulky in a parka, standing in deep shadow. He suddenly turned and headed round the back of the bungalow. Samantha moved closer.

A harsh whistling changed pitch as it raced across the sky, explosions rattled windows, then cascading stars bathed everything in a cold, white light. It illuminated two men, stooping as they emerged from a greenhouse, shirt-fronts and cuffs startlingly white in the glare. When they saw her, their eyes widened. She squeezed the trigger, then squeezed it again. They fell into long grass and weeds, the muffled thuds of the silenced gun lost amongst the cracks and bangs that were rippling across the sky.

Samantha advanced down the side of the bungalow, paused at the rear corner, then slowly leaned out and glanced across an unkempt lawn. Two lookout men were standing by a low hedge that marked the boundary with open fields, gazing up at the firework display. She aimed the gun, waited for a fresh wave of explosions, then fired two shots. The bodies disappeared in the shadows beneath the hedge.

She turned around the back. Thick curtains had been drawn across a French window, but a door that led into an unlit kitchen was open. Perhaps they'd hidden Ronald here for the night while they worked on their alibis at the charity ball. But why the open door? After being banged-up in jail for a year, maybe Ronald liked it that way, and they had posted lookouts. The noise of the fireworks faded for a moment. Faintly, from beyond the tennis courts, she could hear the talk and laughter of guests crowding the terrace. Close at hand, the muffled sound of a television newsreader.

The silencer made the barrel of the gun long and easier to grab. Samantha unscrewed it as she stepped into the dark kitchen. Tiptoeing over tiles, she passed through to a carpeted hall. On her left, the voice of the newsreader was loud through a half-open door. Further down the hall, light from an opening was spilling across blue, floral-pattern carpet. Samantha crept towards it and looked inside; saw a woman astride a bidet, bathing herself. Tousled black hair fell onto brown shoulders; a slender waist curved out over broad hips and rounded buttocks. She spun round when Samantha stepped on to the tiles. The sudden movement made her heavy breasts sway.

Pressing a finger to her lips, Samantha closed the door and sat on the rim of a green bath that didn't quite match the green-tiled walls and floor.

Brown eyes, huge with fright, stared at the gun, then looked at Samantha. 'Who the hell are you?' The woman spoke in a hoarse whisper. Water was hissing up between her thighs.

Samantha reached into her bag, took out an ID wallet and flicked it open.

The woman glanced at it. 'Special Crime. Hell, you've been quick, he's only been out a few hours.'

'And may I ask your name?' Samantha smiled.

'Ingrid: Ingrid Umbassa.'

Samantha gestured with the gun. 'Is Ronald in the room down the hall, Ingrid?'

'Yeah, watching the news to see if he's mentioned.'

'I suppose you're spending the night with him?'

The corners of Ingrid's rather generous mouth turned down. 'That was the idea.

Might not have lasted that long.'

'Dry yourself. I want you to walk in front of me and when we get inside the room stand where I can see you and do as I say.'

The woman rose from the bidet, turned off the taps, then drew a towel from a rail and crouched, legs parted, while she wiped herself. She kept glancing at the gun. She seemed too nervous to be concerned about the intimacy of her actions or her ungainly posture. 'Can I put some clothes on?'

'Is there anything he hasn't seen?'

Brown eyes rolled upwards. 'Seen, licked, fingered and fondled; guess not, girl, but he likes doors open and it's draughty.'

Samantha nodded towards a white bathrobe hanging behind the door. 'Put that on.'

'It's his. He could get nasty. He goes crazy about the stupidest things.'

'He's not going to bother about his bathrobe. Put it on.'

Samantha followed her down the hall. When they reached the sitting room the woman laid her hand on the door and glanced over her shoulder at Samantha. Samantha rested the muzzle of gun in the hollow of her back and nodded. They stepped inside.

Ronald Bassinger was sitting with his back towards them. His huge head, massive shoulders and long legs made the armchair with its chintzy covers seem like nursery furniture. Completely naked, cigarette between his fingers, he was drinking Bollinger champagne from the bottle. The television was loud enough to be heard above the crackle and bang of the fireworks; the room hazy with tobacco smoke. Swathed in the white cotton robe, Ingrid stood, motionless, behind Ronald Bassinger. Fear had widened her eyes and the whites gleamed. Samantha gestured with the gun, directing her to go and stand in front of his chair.

'Ingrid!' Ronald held out the bottle. 'Have a swallow. And take my robe off. Who said you could wear my robe?'

Samantha was close behind him now. The newsreader began to talk about Benjamin, then Paula Hamilton, flanked by police officers, appeared on the screen. She started her faltering, almost incoherent appeal for her missing child. Ronald Bassinger leaned forward, listening intently. The newsreader appeared again, talking about the number of days, about the continuing efforts of the police, then her voice brightened as she moved on to the sporting news.

When Ronald sank back in the chair

Samantha pressed the cold muzzle of the gun behind his ear. 'Where's the boy, Ronnie?' she whispered huskily. 'Where's Benjamin?' His body tensed and his grip tightened on the neck of the bottle. 'I'm tired, Ronnie, nervous, crazy as a couple of cats in a sack. Make any sudden moves and your brains are going to be all over the room. Just lay the bottle on its side and roll it over to the wall.'

The bottle left a foaming trail across the carpet.

Samantha prodded him with the gun. 'Aren't you talking to me, Ronnie? I said, where's the boy?'

'You tell me,' he growled, turning so he could see her.

'Bassingers!' She injected contempt into her voice. 'Put your hands behind your head and stand up.' Glancing at Ingrid, she gestured with the gun and the woman backed into the corner of the room. She was bending forward and squeezing her thighs together. She seemed to be struggling with an incontinence moment. Ronald crushed his cigarette into a pile of butts in an ashtray on the arm of the chair; then slid his hands behind his head, linked nicotine-stained fingers, and rose to his feet. His movements were slow and unhurried.

'One sudden move and you're dead,

Ronnie. Go over to the television, then turn and face me.' Gripping the gun in both hands, Samantha stood, feet apart, pointing it at him.

Tall, he made the ceiling in the room seem low. He wasn't young, but his body was muscular and hard; the flesh tight over a face that had big, craggy features and a mouth like a jagged scar. The year in jail had leached the colour from his skin and his hairless body had an albino-like pallor. A flaccid, uncircumcised penis was hanging between his thighs like a huge, brown slug.

Samantha held his gaze, watched his expression, as she said, 'Benjamin's with Rachel Tyminski. Didn't you know that, Ronnie? Didn't Austin tell you? When Austin found out you were sending men to look for the boy, he collected him from school and took him to Rachel. They've been playing happy families. Austin's known all along where the boy is.'

Deep-set eyes hardened when she said that, and his scar of a mouth almost healed. Her lie had touched a nerve. The Bassingers *were* searching for the boy, and he was infuriated by the deceit, by the disloyalty. 'You're lying,' he snarled. 'Austin's the last man to play daddy for another bloke's retard.'

'Rachel's got him where she wants him,

Ronnie. He's besotted. He'd do anything for her.'

The sound of the television, the explosions rippling across the sky, almost masked the respectful knock on the door. Samantha squeezed the trigger, then swung round and ducked clear as a cardboard box came hurtling towards her. The man framed in the doorway was reaching inside his jacket. She fired two shots, he staggered back into the hallway, then lurched into the kitchen.

Heart pounding, she leaned against the frame of the door and listened. She heard a chair scrape across tiles, a plate fall and shatter, some laboured breathing. She glanced back into the room. Ingrid's eyes were huge with terror; one hand was pressed into her groin, the other was clutching at her throat. She cowered when Samantha crossed the room towards her. Touching her arm to move her aside, Samantha parted curtains, exposing the French window. When she pressed the handle and pushed, it creaked open. Multi-coloured lights went spinning across the sky as she stepped down on to the path. In the sudden glare she saw him, clinging to a rainwater pipe at the corner of the bungalow, an automatic pistol dangling from his hand. Samantha lifted her gun.

Explosions began to rattle overhead; she pulled the trigger, saw his body jerk and drop. She walked over, knelt beside him, opened his jacket and removed his wallet and an envelope containing what felt like a bunch of keys.

Remembering the bodies beside the dilapidated greenhouse, she continued down the side of the bungalow. Suddenly the sky lit up again, and blond hair, as long as a girl's, gleamed in the grass. She stepped over and took a wallet from the younger man, then found the father, sprawling beside a water butt. Man-made thunder rumbled as she searched inside his jacket. She decided to ignore the bodies by the hedge. They were only minders; checking their identity wasn't crucial, and Ingrid had been left alone too long.

Back in the sitting room, she found the traumatized Ingrid still cowering in the corner. 'Get dressed. If the Bassinger's find you, they'll kill you. Have you got transport?'

Ingrid shook her head and whimpered, 'Stanley drove me here from Manchester.'

'Get dressed,' Samantha insisted. 'And collect your things. You'd better leave with me.' Body shaking, Ingrid just stared at her. 'Dressed!' Samantha waved the gun. Ingrid scampered out.

Samantha bent down, lifted the flaps on the cardboard box that had been thrown at her, and began to unwrap neat little parcels: vol-au-vents, sausage rolls, tiny crustless sandwiches; one of the Bassingers had raided the buffet and brought Ronald a little supper over. It was hours since she'd eaten. She picked out a few sandwiches and a chicken leg, then turned towards Ronald Bassinger. His naked body was twisted, his head forced back against the base of the armchair. Digging a stiletto heel into his shoulder, she rolled him on to his back. Half-closed eyes, vacant in death, stared up at her. She bit hungrily into the chicken leg. It was time to part with Clifford's Audi. She found the keys, opened Ronald's mouth with her heel, and dropped them inside.

Footsteps approached down the hall and Ingrid came into the room wearing a white woollen coat and white high-heeled shoes. She was carrying a white-leather overnight bag. Samantha waved towards the cardboard box with the chicken leg: 'He brought a supper hamper over. Have a sandwich.'

A look of disgust spread across Ingrid's face. 'Jesus, girl! How can you stand there eating with his blood all over the wall? How can you . . . ?' She began to retch, turned towards the wall and vomited down the side of a delicate little china cabinet.

Samantha took her arm, led her out of the bungalow and across the lawn, back through the long grass and bushes that bordered the side of the tennis courts. Darkness concealed them. The guests were still crowded on to the terrace, making collective oos and aahs, their upturned faces ghostly white in the magnesium glare of the fireworks.

Having abandoned Clifford Bassinger's Audi, she had to find transport. Instructing Ingrid to wait in the shadows, she climbed the sweeping flight of steps at the front of the house and looked out over the rows of cars. Some official-looking Bentleys and Daimlers were parked close by. She descended the steps and crossed the tarmac, making for a Daimler registered BARF1. A chauffeur was dozing behind the wheel. She opened the door and shook his arm until his eyes began to blink. 'You're the Mayor of Barfield's chauffeur?'

He nodded, suddenly alert.

'Mr Dexter's sent me to tell you he's unwell.'

'You mean he's piss . . . Sorry, Miss. Drunk?'

'Very.'

'Can he stand?' The chauffeur was climbing out of the car.

'With difficulty. They'll get one of the staff to help you with him. He's being very offensive to the waitresses. Some of them have complained.'

'Not again. Where is he?'

Samantha pointed. 'Go down the side of the house. There are some steps leading to the kitchens. You'll see the catering staff through the basement windows. They've taken him there. I'll wait here and mind the car for you. Mr Dexter told me to see him off the premises.'

The man trotted off, muttering under his breath. When he'd disappeared around the corner, Samantha slid behind the wheel, keyed the ignition and moved the big limousine out. She slowed in the shadows beyond the entrance steps. Ingrid Umbassa climbed inside, then they whispered off down the driveway and swept out through massive ornamental gates, heading towards Leeds. Samantha risked a glance at Ingrid. 'You ought to make yourself scarce. Bassingers are lying dead back there. The family's going to come looking for you.'

'Hey, I didn't kill 'em, girl! I'll just tell 'em it was some blonde with a Shirley Temple hair do. Shit!' she muttered, talking to herself now, 'I still can't believe it: his body on the floor, his blood all over the wall. You murdered the mean fucker, you shot Stanley, then you just stood there eating a chicken leg.'

'Have you been paid?' Samantha asked.

'Stanley gave me a thousand; told me I'd get another if Ronnie was happy. Happy! You'd have to die to make that sick bastard happy. All he wanted to do was humiliate me. I was thinking about quitting when you came.' She turned and looked at Samantha. 'I've got my passport in my bag. Stanley told me to bring it in case Ronnie wanted to take me with him to Spain. Could you drive me to Leeds-Bradford airport? I'll go and stay with my mother for a while: Eskilstuna, it's about fifty miles from Stockholm.'

'Why not?' Samantha said. 'And I'll give you the bonus Stanley promised. Just forget what you've seen and take your time coming back to England.'

* * *

Samantha steadied herself against the swaying motion of the Trans-Pennine Express and stared into the mirror. Shirley Temple was right: tight blonde curls were massed around her head like a halo. She peeled off the wig, began to remove grips from her hair and brush it out. A blocked pan was making the toilet compartment smelly; the wash basin was badly stained. She grimaced with disgust, then smiled at her reflection. She'd parked the Mayor of Barfield's Daimler on a double-yellow outside the railway station in Leeds, and by now the traumatized Ingrid Umbassa would be calming herself with a drink on her flight to Stockholm.

Samantha gathered up the wig and hair grips and glanced into her bag. The wallets she'd collected at Frampton Hall were filling it. Taking them out, one by one, she leafed through the contents, searching for names to confirm what she already knew. Stanley Bassinger had brought the hamper over; James and his son, Austin, were the two men she'd killed before going inside the bungalow. She removed the bank notes, gathered them into a bundle, and tucked them under the gun in her bag.

Moving carefully over the rocking floor, she turned towards an opaque window and slid open a vent above it. Cold air began to blow into the cubicle, diluting the stench. Standing on her toes, she brought her eyes level with the aperture and peered out. Distant lights, embedded in darkness, were drifting slowly past. She tore up documents, fed fragments and credit cards through the narrow opening and let the slipstream snatch them away.

When everything had gone, she tossed out the wallets. There was space in her bag for the wig now. As she laid it on top of the gun she noticed the envelope she'd taken from Stanley Bassinger's pocket. She tore it open and shook out a bunch of keys and a note. Unfolding the slip of paper, she read:

Henry,
Keys to the Montrose Tower penthouse, as promised. The sample is in the bathroom cabinet. Could you ask Lewis to collect it and take it, a.s.a.p., to Broxholme Laboratories in Rochdale. A guy called Stephen Shayler is expecting it and he's going to give the DNA test priority. Tell Lewis not to shake the jar. Shayler said they prefer an intact sample.
Stanley.

P.S. I left the master bedroom and the ensuite in a bit of a mess. If Lewis wants to stay over in Manchester with Emma, he ought to give Jenny Mathews a ring and ask her to go in and change the bed and tidy the place up. He's got her number.

Samantha put the keys and note back in the envelope and dropped it in her bag. Henry had survived her onslaught, but

Stanley hadn't lived to hand it over.

She closed the vent, glanced around the tiny cubicle, making sure she'd not left anything, then slid the door open and began to walk back through deserted, swaying carriages to her own compartment. She'd snatch some sleep on the train, be in Carlisle by seven; bathe, breakfast, then check out and collect the Ferrari from the hotel car park. She'd done all she reasonably could to cripple the Bassingers: Vincent, Carl, Clifford, James, Austin, Ronald, Stanley. What was left of the family would be in disarray, hopefully too busy arranging funerals and helping the police with enquiries to compete with her in the search for Benjamin.

13

The nurse asked Samantha to follow her into the private room. Blinds had been drawn to subdue the morning light, and the coloured displays on vital-signs monitors were vivid in the gloom. Bending over the head on the pillow, the nurse murmured, 'Mrs Tyminski . . . Rachel . . . Miss Grey's here to see you.'

Samantha heard laboured breathing quicken. After a dozen gasps, a weak voice mumbled, 'Miss Grey?'

'We called the number on the slip of paper in your bag; you asked us to, don't you remember? And Miss Grey's here now.' Moving back to the end of the bed, she whispered, 'She's very poorly. I can't let you stay long: five minutes at the most.'

Samantha nodded. 'Have the police interviewed her?'

'They left half-an-hour ago. She was able to tell them the name of one of the men and she could describe the others.' The nurse gave her a bleak little smile. 'Five minutes, then you must come out.'

Samantha took Rachel's hand and gazed down into a puffy, blackened face she could no longer recognize. 'Was it the Bassingers?' she asked softly.

'Yes,' Rachel breathed.

'When?'

'Early this morning.' Samantha put her ear close to Rachel's mouth so she could hear the faltering, whispered words. 'They woke me up. The man said he was Morris Bassinger, Austin's uncle; said Austin had had an accident. I let him come up and when I looked through the spy-hole I recognized him. Two other men followed him in when I opened the door. Identical twins: it freaked me out. They wanted to know where Benjamin is, where Janos is living, whether you'd been to see me.' Narrow slits in bruised and battered flesh closed and lights that had been reflected from Rachel's eyes suddenly disappeared.

Samantha stroked her hand and waited. The laboured breathing began to quicken, then a faint voice was croaking, 'I kept begging Morris Bassinger to make them stop, but he just sat there, grinning. He was enjoying watching them do things to me.' Her eyelids had parted; the wetness between was reflecting the monitor lights again. 'Austin,' she breathed. 'How could Austin let them . . . '

'Did you tell them where Benjamin is?' Samantha asked.

'Couldn't, because I don't know. That's why they were hitting me.'

'Janos,' Samantha said. 'Did you tell them where Janos is?'

'When they started to cut me,' Rachel sobbed. 'I'd have told them anything to stop them cutting me. I told them where he lives. I couldn't tell them where he works, because I don't know. He'll be dead now. They'll have murdered him.'

'They won't find him,' Samantha said. 'I saw him yesterday. He was scared because I'd traced him. He probably walked out of his job and left the house in Friary Road.'

'Am I going to die?'

Samantha stroked her hand, injected more conviction into her voice than she felt when she said, 'You're going to be fine. They'll make you like new.'

The tiny points of reflected light vanished. 'They cut me,' Rachel whimpered. 'I'll never be . . . '

'As good as new,' Samantha murmured. She stroked the cold, limp hand, then asked, 'How do you contact Janos? Do you have a phone number?'

'Got a special mobile number. Written inside a matchbox, under the matches. It's in the desk in the spare room.'

'Can you remember it?'

Rachel's breathing slowed and began to falter. Samantha let go of her hand, tugged open a bedside cabinet and saw a handbag and a pair of scuffed shoes resting on some underwear and a neatly folded skirt. Opening the bag, she pushed aside a bulky purse, then rummaged amongst the things beneath until her fingers touched a bunch of keys. She took them, replaced the bag in the locker, then left the room and went to the nurse. 'Rachel's breathing's become very irregular. I think you should take a look at her.'

The nurse rose to her feet and stepped from behind the reception desk. 'She's very poorly. That's why we contacted you as soon as she asked.' She hurried across the corridor and disappeared into Rachel's room.

Samantha walked past some four-bed wards, pushed through double doors, then crossed over to the lifts and pressed every call button. Seconds later she was bracing herself against an icy wind as she ran across the car park towards the Ferrari.

* * *

'Has the bull caught the bunny, Magda?'

'He's not caught her, Benjamin, he's cuddling her, because he likes her. And it's a minotaur and a hare, not a bull and a bunny.'

Every time they came down the Promenade they had to stop and stare at the huge bronze figures that towered over the pavement outside Waterstone's bookshop. In truth, she found the sculpture rather sinister: the minotaur with it's massive shoulders, the startled hare with its long erect ears and extended paws. She squeezed the child's tiny hand. 'Shall we go, Benjamin, back to Rafal, have cocoa and cake?'

Benjamin didn't answer. He was frowning thoughtfully at the bronze figures, sitting together on an ornamental chair. Presently he said, 'I think he's holding her. He's taken her prisoner.'

Magda laughed. 'He's only holding her around the waist, and hares can run fast. I'm sure she'd run away if she wanted to.' She tugged at his hand. 'Cocoa and chocolate cake?'

Benjamin looked back over his shoulder as they walked on past the council offices. Such a strange child, Magda reflected. She'd been afraid she wouldn't be able to cope at her age, but he'd been no trouble, no trouble at all. In fact, he'd been a help to Rafal, sorting all those eyes into pairs. But the situation frightened her and she'd still not got over the shock of hearing Janos's voice on the telephone. She'd thought it was a cruel joke until he'd actually walked into the shop. And the story he'd told! The police staging his death, changing his identity, and even then the Bassinger people had managed to find him. Strange the way he'd discovered they were looking for little Benjamin. Guardian angels: everyone had a guardian angel, she was sure of it. But the situation really scared her. Benjamin had been with them for a week now and his mother kept going on television. She'd had to switch it off. She couldn't bear to watch it. No matter how much danger Benjamin was in, Janos should have told Paula that her child was safe with them. No matter how good their intentions, she and Rafal were implicated in a child's disappearance, and the longer Benjamin stayed the worse it would be. Those wicked Bassingers were the cause of it all. Janos was absolutely terrified of them. And the police had been telling the Bassingers where he was living and giving them keys to his house! No wonder he daren't trust the police. But he should have confided in Paula. The situation couldn't go on. She'd talk to Rafal about phoning Janos on that special number tonight. He'd told them not to unless there was an emergency, but this *was* an emergency. And if they couldn't get hold of Janos, she'd phone Paula, no matter what the police did to them.

She felt Benjamin tugging at her hand and looked down at an upturned face framed by the fur-lined hood of his jacket. The weak, winter-morning sunlight was reflected by his spectacles, obscuring his eyes. 'Church, Magda. Let's go to church and light candles for Mummy and Janos.'

'It's out of our way, dear. Tomorrow, when we go and buy the fish; we'll go then.'

'Has mummy gone to Jesus?'

'I don't think so, dear. Didn't Uncle Janos say she's gone to see your Aunt Rachel?'

'Janos went to see Jesus.'

Magda sighed. 'I know, dear.' They had this conversation two or three times a day. Beaming at him, she said brightly, 'Cocoa and cake? And then you can go up to Rafal.'

'Do some more eyes?'

'Yes, dear, do some more eyes.'

They were walking up Montpellier now. When they reached the top he'd want to stop again and look at the Grecian statues that decorated the shop fronts; ask her if the buildings would fall down if they walked away. Such a strange child, confusing the animate and the inanimate, the living and the dead. He seemed to live in a world of his own that had its own mysterious logic.

* * *

Samantha switched on the wipers to clear the mist of fine rain from the windscreen. She'd parked at the end of Brook Street. Napier House, the building where Rachel Tyminski had a flat, was clearly visible. Some plain-clothes officers had driven off in a police car an hour ago, but the white van used by the scene-of-crime people was still parked outside. She'd rejected the idea of just walking in and flashing one of her ID cards. She was no longer a member of the service, no longer on the payroll. A smart policeman might have dialled the number on the card. It would have got him through to Marcus, and Marcus would almost certainly deny any knowledge of her. Fallon would have given explicit instructions that the department and its political masters must no be embarrassed in any way.

While waiting, she'd leafed through the items in the folder she'd taken from Janos Tyminski's house: photographs of a Lourdes pilgrimage; altar servers; the church choir; a few pictures of his wedding and some family snapshots. Certificates of baptism and confirmation were folded amongst birthday cards, and there were a couple of letters from Rachel. The memorabilia of a very ordinary life. One image caught her attention. It was of a younger Janos, standing between an elderly man and woman outside a small shop in a sunlit street. The man was bald; the woman's white hair was drawn back and arranged in a chignon. Both were tall and slender, and the woman wore wire-rimmed spectacles. Samantha peered at the photograph. The shop was sandwiched between a confectioners and an ironmongers, its tiny display window filled with dolls. Buckets and brooms had been arranged on the pavement outside the ironmongers. Something about the scene was familiar to her, something she couldn't quite place.

White-suited figures emerged from the block of flats, threw a box and some plastic sacks into the back of the van, then climbed into the cab and drove off. She pulled out, cruised down the street and turned into the space they'd vacated. A canopy over the entrance sheltered her from the drizzle while she tried the keys she'd taken from Rachel's bag. Eventually she found one that fitted, stepped into the communal hallway, and climbed concrete stairs to flat six. Yellow crime-scene tape had been stretched across the doorway. She worked through the keys until the lock clicked, then tore away the tape and stepped inside.

Morris Bassinger and his enforcers had already made a search. In the bedroom, drawers and wardrobe had been emptied over the bed; in the kitchen, the contents of cupboards had been scattered across work-tops. The police had been busy, too. Fingerprint powder clouded all the places the intruder's hands might have touched. Squeezing through the jammed door to the spare room, Samantha trod over files and papers, pens and other office things, that had been tipped out of desk drawers on to the floor. Dropping to her knees, she began to search for the matchbox, eventually found it under a radiator beneath the window. She shook out the matches and peered into the tiny cardboard tray. There seemed to be nothing written there. An overcast sky was making the room almost dark. Rising to her feet, she turned the tray to catch the light. She saw it then, a phone number, written faintly in pencil. Even by the window it was barely visible.

Back in the Ferrari, she keyed the number into her mobile. Almost immediately a voice snapped, 'Who is this?'

'Georgina Grey, Janos. We met yesterday. I must see you again. We have to talk.'

'How did you get this number? Only Rachel and Rafal have — '

'Your wife's been badly hurt by the Bassingers. She's in the Cumberland Infirmary, in intensive care.'

'She's dead.' It was as if he'd spat the words into the phone. 'And she died alone. They wouldn't let me see her because I'm dead, too, aren't I? I'm called Keating now, not Tyminski.' Anger and distress were making his voice harsh, almost shrill.

'How did you find out?'

'Local Radio station. Heard about the assault when I was driving for a job interview.'

'Janos,' she made her voice urgent, trying to keep him talking. 'I have to find Benjamin. He must go back to his mother. The police are all around her. He'll be safe with her.'

'Liar! You're a Bassinger woman. You appear on the scene and the next day Rachel's beaten to death. And if I hadn't left the job at Azam Autos and moved to another flat they'd have killed me this time.'

'This time?'

'You know what I'm talking about,' he snarled angrily. 'I'm talking about when your people searched the safe house a week ago. I'd gone there for a duvet and some pillows. They got inside with a key. Where did they get a key? When we got the house, the keys were handed to me by Detective Inspector Lacey. Maybe he gave copies to you when he told you the address. And if the men you'd sent hadn't been so careless, if they'd really tried to search the place, they'd have found me. I was hiding behind the door in the downstairs toilet and I could hear them talking. They were saying Ronald Bassinger had told them to forget me for a while if they didn't find me, and concentrate on getting Benjamin. He'd told them drive over to Stockport that same day. And that's what you're doing: trying to get Benjamin. The only reason you didn't kill me yesterday was because you thought you could trick me into telling you where he is.'

'OK, Janos, you don't trust me. You don't trust anyone. But if you won't let me take him back to Paula Hamilton, you take him back.'

Fear suddenly replaced the anger in his voice. 'I'm going to get off this phone. You're using the call to trace me, aren't you? You're — '

'Janos . . . Janos?' Samantha took the phone from her ear, stared down at it for a moment, then keyed it off.

The rain was heavier now, drumming on the roof of the car and pouring down the windscreen. Sighing out her exasperation, she began to sift through the folder of photographs and papers that lay on the passenger seat while she considered the situation. Janos had taken Benjamin, she was sure of it now.

But he couldn't care for a child. He was a man in constant fear of the Bassingers, a man on the run. He'd have to place him with a friend or a relative, someone a frightened and difficult child would trust. The addresses Paula Hamilton had given her were all in and around Stockport, and Father Ryan had said the family hadn't drifted away. He wouldn't attempt to hide him so close to home. She suddenly remembered something Father Ryan had said, about a relative with a special skill, a clockmaker perhaps. She picked out the photograph of Janos with the old couple in front of a shop that had a tiny display window, filled with dolls. It was cropped across the black and gold signboard and only the lower edges of the letters were visible. DOLL: the second word had to be DOLL. The third word . . . The third word was probably DOCTOR: THE DOLL DOCTOR. A man who repaired dolls, a man with an unusual skill.

Samantha flicked through the notes she'd made when she met Paula Hamilton, found the telephone number of one of the Stockport Tyminski's and dialled it. A woman answered.

'Mrs Tyminski?'

'That's right.' The voice sounded wary.

'I have an antique German doll that needs some attention, I understand you — '

Laughter sounded in the earpiece. 'You've

got the wrong Tyminski. You need my husband's brother, Rafal Tyminski. He has a shop and workshop in Cheltenham, in the Montpellier area.'

Rafal: Janos had just said Rachel and Rafal were the only people who could contact him on his mobile. 'Sorry to have troubled you,' Samantha said. 'You don't happen to have his telephone number, do you?'

'It's no trouble. I've got it here.' She recited the numbers and began to laugh again as Samantha was nothing them down. 'This is so strange. A man phoned my husband about an hour ago asking if he could repair a doll, and he directed him to Rafal.'

'A man phoned an hour ago?'

More laughter. 'That's right. My husband said he didn't sound the least bit like a doll collector; said he sounded more like a man who yelled at the crowd while he sold things from a market stall.'

'Thanks, Mrs Tyminski. You've been very helpful.'

Samantha dialled the Doll Doctor's number, then listened to the bleep-bleep of the ringing tone while the rain drummed on the roof of the car.

14

Benjamin dropped the eye into the sizing cup. It was a snug fit, so he transferred it to the tray. 'Check size first,' Uncle Rafal had said. 'Then match colour.'

He was doing the twenty-fours now. They were the big ones. He'd finished the sixteens and eighteens. They were arranged in neat rows in shallow trays: browns, greys, blues and greens; a matching pair in every tiny compartment. He liked it here, helping Uncle Rafal. It was quiet and peaceful, no shouting and jostling like there was at school. He liked sorting things for him, arranging them in order. When he'd finished the big bag of eyes, he'd sort out the hands. Uncle Rafal had said he could.

Benjamin could hear the telephone ringing, faintly, in the living room below. Turning on his high stool, he looked at Rafal. Rafal was frowning through battered spectacles at a doll's head, his tongue between his teeth, concentrating on painting the mouth. 'Uncle Rafal!' Benjamin spoke loudly, but his uncle couldn't hear. Rafal was deaf. Magda kept teasing him about it, telling him to get a hearing-aid. When Magda was out, the phone never got answered. It had been ringing when they came back from the shops, but it had stopped before Magda could get to it. It had been ringing, on and off, all afternoon while Magda was out. Benjamin daren't touch Rafal while he was painting. He watched him finish the upper lip with a deft sweep of the brush, then reached over and nudged his arm. 'Telephone, Uncle Rafal.' He almost shouted the words.

The old man looked over his spectacles and grinned. 'Magda will get it, Benjamin.'

'She's in the bathroom, Uncle. She's singing.'

Rafal laid the doll's head on the bench, rested his brush across the jar of paint and listened intently. 'I can't hear it, Benjamin.'

'That's because it's stopped, Uncle.'

Rafal chuckled and squeezed Benjamin's knee. 'That's OK, Benjamin. If it's important, they'll call again.' He leaned over the workbench and peered into the tray. 'How are the eyes going?'

'I'm doing the twenty-fours now.'

'The twenty-fours!' Rafal gave Benjamin's knee another squeeze. 'Marvellous! Marvellous! I've never known a boy who worked so hard.' Picking up an eye, he muttered, 'These are German, so brilliant, so lifelike; much too good to be lying in a bag under the bench.' He leaned back and sniffed the air. 'Beef stroganoff: we're having beef stroganoff for dinner, Benjamin.' He sighed with contentment. It had been good having the boy for company. Such a strange child, always wanting to sort things, to arrange them in order. Magda was becoming very scared about him being here and he shared her fears. But he believed what Janos had said. Janos had always been so serious, so level-headed. And why would he lie to them about the danger the child was in? He didn't like using the phone because he could hardly hear what people were saying, but he'd call Janos after dinner, tell him he had to collect the boy, tell him that if he didn't they'd tell Paula. God knows what would happen if they had to do that.

Rafal pushed his chair back. He'd string the doll tonight, when the lips and eyebrows had dried. At one time he could string a doll in ten minutes. Two old shillings he'd charged. You could buy a decent meal for two shillings then. He couldn't string a doll in ten minutes now. The arthritis had made his fingers too stiff. And he couldn't buy any sort of a meal for ten new pence. Pressing his hands on the arms of his chair, he heaved his thin frame upright, then rolled down the sleeves of his red check shirt. He smiled at Benjamin. 'Magda's taken you for a hair cut.'

Benjamin nodded. 'My head feels cold.'

'I'm not surprised.' Chuckling, Rafal ran his hand over the light-brown fuzz. 'You've not got much more than me now.'

'Rafal?' The voice floating up the stairs was loud enough for him to hear. 'Come down and lock up the shop. Dinner will be ready in ten minutes.'

'Coming, my love.' When he'd ambled over to the door, he looked back at Benjamin. 'Dinner, Benjamin. Come and wash your hands.'

Benjamin held up an eye. 'Let me finish these, Uncle. There're only six left.' He dropped the eye into the sizing cup.

Rafal passed Magda on the lower landing. Fragrant from her bath, her hair had been loosely pinned up and she was wearing her black velvet dress. He slid an arm around her waist and kissed her cheek. Laughing, she pushed him away. 'Lock-up, Rafal. Dinner's almost ready. Where's Benjamin?'

'Still in the workshop.' Rafal started down the lower flight of stairs.

'That boy!' Magda said, loud enough for Benjamin to hear. 'He'd better be down in five minutes.'

Hitching up his baggy corduroy trousers,

Rafal lifted the counter flap and ambled across the shop. He locked the door, turned the card to CLOSED, then switched off the lights and headed back towards the stairs.

The sudden pounding was loud enough to make the glass shake. Rafal glanced over his shoulder. A heavily-built man with close-cropped red hair was peering into the shop. His zip-up car coat was badly stained with what looked like blood. He was gesturing for him to open the door.

Rafal waved his hands from side to side and pointed at the CLOSED sign. Then he saw it: the big black car parked outside the ironmongers. A tall man in an expensive-looking fawn overcoat was climbing out of the passenger side. They'd come. They'd come for Benjamin. Janos had warned him they might. Rafal looked out through the display window, his gaze moving nervously over the shops on the far side of the road. They were closed and unlit. No one lived above them any more. And the dark, rainswept street was deserted. The tall man was standing behind his companion, gesturing, mouthing, 'Open up. Open the door.'

Rafal turned and hurried back to the stairs, slammed the door at the back of the shop, then climbed up to the living quarters and tottered into the kitchen. Magda had heard the banging. She was staring at him, wide-eyed. 'Men,' Rafal panted. 'Two men. I think they've come for Benjamin. Go up and hide him in the house.'

Magda didn't speak. She threw down her oven gloves, brushed past Rafal and hurried up the narrow uncarpeted stairs to the workshop. She could hear them pounding on the door again; hear her husband descending to the shop. Benjamin was sitting on his stool, an eye in one hand his measuring cup in the other, staring towards her down the gap between the storage racking. Lifting him into her arms, she kicked open a door and swept him into a crumbling attic room above a projection at the back of the building. She flicked on the light, made her way through boxes and bric-a-brac towards the biggest thing stored there. It stood on a bench against the wall at the end of the roof; a huge, four-storey dolls' house in the Regency style. When they'd first come here, Rafal had spent months making it, then he'd realized he couldn't get it down the stairs in one piece. Its front was formed into three doors, and the floors slid in, like shelves. Magda swung open the right-hand door, tugged out the floors, then sat Benjamin inside. He seemed unperturbed, as if they were playing a game. His strangeness was a blessing. 'The hare has run away from the minotaur,' Magda whispered. 'He's searching the town for her. Can you hear him banging on the door?'

Benjamin nodded. His knees were under his chin; his fingers were curved around his ankles.

'I'm going down to help Rafal chase him away. You must stay here and not make a sound. If anyone comes calling your name, don't answer. The minotaur is full of clever tricks. So don't move, don't make a sound, until I come and let you out. Do you understand?'

Benjamin nodded.

'I'll have to turn out the light,' Magda said. 'Be brave.'

She swung the front of the doll's house shut, engaged the hooks that secured it, then hurried back to the narrow, uncarpeted stairs. On her way down she heard the shop door splinter and Rafal's thin, wavering voice shouting, 'Get out, get out. You cannot behave like this.'

'Where's the boy?' a voice snarled.

'What boy? My wife and I are old. We have no children.'

'Don't piss me about, you Polak bastard. The kid who's missing. Benjamin Hamilton.'

'I know no Benjamin,' came her husband's wavering voice.

Magda was on the landing now, looking down at the door to the shop. She heard a thud, a low groan, then Rafal appeared, staggering back. He tripped and fell on to the stairs. A heavily-built man followed him and swung a kick, then someone taller, with greying fair hair and massive shoulders, was pushing the heavily-built man aside and bending over her husband. 'You're a Tyminski.' The tall man's voice seethed with anger. 'I hate all fucking Tyminski's. My son and half my family are dead because of you. Where's the boy?'

'No boy,' moaned Rafal. 'I know nothing about a boy.'

'Bring him to me. I know he's here.'

Heart pounding, pains lancing through her chest, Magda gripped the handrail with a shaking hand and began to descend the stairs. When the intruders glanced up, the tall man's mouth widened in a chilling smile. 'Mrs Tyminski,' he crowed. 'Where's the boy, Mrs Tyminski? Where's Benjamin?'

'You heard what my husband said. We have no boy.' Magda sat down beside Rafal on the stairs, tried to cradle his head in her arms, but he struggled up and wrapped a protective arm around her shoulders. He could feel her body shaking.

Huge hands darted out, grabbed Magda

and lifted her to her feet. Her loosely pinned hair came undone and swirled down, long and startlingly white in the gloom of the stairs.

'Please!' She screamed. 'My husband was telling truth. There is no boy.'

Rafal scrambled up, tugged at the man's arm and tried to pull his wife free. A fist smashed into his face. He collapsed on to the stairs and the tall man trampled over him as he began to drag Magda up to the flat. 'We'll search the place,' the man called to his companion. 'Get Bennie out of the car, check the shop and the back room, then come up.'

'What about granddad?'

'Shoot the stupid old bastard. It might make his wife see sense.'

The pain in Magda's chest and arm was unbearable now. She could hardly breath for it. Suddenly her legs sagged and the man had to bear her weight. Everything was becoming shadowy and dim. Sounds were echoing. From a great distance she heard a voice saying, 'Useless old bitch,' then the grip on her body relaxed and she slipped into the icy darkness.

* * *

Paula Hamilton lit the candles beside the improvised shrine to Our Lady of Fatima, picked up her rosary beads, then stepped back from the dressing table and sagged on to Benjamin's bed. Why should she bother any more? God hadn't bothered with her. He'd forsaken her, left her prayers unanswered, oppressed her with even more grief. That knock on the door this afternoon: she'd thought, as she always thought, that it was news of Benjamin, but it was the police calling to tell her that Rachel had been murdered. Murdered! And the last time she'd seen her daughter alive she'd called her a slut and a whore. Her last words to her child had been ugly, angry words. God was punishing her. Derry had gone; Benjamin had gone; Rachel had gone. She had to live out her life on her own now. Go on living in this dreadful street where no one spoke English and neighbours chanted noisy prayers. Did God listen to *their* prayers?

And Lawrence Cosgrave had only sent that Georgina Grey to pacify her and keep her quiet. The woman hadn't done a thing. What could she do? Benjamin was dead. He was dead before she'd even started looking. And what had the people who'd taken Benjamin done to him before he died? She began to sob. She couldn't bear it any more. The black-haired woman was such a cruel liar. How dare she give her hope? How dare she take hold of her hands, look into her eyes, promise her she'd find Benjamin and bring him back? Liars! Lawrence Cosgrave, the Grey woman, the Bassingers: the world was full of cheats and liars, wicked people who thrived and prospered while the likes of her suffered.

* * *

Rain was still falling when Samantha reached Cheltenham; icy rain, driven by a wind that swept over the surrounding hills and came swirling down through the town. She saw the terrace of shops when she cleared the roundabout at the end of Lansdown Road, windows darkened, the sculptured female figures gazing out over the park. She'd visited the town and these elegant shops before. Montpellier: it was all as she remembered it. And the Doll Doctor's, the ironmonger's, and the confectioners, were in a narrow street a little further down the hill. She parked the Ferrari outside a jeweller's. The place was deserted. There were no other cars, and no pedestrians were braving the dark and the rain.

She'd tried the Doll Doctor's number a dozen times during the drive down, but there'd been no answer. Perhaps Janos had warned him; told him to flee when he'd learned what had happened to Rachel. The alternative was too unpleasant to contemplate. Morris Bassinger must have discovered something: something that had prompted him to find the Tyminski who called himself the Doll Doctor. And Morris wouldn't come alone. He'd bring the enforcers who'd murdered Rachel. They could be in there now: three, possibly four men. She needed something more deadly than the pistol.

Kicking off her shoes, she drew on rubber-soled boots, laced them up, then reached behind the seats and lifted over her heavy raincoat and the Heckler hidden beneath it. She climbed out of the car and sheltered from the rain in the jeweller's doorway while she drew the coat over her suit. After covering her hair with the hood, she headed for the narrow street beyond the terrace of exclusive shops, holding the gun by its stock, letting it hang down beside her thigh.

A car was parked outside the ironmonger's: a Mercedes, not the usual Audi or BMW, but it was big and black. Samantha approached, drifting like a shadow past darkened windows. The head and shoulders of a man appeared out of the Doll Doctor's doorway, an arm gestured, then a car door swung open and a stocky figure climbed out and darted into the shop.

Drawing close now, Samantha lifted the Heckler and slid the status catch to single shot. The shop door was open; its frame and jamb splintered where the lock had been forced. She peered inside. The counter flap was up and resting against the wall. A door at the back was open and light, escaping from an upper room, was casting shadows down a steep flight of stairs. A man was crouching behind the counter, savagely beating what looked like a pile of old clothes. The man who'd just left the car was standing with his back to her, watching the assault. Samantha swung the Heckler up and fired from the hip. As the watcher fell, the crouching man turned and stared at her through the gap in the counter. The second bullet tore through his left eye, jerking his head back. He rolled over on to the floor.

When she stepped inside Samantha could hear the thud of heavy feet on the floor above; the sound of things being thrown about in a hasty search. The footsteps quickened, became purposeful, then a voice was calling down the stairs, 'Don't spend all night down there. If you've shot the Polak bastard, come up and take a look around while I search the attic.' The footsteps retreated, a door opened and the voice, fainter now, called, 'Benjamin . . . You up there, Benjamin?' Shoes began to tread on bare wood. 'I've got a present from your mother. She's sent you . . . ' A door slammed and the gruff voice became inaudible.

Samantha bent over the body of an old man. Glass from his spectacles had been pounded into his eyes and his face was covered in blood. She unbuttoned his shirt and slid her hand inside. His heart was no longer beating. Rising, she moved through the door at the back of the shop and began to climb the stairs. Halfway up she stumbled. Kneeling, she touched the body of a woman. Her black velvet dress had made her almost invisible in the shadows. There was no discernible pulse when Samantha pressed her fingers against her throat. When she lifted the woman's shoulders and turned her face towards the light, white hair spilled across the stairs. Her lips and cheeks were blue; the flesh around her eyes dark. Samantha gently lowered her, then continued up to a landing where light was pouring from a kitchen, a bedroom, the half-open door to a bathroom, and what looked like a living room. Feet were shuffling around on the floor above and a deep, urgent voice, in a parody of gentleness, was calling, 'I've got a present from your mother, Benjamin. It's a car: a red car. Look, it's right here, Benjamin.'

The sound seemed to be coming from a doorway at the furthermost end of the landing. Samantha crept towards it and peered through; saw a narrow, much used flight of bare wooden stairs. He hadn't found Benjamin yet. Benjamin might not be up there, but if he was she had to stop Morris Bassinger searching. She had to entice him down before the frightened child revealed himself.

She called, 'Morris? Are you up there, Morris?' Stepping back from the door, she made her tone mocking as she went on, 'You're wasting your time, Morris. Benjamin's in my car, waiting for me to take him home.' She listened to the silence, straining for any sound. All she could hear was water boiling in a saucepan; rain whispering over slates. She swept her thumb across a lever, changed the status of the gun from single-shot to automatic, then said, 'I killed your boy, Morris. I killed Carl. He's in a derelict house in Stockport. I shot him, kicked his body down cellar steps, left him for the rats to feed on.' She held her breath, listening intently. A saucepan lid was dancing on steam, water was rippling along gutters, blood was beating loudly in her ears.

'Ronnie's dead, Morris. Have they told you that yet? And James and Austin and Stanley. I killed them at Dexter's place.' She listened to the silence for a few heartbeats, hoping that the taunting, the news of the deaths, would enrage and distract him, make him reckless. 'Ingrid Umbassa, the woman you found for Ronnie: she was beautiful, Morris. They made quite a contrast on the blood-soaked bed: brown velvet and prison pallor. What will Alice say when she finds out her husband died in the arms of a whore? Didn't she visit him twice a week in jail? The police will make sure she gets to see the crime-scene photographs. What's left of the dysfunctional bunch of morons you call a family might not mean much to her then. She might — '

Feet thudded overhead. 'Whore!' He half-screamed, half-sobbed the word down the attic stairs. 'You dirty, murdering whore.'

Samantha took three paces back into the kitchen, saw a big green apple in a rack and snatched it up. 'I'm going to leave you now, Morris. I'm taking Benjamin back to his mother. Why don't you drive up to Stockport and take a look at what's left of your boy?' She crept to the head of the stairs, set the apple thudding down from tread to tread, then darted back to the kitchen and stood behind the door.

'Whore!' He bellowed. 'You filthy little whore.' The flimsy partition wall shook as he stamped down from the attic. 'I'll kill you,' he screamed. 'I'll fucking-well kill you.' A tall figure pounded past the kitchen doorway, moved out of sight, then reappeared on the turn of the landing. Samantha squeezed the trigger, felt the Heckler shudder as bullets punched black holes in his fawn overcoat. Morris Bassinger's body folded, toppled forward, and crashed down to the shop.

Samantha climbed up to the attic, passed through a narrow space between storage racking, then stepped into a brightly-lit workshop. A high stool and an oak office chair were arranged in front of a scarred workbench. Trays of glass eyes, a dolls head, tools, paint and brushes, were laid out on top of it. 'Benjamin?' She called his name softly; kept her voice low. Glancing under the bench she saw packages and boxes, but no spaces for a child to hide.

She moved towards another door at the end of the room. Low, badly fitting, covered with crazed brown paint, she pushed it open, found a switch, and a fluorescent strip flickered on. The void beneath the sloping roof was littered with dusty packing cases, broken cots, prams of ancient vintage: the forgotten remnants of Rafal Tyminski's doll-doctoring days. A boy could be hiding behind the discarded things, in the deep shadows where the roof ran down to the floor. 'Benjamin?' she called softly. 'Are you here, Benjamin?' She listened to the rain pattering on slates inches above her head. Suddenly the wind gusted and sagging rafters creaked. She shivered. It was cold up here beneath the roof. 'Benjamin,' she murmured softly. 'I'm here to protect you. I won't hurt you. Call out to me if you're here.'

Samantha moved across the rough wooden floor, stepping around things made unrecognizable by cobwebs and dirt. At the end of the attic, on a bench built against powdery old brickwork, stood a massive doll's house; elegant, classical; its cream paint grimy and yellowed by age. Pausing beside it, she glanced down at the floor, saw in the dust the faint impressions of another woman's shoes. A glass eye, startlingly white, was staring up at her from a gap in the boards. 'Benjamin,' she whispered. 'Where are you, Benjamin? It's time to go home to your mother.' She heard a sigh, a sudden intake of breath. Lifting hooks, she swung open doors that formed the front of the house, then saw small booted feet and tiny hands clasped around knees that were tucked under a quivering chin. Leaning forward, she looked up. Wide blue eyes gazed at her through wire-rimmed spectacles. 'Benjamin,' she murmured, and her crimson lips parted in a smile.

'Have you killed the minotaur?' The child's high, thin voice wavered with fear.

Strange, Samantha thought. She stopped smiling and frowned up at him. It was a time to be serious. 'I've killed the minotaur,' she said. 'You're safe now.'

'Did the hare get away?'

'I'm afraid so. Your uncle and aunt are chasing it across the park.'

Benjamin unclasped his hands from around his knees and swung his legs out of the doll's house. Samantha lifted him down. He was gazing, awestruck, at the Heckler; at its oily blackness, the sweep of its magazine, its muzzle extended by the heat-scarred silencer. 'Did you kill him with that?'

Nodding, Samantha took his hand and began to lead him through the attic and down to the kitchen. 'It needed many bullets. He was very big, very strong.'

She fed him from a tureen of stew and a saucepan of potatoes that had been simmering on the stove; ate some herself, then helped him into his coat. After she'd dragged the bodies into the shop and secured the splintered outer door with a chair, she carried him down the stairs and through a back room where Magda had kept her sewing machine and made dolls' clothes. They stepped out into a dark passageway.

'Where are you taking me?'

'Home, to your mother. She's waiting for you.'

'I want to say goodbye to Rafal and Magda.'

They were walking along the terrace of ornate shops, heading for the car. Samantha pointed across Montpellier Park. 'They're just beyond those trees, still searching for the hare. Can you see them?' She lifted him higher.

Benjamin ran his arm around Samantha's neck and clung to her. 'The rain's on my glasses, I can't . . . '

'They're looking and waving,' Samantha said. 'Wave, say goodbye.'

'Bye, Magda. Bye, Rafal.' He waved frantically.

'Louder, Samantha urged. 'As loud as you can.'

He shouted out the words. The gusting wind caught them, carried them over the road and tossed them into the darkness of the winter night.

* * *

Samantha stopped the Ferrari at the junction of Spandyke Street and Atherton Road, positioning it so she could see Benjamin's house. She stroked the sleeping child's cheek, then shook his shoulder until he woke. 'We're here,' she whispered.

He sat up and blinked through the windscreen. 'Where's mummy?'

'In bed. It's very late: after one o'clock.' She drew him close and briefly held him in her arms before handing him a carrier bag that contained his few possessions and a package for Paula Hamilton.

Benjamin gazed up at her. 'Did Jesus send you?'

Samantha smiled. How should she answer? Deciding to go along with his perception of things, she said, 'Yes, Benjamin. Jesus sent me.'

He frowned thoughtfully. The woman with the green eyes had only confirmed what he already knew. He'd worked it out while they'd been roaring home in her racing car. Nodding, he said, 'Jesus sent Janos back to take me to Rafal and Magda.'

Samantha reached over and opened the passenger door. 'Time to go home,' She said. 'Knock hard and mummy will come down.'

Benjamin slid out of the car and pulled his carrier bag off the seat. 'Are you going back to Jesus now the minotaur's dead?'

Deciding to continue humouring him, she

murmured, 'Yes, Benjamin, I'm going back to Jesus.'

He stepped clear, slammed the car door, then turned and walked off down the dark street, dragging his carrier bag through the puddles. He crossed the pavement, climbed on to the step and began to beat the shiny blue door with his fist.

A bedroom light went on. Seconds later, a light appeared behind the transom above the door, and then it opened. A stunned Paula Hamilton gazed down at the child she'd given up for dead. She fell to her knees and drew him into the house and into her arms.

Samantha released the brake, let the car roll back from the junction, then keyed the ignition and turned in the road. Manchester city centre wasn't much more than five miles away: close enough for her to take a look at the Bassinger's penthouse flat in Melrose Towers; recover the sample Stanley had mentioned in his note to his brother Henry. After that she'd book into a hotel, bathe, have breakfast brought up to her room, and catch up on some sleep. Then it would be time to begin her own journey home.

15

'Miss Fallon . . . Loretta!' A beaming Lawrence Cosgrave gestured for her to enter. Loretta closed the door and began to walk down the long table in the Cabinet Room. She pulled out the chair opposite his, dropped her battered briefcase beside it and sat down.

'I presume Georgina Grey's submitted her report?'

'She has no duty to report, Prime Minister. She's no longer a servant of the Crown. If you remember, I took the precaution of discharging her from the service. But she has let me have an event log for the investigation.' She clicked open the briefcase, plucked out a sheet of paper, and slid it across the table. 'It's mostly times and dates of death for the men she killed, and the location of the bodies.'

'Good God!' He began to count, found it too much of an effort and glanced up. 'How will you deal with this?'

'Special Crime has been notified. They're all Bassingers and their hangers-on. We're saying it's gang-land killings.'

‘Do we know who murdered Rachel Tyminski?’

‘Morris Bassinger and his two enforcers. Grey killed them in Cheltenham. I had a call this morning; the police have DNA matches linking the men to the assault. I understand they were called the Thomson Twins.’

Lawrence Cosgrave touched his finger tips together and shaped his distinguished features in a grave expression. He didn’t quite know what to make of all this. He wasn’t sure how he should respond. Gazing across the table at Loretta, his thoughts began to wander. She’d never been beautiful, and was no longer young, but she was still attractive. If her hair weren’t drawn back so tightly, if she wore a dress instead of that navy blue suit and white blouse, she’d . . . He brought his attention back to the meeting. ‘What’s happened to Rachel’s husband?’

‘Jacob Tyminski?’ Loretta smiled. ‘You obviously know the police staged his death and gave him a new name?’

Cosgrave nodded.

‘He’s in the psychiatric ward of some hospital in Carlisle; I think they said the Cumberland Infirmary. He’s been sectioned. Seems he went into a church asking for the priest, started telling some nuns he’d returned from the dead, raped and murdered his wife and killed half his relatives. They gave him a cup of tea and called the police.'

Making his expression sympathetic, Cosgrave murmured, 'How unspeakably sad.' He frowned over Loretta's shoulder at the inept portrait of The Queen while he reflected on the situation. Rachel had always been something of a worry and a threat to him, but she was dead now. Silenced. Her mother and the Grey woman wouldn't talk. The priest knew, but he didn't count; he'd take everyone's secrets to the grave. It was unlikely Rachel had told her husband, and even if she had he was tainted with mental problems so he'd have no credibility. It had been a nerve-wracking ten days, he'd had a few sleepless nights, but he'd emerged unscathed and far less vulnerable. He flicked his gaze back to Loretta, cleared his throat and smiled. 'I gather from press reports that the child's completely unharmed.'

Loretta nodded. 'So the doctors say. The police can't make any sense of his story. He talks about Jesus sending Janos back and a woman with green eyes killing a minotaur. And he keeps asking if Magda and Rafal have caught the hare. Child psychiatrist said he has a very high IQ and he's trying to come to terms with the loss of his Uncle Janos. Seems Janos Tyminski was the father-figure he was strongly attached to.' Loretta studied Cosgrave's expression closely when she said that, but his face was a mask. She went on, 'Grey let me have a statement of monies and other items she seized from the Bassinger's. She took a case containing just over three hundred thousand from Vincent Bassinger's flat, a case containing one hundred and thirty thousand from the boot of Clifford Bassinger's car, and she found rather more than two-thousand pounds in the wallets of the men she killed. She sent the money recovered from the car and the wallets to Paula Hamilton with a note saying it came from you.'

'From me!' Lawrence Cosgrave exploded. 'What possessed the woman?' He saw Loretta Fallon's lips curving in a smile. She knows, he thought. She bloody well knows.

'Perhaps she felt that making the ex-gratia payment in your name would give it validity, Prime Minister.'

Swallowing hard, he decided to move the conversation on. 'And the money from the flat?'

'After deducting expenses, she took the balance as a fee.'

'Expenses! Fee!'

Loretta's smile widened. 'She's no longer in our employ, Prime Minister. She's not salaried, and if you think about the risks she ran and what she accomplished, it's not an excessive amount. And it was Bassinger money.'

Lawrence Cosgrave scowled across the table. He wasn't happy. No matter what the woman had done, she didn't have the authority to appropriate and distribute funds like that. She certainly didn't have the authority to do it in his name.

Trying to end the angry silence, Loretta added, 'Grey also mentioned three cases of money still in Vincent's flat, and she noticed a room had been bricked up. We passed that on to the police. When they broke through they said it was an Aladdin's cave: Renoirs, a Monet, a couple of Picasso's; it was crammed with stuff Ronnie Bassinger was trying to hide from the sequestrators.'

Loretta began to rise, then, suddenly remembering, said, 'The Bassinger's have a company flat in Manchester. Grey found the keys and searched the place; left watches and rings, all the personal things she'd taken from the men she'd killed, in one of the bedrooms.' Loretta reached into the briefcase, lifted out the glass sweet jar and lowered it gently on to the table. She was tempted to say, 'Yours, I think, Prime Minister,' but she just gave him a tight-lipped little smile and slid it across the polished surface with her fingertips.

Surprise, embarrassment, and then revulsion chased one another across Cosgrave's features. 'I . . . I don't understand. I really don't see what . . . '

'I think this note explains things, Prime Minister.' Loretta pushed a square of paper towards the jar. 'Grey found it with the keys.'

Cosgrave reached out, snatched up the note, and began to read. 'Sample . . . Broxholme Laboratories . . . DNA.' When he glanced up at Loretta there was something close to fear in his eyes.

'The Bassingers had an agenda, Prime Minister. I presumed you realized that. I presumed that's why you asked for the most ruthless operator we've ever had.'

THE END

Other titles published by
The House of Ulverscroft:

KISS AND KILL

Raymond Haigh

Private eye Paul Lomax expected trouble when Velma Hartman said she needed a big, strong man. But it's hard to say no to a woman alone. And the formidable Mrs Pearson is demanding intimate pictures of her husband with his lover: another unwanted case when all Lomax wants to do is cultivate his relationship with the irresistible Melody Brown . . . The police are interested in what Lomax knows. Two killings later, Lomax makes the connection between Velma and Mrs Pearson and the corruption that blights the town. But then he's staring death in the eye himself, and there seems to be no way out.

DARK ANGEL

Raymond Haigh

The Prime Minister and the Home Secretary are scared — very scared. Terrorists, riots, the plague sweeping over the country, these are not the cause of alarm. Their concern centres on the documents held by a biochemist, which implicate the Government in a grave crime. Now, the biochemist is missing, as well as his wife and child. Government agent Samantha Quest is searching for them — but soon she is also being watched and hunted. A trail of death follows. Can Quest find the missing family and protect them from powerful men who will stop at nothing to conceal their crimes?

CRIPPLEHEAD

Raymond Haigh

Private eye Paul Lomax never wanted the case. Checking on errant wives wasn't his scene, but keeping an eye on Rex Saunders' ex-fashion-model wife, Mona, promised to be all profit and no pain. How was Lomax to know that foxy old Rex was keeping so many secrets? And then there was the problem of Lomax's budding relationship with the irrepressible Melody Brown. Taking the case didn't help the romance along, especially when Mona dumped her inhibitions. Now Mona is terrified by sickening threats and the local morgue is filling up fast. When a hit man moves in and the police don't want to know, Lomax and Mona find themselves on their own.